INNOCENT
BYSTANDER

Robert J. Christophè

authorHOUSE®

AuthorHouse™
1663 Liberty Drive
Bloomington, IN 47403
www.authorhouse.com
Phone: 1 (800) 839-8640

I used actual names of places of which I have personal knowledge and
expierience. All of the names of persons in this story were fabricated.
Any similiarty to actual persons is purely coincidental.

Published by AuthorHouse   09/08/2015

ISBN: 978-1-5049-2577-8 (sc)
ISBN: 978-1-5049-2578-5 (e)

Library of Congress Control Number: 2015912044

Print information available on the last page.

Any people depicted in stock imagery provided by Thinkstock are models,
and such images are being used for illustrative purposes only.
Certain stock imagery © Thinkstock.

This book is printed on acid-free paper.

DEDICATION

To Roxanne Johnson who has become a very dear friend. After she read the manuscript she prodded me to get the story published. She has helped in many ways. Most importantly by offering to do whatever I needed to get it done. Our many walks through Northern Idaho's forests and parks further inspired me to publish what I started and finished, then laid to rest at the bottom of a desk drawer for many years.

To my family all of whom have encouraged this work, namely, Janice, Cynthia (Cindy), Bradley and Jason. Thank you. Dad.

TABLE OF CONTENTS

CHAPTER 1

It was mid October in the Sierra Nevada Mountains. That time of year when afternoons are warm, nights are cool, summer temperatures just a memory. Before winter snows blanket the mountains. The air was still and icy this early morning. The sun, peeking over the eastern periphery, just now striking the trail, warmed the mist and eased the chill on the back of his neck.

Only a few drops of rain had touched this part of California in three months, causing the dry trail to stir up wispy billows of dust from under his heavy footsteps making it difficult to breath. A musty aroma of dried and decaying pine needles, carpeting the forest floor, rekindled his memory, reminding him of the first time he walked this path, some years before. The tranquil atmosphere broke momentarily with the sweet melody of a Western Tanager that illuminated his spirit, announcing one of nature's wonders. He looked up but could not see the elusive yellow and brown bird that welcomed the morning from within the thick woven foliage.

Mark Baxter, in his early forties, was as healthy and robust as a man could be at this stage of life. A ruddy tanned complexion graced his clean shaven face. A square dimpled chin complemented a neatly trimmed graying mustache. The small pack slung over his back hung tightly around broad shoulders. In shorts, his muscular legs produced a steady gait that gave the impression of self confidence and determination. Azure blue eyes high lighted this youthful handsome man.

He was in his element. He loved the mountains, the isolation, the secret forest meadows, the steely granite cliffs and steppes he'd traverse on his outings. Out here he was free. Devoid of all the problems that plagued him, back there. Back there, was civilization. Back there sucked. In the mountains his problems ceased to exist. Not that he had many, but enough to trouble him. His only concerns out here in the wilderness amounted to concentrating on keeping track of his direction and how much energy he would need to return safely. The views, he knew would always be spectacular, the solitude quieting, his healing complete before returning. Just being able to be here was the world to him.

He was approaching Desolation Wilderness from Wrights Lake. Wrights is at an elevation of eight thousand feet, surrounded by fifty or so square miles of granite domes and depressions, ringed by nine to ten thousand foot peaks, one of them being a rocky strewn prominence called Blue Mountain. His goal for today. This was pure pristine wild land clustered with crystal clear lakes, some hundreds of yards across, some just potholes. Up here, alone, you became a part of the whole. Rarely crossing the path of another.

Glancing down the trail through stands of Fir, Pine and a scattering of Aspen, he spotted the nine thousand five hundred foot rocky top of Blue Mountain. From up there on a clear day you could see the faint curvature of the earth indicating the Pacific Ocean some 300 miles away. On any given day Mount Diablo in the Coast Range near San Jose could be seen rising up through the haze near the western edge of the Sacramento Valley. He had been on Blue Mountain before. Twice before.

He labored over a fallen snag on the trail. Too large to straddle easily. The mist from his breath partially obscured the face of his watch as he glanced at it to estimate the three hours it would take to reach the top. That's where he wanted to be at ten thirty this sun filled but very cool morning.

It would not be easy, but reading the drainage pattern on the side of the mountain he could tell where the bogs and swampy areas lay in the meadows ahead and the formidable low cliffs that he would have to navigate to get to the base of the mountain, some two miles away. He remembered too, the thick stands of Firs, Lodge Pole Pines, Willows and the waxy leafed Manzanitas that would challenge his energy and determination. He slowed his pace considering what lie ahead.

Working his way toward the base of the mountain he reflected on the reason he was here this day. It was important, he thought. It was important because it would give him the peace that he needed. He paused in his tracks as his mind flashed back to the days as a DEA agent, plying his skills throughout Mexico and Columbia. I was the best he thought to himself And he was. His cunning and survival instincts would keep him alive and safe today just as it had in those stormy times.

The warmth from the rising sun had evaporated the moisture and the chill from the air. He glanced down at his watch once more, the mist from his breath had all but disappeared. Standing alone in the alpine meadow he took out his compass and shot a line directly to the top of Blue Mountain, reading the number of degrees on the facing scale. This is where he would leave the overly worn trail and make his own. Bushwhacking. The way he liked it. The challenge. The way he always did it. Making it on instinct. There wasn't much he had left of himself but the fact that his daring in the past allowed him to keep some semblance of self esteem and respect. That was the most crucial thing about his being. His existence. They couldn't take that away. Not the government, not his parents or anyone, anymore. He was his own man out here.

Again his thoughts wandered back to the past. The early years growing up on his fathers dirt and rock farm in the heart of the Appalachian Mountains. Always exploring in the thick woodlands. Always catching hell from his widowed father for not paying attention to his responsibilities. But his heart was in the depths of the wilderness. Sometimes staying out overnight, returning early the following day to bear his father's wrath, berating him for what he called his dereliction and laziness. Once too often he stood and tolerated his dad's tirade. Once too often, prodding him to lie about his age when he ran away and joined the Navy.

It was there that his mettle and fearless demeanor led him into the Special Forces. The navy Seals. It was his calling, he surmised, a few months out of basic training.

He removed the backpack to move the binoculars that had been digging into his back to a more comfortable position. At the same time he retrieved his compass and clipped it to his belt for easy access. He looked ahead and started out across the meadow toward a stand of tall white bark Fir trees.

He felt good, strong, as his second wind kicked in. Second Wind was his way of fooling himself that he had renewed energy. His muscles relaxed, the tightness had disappeared. He was now more than a mile from where his rust bucket, an old 1967 Plymouth, sat parked and partially hidden under a stand of reddish orange, and yellow Aspens displaying their fall colors.

Nearing the stand of Firs he had spotted minutes ago, he inadvertently found himself surrounded by tall reeds growing out of a marsh. The underlying water engulfed his boots saturating him to the skin. Refusing to backtrack he continued sloshing on to the granite shelf some twenty five yards distant. Thick marsh grass heavy as corded fabric wrapped and entwined its tentacles around his ankles impeding his progress. He cursed his mistake and for a minute his enthusiasm faltered. Damn, he muttered while looking for the easiest way out of his predicament. The Willows on the edge of the bog were within a few yards and a promise of dry ground.

Stepping out onto solid granite he spied a fallen log where he sat struggling to remove his water logged shoes and socks. He cursed the experience while wringing out as much water as possible from his socks. There was a stillness in the air. He was loving it and at the same time resenting that he had allowed himself to fall into the water trap. That was unusual for him. The socks went back on hesitatingly. He shivered against the cold. He entered his boots with more ease. Soon the warmth of his body neutralized the cold surrounding his ankles as he threaded his arms through the straps on his pack. Snug now against his back he examined the area ahead looking through the heavy undergrowth. The mountain was not visible from his position prompting him to check his compass to take a reading. Dead ahead on the scale.

He stood silent for a minute, relaxing from the experience. His thoughts wandered again, this time to that hot muggy summer night in a Vietnam harbor. The night he and four other Navy Seals were to infiltrate, assault and sink an enemy freighter docked and loaded with ammunition destined for the Viet Congo. Their mission was to attach explosives to the hull of the ship, dive deep and escape the detonation. All went well, completing the first segment of the foray successfully. Some distance away from their victim, swimming together, Mark noticed one of his comrades struggling with his mouthpiece. He had prematurely exhausted his oxygen supply and was suffocating for lack of air. Mark hurriedly swam toward him, shared his mouthpiece and together they both reached the surface safely. Their timing could not have been more disadvantaged as they were confronted with a patrolling gun boat. A burst of fire from the fore deck quickly dispatched his mate. Mark dove for the safety of the depths but was struck several times in the legs and once in the abdomen. He and his three remaining companions struggled diving deeper into the murky waters, eluding their pursuers. Mark recovered slowly over a period of months. The wounds were serious enough to award an Honorable Discharge for medical reasons. Only the scars are left to remind him of that terrible experience. The Purple Heart and Distinguished Service Cross are stowed out of sight and purged from his memory.

He struggled through the obstacles in the underbrush keeping the sun at his back. Reaching the second set of granite shelves, he delighted at the sight of the smooth chiseled surfaces of the rock under his feet. Where once a powerful glacier had methodically ground its way down the rugged landscape shearing off the edges leaving behind these expansive denuded areas. Here, the retreating ice deposited boulders, some the size of houses, leaving them behind as the glacier retreated. A testimony to that awesome raw force that belies nature.

The sun was now nearly overhead, the heat bearing down excessively in the open. He removed the small pack from his shoulders, pulled off his sweatshirt and crammed it into the pouch. The respite was immediate. The cool breeze flowing gently across the expanse of the granite cooled his body and kept him from cursing his earlier discomfort. He continued a solid pace across and up-ward on the shelves. He ascended higher and higher over the plateau. The topography varied, unforgiving from time to time. Descending a short distance crossing a small stream then back up again. Over and over this routine repeated itself. On occasion discovering a small tarn hidden in the depression of the shelves. Crystal clear water. The bottoms of which were littered with fallen trees, rotting in the water. Ancient, completely saturated.

The mountain was in sight but still some distance off. He remembered his last climb up Blue, thinking of it as an old friend and thinking also of the airplane wreckage he'd found buried in the large rocks that covered the upper top quarter of the mountain. Parts of a fuselage, engine cowling. He remembered being concerned about the fate of the occupants. He wondered momentarily if he could find the location again. Probably not.

He did however find the stream that originates near the summit of Blue Mountain, which cascades down to Wrights Lake. Following the stream to the top, he knew was the easiest, safest and quickest way. He climbed along side the rushing water for a time then veered away to another pathway, all the while keeping the sound of the waters within hearing range. The assent was steep. More so than he'd recalled. His breathing was labored becoming more difficult with each step. He paused to rest to ease the pounding in his ears. Once more beside the stream, he knelt and drank, using the palm of his hand as a makeshift cup. He was approaching the eight thousand foot level, nearing tree line. The air was thin, making it more difficult to breath, without periods of rest. Thinking out loud, he said, "Got at least two more hours to reach the summit."

The most troublesome and labor intensive part of the climb lay ahead. Like most of the Sierra's, the mountain tops are constructed of large boulders stacked one on top of the other with deep crevices separating the olio. But his goal was within sight and reach, spurring him on. Picking his way up through the rocks, hopping over the crevasses, he reached the point he had envisioned from below. It was an exceptionally clear day. And there, far off in the distance he spied Mount Diablo poking it's head up through the haze. In the distance his hearing tuned in on the distinct repetitive drone of an aircraft. Nothing unusual. He had heard that sound many times before on any number of outings in the mountains. As he listened, his exhausted lungs were begging for a rest. The thumping from his heart beat in his ears and the aching in his calves and lower back demanded a respite. He glanced up into the Eastern sky, once more, to locate where the sound was coming from. He could see nothing but endless blue expanse but the drone grew louder as it came closer.

Still fifty yards from the summit he looked up once more and spotted the craft through the saddle between Blue Mountain and Pyramid Peak. He casually estimated it to be about ten miles to the east heading in a southwesterly direction toward San Francisco. Just as he knew it should be.

It was flying low. Too low, he thought, to pass over the crest of the range safely. He watched the flight intently hoping that his line of sight might be distorted and that the plane was in no danger. The left wing dipped as if to indicate a defensive maneuver. It then righted itself to level flight and flew through the saddle safely.

It appeared as if he could almost reach out and touch the ship. Suddenly without any warning a flash of bright light emanated from the craft, then a low rumble. The plane seemed to shudder in mid air. The nose dipped downward. The pilot, obviously struggling to right the ship managed to bring the nose up allowing the craft to slam belly first into an elongated ravine of decomposed granite. The craft skidded, bounced, twisted, grinding its way through the narrow passage. The wings striking the granite cliffs on either side, sheared off in screaming agony. He watched in awe as the engines exploded with a roar, rolling then bouncing into the air, careening into oblivion and a thousand pieces flying in all directions. The fuselage split open and came to rest in a crescendo of flying debris. A vapor of steam began rising from the underside, but no fire. It was eerily quiet.

Instinctively, his adrenaline peaked, Mark began descending through the crevices caused by the piled boulders. Leaping from one to another trying to avoid the deep chasms in between. At the same time glancing out onto the crash site, he fell several times, splitting open the skin on his knees, thigh and elbows. In his excitement he was unaware of the pain and damage to his body.

The stillness below at the crash sight spooked him. A sliver of blue smoke began to rise from the under belly of the craft. The solemnity of the scene was abruptly interrupted by an agonizing groan belched up from a piece of the wing breaking loose from its position sliding down the mountain to a new location. It was caught by and wedged between two ancient wind swept Junipers. The wisp of blue smoke became more profuse. Twisting and swirling in the light breeze upwards into the rich blue sky it bore signs of flashing yellow light within the column. Mark froze in his descent waiting for an explosion. Minutes passed as he crouched in the safety of the protective boulders. Peeking out from behind his shelter he noticed that the smoke was subsiding. He proceeded. Now within a few yards of the wreckage, down out of the rocks, standing in the opening were the plane had grounded, the wreckage looked even more devastating.

The stench of fuel permeated the air. He scurried back to the safety of a rock outcrop at the base of the cliffs expecting a holocaust. After what seemed a long suffering time to wait to get to the scene to see if anyone or anything had survived, he approached the aftermath.

He stepped warily toward the remains of the silver remnant and began looking into each of the three shattered windows of the fuselage while working his way down the side of the aircraft. More than anything he was keenly aware of the smoke and flames he had seen earlier. Reaching the cockpit, the window at eye level, revealed the pilot pinned between the seat and the instrument panel, impaled on the steering column. His face was covered with blood obliterating any recognizable features. The side of his skull crushed and caved inward, left no doubt as to his fate. He reached in through the open windshield and nudged the body. Nothing. He pressed his index finger to the neck. There was no pulse. He was alone in the compartment.

Entering the smoldering wreckage through a gaping split in the fuselage, he glanced down towards the cockpit, then back to the rear into the tail section. Debris was strewn throughout. Two individuals were lifeless still strapped to their seats. The odor of fuel was stronger inside than he had experienced outside. A tingling sensation ran through him. His intuition told him to get out, but his curiosity prevailed.

Packages of white powder lying about caught his attention. Many were broken open. He knew instinctively what it was. Dipping his finger into the substance and tasting it, refreshed his memory to his days in Latin and South America. Cocaine.

It was a small aircraft. Looking around he determined that everyone on the craft was accounted for. Dead or alive. His trained eye continued surveying the interior. Two of the overhead storage compartments had opened. In one he saw three briefcases, in disarray. He reached upwards over one of the deceased passengers, nudging him aside. Tugging at one of the brown valises, the latches which also had broken on impact, caused the lid to open as he pulled it toward him. Lying, neatly stacked, one atop the other were packets of one hundred dollar bills, some of which fell on one of the passengers below. He stared excitedly. Like a shot he speared the other two cases from the compartment, examining each one in turn. The same contents. Mark tried to estimate what he was looking at. The situation was overwhelming. His excitement soared, heightened. He knew it was a very large amount of money.

Unconsciously staring at the gigantic sum of money, he felt transfixed in time. In a surreal mind boggling fog. For a moment he lost his sense of place. The dead and the white powder became a blur in his mind. All he could behold was the briefcases with their contents. He did not feel remorse for the deceased or the trauma that had occurred just minutes before. Mark stood silent for what he thought, a long time. Slowly he began to recover from the twilight that had overcome him. He looked inside to his conscious. He searched for an answer. He wanted to walk away from the scene, but nothing could or would deter his overwhelming desire to embrace the money. He clutched a packet of bills. He fanned the stack, mentally counting it. He was looking at riches beyond anything he could have imagined an hour earlier.

His rationale now became more acute and into focus. He felt electrified, his skin experienced a prickling sensation. The smell of the fuel caused nausea. The aura surrounding the past few minutes caught up with him. He knew too, that his thinking was out of kilter with his principles and lifestyle. Honesty, play the game by the rules had always been his forte.

He knew also that the crash would not go undetected much longer. There would be knowledge of its occurrence. Someone or a party would be on their way to investigate.

Fifteen minutes had passed before he finished examining the interior and erasing as much of his presence as possible. Time, he thought was running out. Then, without further consideration he seized the three cases, tucking one under each arm and clutching the third he departed the craft ducking his head at the exit. A few yards down and away from the wreckage he stopped, looked back toward the destruction, gave a heavy sigh, turned and continued down and away from the scene.

Running, dodging around, down through the mountains natural obstacles, he plunged forward headlong at breakneck speed to what he hoped would be a successful escape.

Not long into his descent he began to feel the weight and burden of the money filled satchels. His underarms ached, stinging painfully with the tightness. He dropped one then the other time and again. The money spilling out and scattering over the ground. Gathering the packets for the third time and placing them back into the satchels, Mark dropped to the ground, out of breath, exhausted. Again the mental and physical experience of the recent events grabbed and wrapped him in a web of fear. He rested. It was here that he decided to stash the cases one at a time in different locations for later retrieval. He could make better time without the burden of the cases. After all, he knew the mountain and its terrain. He could return later and recover his treasure. He needed time to think things through.

A few yards further down, in the trees, his body soaked with perspiration, he lowered the bags to the ground giving off an utterance of relief. Standing in a shaded area looking at an arrangement of large boulders that formed an obscure cave like structure he decided to conceal the first of the three briefcases. But before he did, he opened up the valise and stared longingly at the money. Second thoughts about abandoning the briefcase was an unforgiving consideration. Using the large red hankerchief that always accompanied him on his outings, he wiped the case clean of any prints, then carefully positioned the case and its contents as deep into the opening as it would go. Hurriedly scraping up pine needles as fast as his energy allowed he covered the body of the case completely.

He stepped back a few feet eyeing the location making sure it was inconspicuous. He was satisfied. He marked the spot on his topo map, scanned the area for any outstanding landmarks, noted them on the map, grabbed the two remaining cases and fled. He worried about finding the spot again, since he knew that the sun at different times of the day can alter the most recognizable places. He'd have to chance that. He was sure he could relocate it later.

A Golden Eagle caught his eye, wings spread, soaring effortlessly on the thermal updraft near the cliffs. He was relieved for the moment by the freedom the bird represented. Without warning the hiatus was shattered by the Whop-Whop reverberations of a helicopters blades slapping against the same thermal the eagle was enjoying. He crouched. The chopper was visible through the stands of pine for a brief second as it approached. Then it disappeared. He listened intently. His heart thumping as loud as the helicopter blades. This time not from exhaustion. He felt a desperation to run. Panic suddenly overwhelmed him. He defied the urge and remained motionless.

The incursion grew louder until the thunder from the blades were the only thing that existed. He thought it was going to settle on top of him. Then as abruptly as it had arrived it faded away. He sighed. He caught another glimpse of the craft as it continued over Mt. Price. It obviously had nothing to do with him or the carnage up above. At least, not for now.

The appearance of the helicopter made him realize his vulnerability. That he had to get out of the mountains and the forest with haste. He continued down the mountain helter skelter, dodging barriers as if in a commando training course. The satchels swinging wildly away then back against his thighs began to take their toll, inflicting more pain and bruising.

He stopped again to catch his breath. He looked for a hiding place for the second case and spotted as good a location as before. Rapidly securing it neatly under some heavy brush he again marked his map and noted the outstanding signposts. The lightened load renewed his spirit and energy, but he wondered if it was all worth it. A fleeting thought. Visions of the money, the excitement, the adventure it represented soon dispelled any regrets.

Some distance from where he secured the second valise, he paused. Mark sat with his back against an old decaying fir. Its trunk smoothed over time afforded a comfort which allowed him to reflect on the tranquil aura that filled his space.

It occurred to him that he had abandoned the stream that he used as a guide to climb the mountain. He realized that if he could find the stream again it would ease and speed his return to the place where he parked his car. Oh man, he wanted to see that old yellow beater in the distance.

In the quiet atmosphere, he listened intently for the sound of running water. He could not hear any resemblance of a flowing stream. The air seemed cold, icy, alien. He shivered, overcome with inadequacy. His thinking muddled. He felt the pain under his arms, on his thighs. He made a fist with his swollen hand. It would not close. He examined his legs. Cuts and scratches crisscrossed in a crazy quilt pattern. Each one burning to a different tempo. Exhaustion and mental fatigue had set in. He took three deep breaths, one at a time, and let them out slowly. He felt an easing for the moment. The stream had to be off to his left, he reasoned. From his direction that's where it was, off to his left. "Yes," he said softly, "I came down to the right of the creek." He grabbed the briefcase firmly and began weaving his way through the brush, ignoring his cuts and bruises. His instincts were rewarded. He stopped and listened, he heard the soft gurgling sound of water rushing over smooth worn pebbles. He realized that he had not gone far before he found the cascading rivulet. It was a rejoicing euphoria. He felt good again. His faith peaked as he ran along side the water keeping pace with it in its rush to the base of the mountain.

He began looking for a site to hide the third briefcase. As he and the coursing water slowed through a meadow, Mark discovered another mass of giant boulders near the stream. The bottom edge of the top most boulder cantilevered out over its supporting base forming a cavernous opening. A fir snag perched on top of the rocks wrapped its gnarly roots around and down into the crevices in a futile struggle to keep the silvery tanned trunk with its eerily twisted branches standing. The tree and the boulders seemed to be acting out a ballet, both balancing on top of a group of supporting rocks and soil. Mark was sure it would be easy to recognize from a distance. He dug furiously, filing the gap under his fingernails with the dirt and moss that clung tightly around the bottom of the outcrop. He dug further until he struck the firm surface of underlying rocks, laced with the roots of manzanita bushes that grew along side the neighboring granite. When he was satisfied with the depth of his efforts, he gathered pine and fir needles, along with small branches and prepared a secure, dry nest for the case. He capped his treasure with more forest debris and tamped all the covering down. It was concealed from casual observation. He then located the spot on his map. He felt a relief from the stigma of being caught with any evidence. A smile on his face and a brightness in his eyes suggested his pleasure when he spotted the rusted yellow Plymouth through the trees.

Standing beside the car he opened the creaking door, winced, and climbed in. He folded back the vinyl rip on the seat, that had torn years before, and settled into the well worn pocket under the wheel.

His trembling hand made it difficult to insert the key into the ignition. Succeeding finally, the engine shuddered, rumbled and bucked as if choking before mellowing out to a smooth even resonance. He patted the top of the dash as if to reward his "Tahoe Cruiser" for its reliability, but more to support and continue a superstition. The shaking continued as he pulled her out onto the dry and dusty road. He ignored the tremors that deviled him, a frightful experience. He drove slowly trying not to raise dust in his exodus. He frequently glanced into the rear view mirror slowing at the slightest sign of billowing dust. Agonizingly and slowly he drove. He continued to listen for any sound of helicopters. He heard nothing but the car's engine and slight thumping from the tires going over rough terrain on the road. Only after reaching the highway did he recognize the trembling. Fortunately it was subsiding. He relaxed now fantasizing his next move.

CHAPTER 2

Mark entered his rented condo, exhausted, excited. Tucked down under a grove of Lodge Pole Pines, the complex of buildings, complete with tennis courts, swimming pool, health spa and enclosed garages hugged the East Shore of Lake Tahoe. From his living room and bedroom he had an unobstructed and expansive view of the lake and the West Shore, with Mt. Tallac showing off its snow sculptured cross. It was an envious place to live. His ability to live there considering his financial situation often amazed him.

He flicked on the television as he headed for the bathroom. It was five 0' clock, time for the evening news out of Reno.

He left the door ajar so he could hear if there was any report on the crash. Nothing. He could not believe that the authorities had no information yet. It was four hours old.

Then, as if it were back page news the anchor casually announced that, "it is believed that an unidentified aircraft has gone down somewhere in a remote area of Desolation Wilderness in California. More on this later."

Mark was disappointed. At the same time he felt relieved. At least to him, at this moment, it meant that no one had spotted him. That was in a macabre way, good news.

The reporting droned on. Sports, weather and a lot of blabber, as he referred to it, about school board in-fighting and lost loves in Hollywood.

The news continued as he stepped into the shower. The warm water soothed his aching muscles as it cascaded down over his back. He hurried. The television blared over the pitch from the shower head. He worked the towel over his body while standing in front of the television. It was the next half hours segment of the news. Surely, by now they have something.

He was right. Excitedly, the reporter, gave the following account. "Just in. The El Dorado County's Sheriff's Department has reported the sighting of the wreckage of an aircraft in the Blue Mountain area. At this time details are incomplete. It is not known where the flight originated nor its destination. No flight plan has been determined. It is not known if there are survivors. A rescue team has been dispatched to the scene. More details as they come in."

He picked up the phone. "Alexis."

"Yes, Oh hi. Where have you been? I've been trying to reach you all day."

"My usual."

"Usual what."

"I took a walk today. A hike. You know."

"Oh that," she said. "You didn't tell me where you were going." He always left a message letting her know where he would be for the day. He didn't this time. "Some day Mark, you're going to get into trouble."

He interrupted. "Not a chance lady, You know I'm careful."

"What are you doing this evening," she purred. "I'm fixing your favorite. Want to come over?"

Just then the news caught his attention. "Hang on Alexis, some stuff on the news 1 want to hear."

"What," she said, disconcerted.

He held the receiver to his waist, listening.

"Wreckage has been spotted as reported earlier, but the onset of darkness is preventing any rescue attempt or further investigation until daylight. A helicopter hovering over the wreckage has reported that no survivors appear to be in evidence."

Mark put the receiver back to his ear and apologized for interrupting the conversation.

"Yes Hon, what's cooking."

"It's one of your favorites, let it be a surprise."

"I'll be there in forty five, that OK."

"Yes, that's fine. I love you." She blew a kiss. He responded in kind and hung up.

Mark was dog tired when he arrived at Alexis's townhouse, a few miles north of his.

They had been a couple, on and off, for three years. Their relationship was warm, gentle, assuring. Alexis Cottier was strikingly beautiful. Silky auburn hair, with a trace of a curl, it flowed gracefully to her shoulders, complimenting her hazel eyes. From her French and native American heritage she was blessed with high cheek bones and full red lips on a backdrop of olive complected skin. At five foot eight inches and shapely, she was desirable from any point of view. She could make Mark change his mind or attitude with just a glance of approval or disapproval. That bothered him somewhat, but his love for her forgave her stubbornness and sometimes stiff posture. She was intelligent, giving, loving and attentive.

They embraced warmly at the door and pecked with a kiss. "You look worn out," she said.

"I am, it took longer to get back than 1 planned."

"Where did you go, and why didn't you tell me," She scolded.

"It was a spur of the moment thing. 1 decided to take off this morning. It looked like it was going to be a great day to be in the mountains. 1 couldn't sleep, the sky was clear at dawn, so 1 headed out. Besides, you were still in the sack."

"How may times," she started.

He interrupted, "I know, I know, I'm going to get into deep you know what someday."

"You needn't remind me."

"How in the world would anyone know where to start looking if something awful happened," she continued.

"I'm careful, very careful," he said. "Anyway don't I always let you know where I go. I slipped up this morning."

"Well, I suppose so, but you know that it can happen when you least expect. Don't go anywhere out there unless you tell me. Promise," again softly reprimanding.

"You mind if I turn on the TV," he asked.

"What on earth for," she asked.

"Ah, I caught a brief report just before leaving the house about a plane crash near Pyramid and I just wanted to see if there was anymore on it."

"Honey, it's seven o'clock, there's no news on now. C'mon let's eat."

Dinner went down with anticipation. Although it was one of his favorites, a Chinese specialty of hers, he wished the time away. With every bite he was absently planning every footstep back into the mountains to retrieve the money. She sensed his absence of mind but made no comment. She was accustomed to his mental wanderings from time to time, paying little heed.

Soon as was polite, Mark excused himself as being exhausted from the days activities. She agreed and he left just as he entered, with a warm embrace, a kiss and a promise to see each other the next day.

Upon arriving home, he went straight for the news again. It was nine o'clock. Maybe CNN would have something on it, although he did not expect a national news organization to report on a local occurrence. He watched the entire report. Nothing.

Lying in bed the ten o'clock report disclosed no more information than that given at five. Mark drifted off to sleep.

He awoke around four AM, the TV quietly chattering. He raised his head off the pillow, squinted and turned the tube off with a swat at the remote. He dozed off once more, abruptly awakening with a start from a nightmare. He dreamed that he was on the aircraft when it crashed and lay helpless, seriously injured in the wreckage. The wealth of the money gone and the authorities descending upon him. He could not fall back to sleep in the darkened room. He threw the comforter back, sat on the edge of the bed for a second and slipped into a pair of sweats he had piled on the floor before retiring. He staggered toward the bathroom, brushing against the chest of drawers that always seemed to put his place and direction in perspective.

A splash of cool tap water to his face brought him around. He forgave the intrusion of light overhead. That too, was part of the cure for grogginess.

He was gaining speed. His eagerness to get at the money wouldn't allow him to wait another minute. He quickly prepared for the day ahead and the challenge, that he knew, would be ever present. He decided to travel light. The briefcases would be enough burden to deal with. They would exact their toll on his strength by inflicting more pain on his already bruised body. At the same time he knew, too, that what they represented, would give him the energy to accomplish his task.

While gulping down coffee, his morning elixir, he prepared a snack and planned the time right down to the hour that it would take to climb to the first briefcase, then turn back to the second and third. Then on to freedom and the fantasies that the money would provide. So he thought.

CHAPTER 3

At five thirty AM, his headlights off, with just enough light, Mark eased the Plymouth along the rutted dirt road he had used the day before to depart the forest. He pulled up under a stand of Jeffrey Pines, this time closer to his jumping off point and nearer the trail leading to the last briefcase he concealed on the mountain.

He wondered if this wasn't all a big mistake. Mark regretted the fact that he hadn't taken at least one of the cases with him yesterday. At least he would have some of the money, safely at home.

His plan was to make a rapid climb to the first case, snatch it, then down to the second and third. Using his compass readings from the day before, he set out through the trees threading his way on the familiar course.

He located the stream necessary to achieve the easiest ascent. He traversed alongside the tributary reaching the hiding place of the third valise. The one nearest to his car. He hesitated thinking that maybe he should take it and leave now, abandoning the other two. After all there was enough money in it to last him a lifetime.

With that idea quickly fading, he set out again continuing the climb, leaving the scene empty handed. He would go on reasoning that he would never again have a chance at such riches.

Forty minutes later, he reached the second hiding place, totally out of breath from the accelerated pace he had maintained. Some minutes before he swore he had picked up the sound of helicopters. With the sun rising, he knew the investigation and rescue up above would soon take place.

It was now or never he mused. Departing again he spurted for the briefcase nearest the top. Stopping briefly he stood and surveyed the area ahead. He worked his way out of the trees and up onto a granite shelf. It was risky being exposed, but it was the shortest route to his quest.

He had gone only a short distance from the last reconnaissance when he abruptly froze in his tracks. Over his labored breathing he heard the mournful wail of a dog, then several, then a crescendo from a pack of hounds.

Combining the eerie dissonance of the bloodhounds with the helicopters he heard earlier meant only one thing. Tracking hounds were working to pursue somebody. But why would they use dogs. Did they know about the missing money? How could they have known that in such a short time? It puzzled him.

Obviously the dogs had picked up a scent. His scent. They would be hunting and he was their prey. He shuddered. Terror stiffened his frame. He swiped his brow. It was cold, clammy. He had never been in this kind of trouble before.

With the quickness of a fleeing deer he turned, giving up the idea of retrieving the briefcase above. He would have to be satisfied with the two below. With a flexibility he hadn't experienced in some time, he descended in an erratic and uncontrolled surge, slipping time and again, falling to his knees, his elbows, his thighs, cutting them producing a blood trail.

He ignored it. The intermittent yelping of the dogs above drowned out any pain he felt. At this altitude his lungs were screaming for oxygen, his pumping heart pounding in his ears. His calves felt as if on fire. He paused, bent over clutching the bottom of his shorts. His eyes bore into the ground while heaving to catch his breath.

It was silent. The bawling of the hounds temporarily ceased. He listened. It was a relief he welcomed. Mark knew it was a false hope. Their relentless pursuit would begin again.

Once again he took flight. The chilling effect from the sound of the dogs quickened his pace. It was louder, closer. He was back down within proximity of the second briefcase, the one he left behind minutes before. Spotting the location he pounced on the debris covering the case. He snatched the handle pulling it towards him, needles, dirt and dust flying in all directions. He lunged forward again, his upper body outdistanced his legs. He lost his balance and fell spread eagle on the hard ground. The briefcase escaped his grasp hurtling forward striking a large rock. The lid snapped open, bundles of cash scattered before his eyes. He looked in dismay and disbelief at the chaos.

Hurriedly, he gathered the packets stuffing them back into the case. Their erratic placement prevented the top from closing completely. In desperation, he forced the lid down, slinging it under his arm clamping it tight against his side.

Descending, he thought back to the time the hounds were silent. It occurred to him that they were probably at the site of the first case he had hidden. He visualized the authorities studying and discussing their find, holding the animals at bay. Mentally estimating the distance between the two locations, he calculated the time it would give him in his escape. He felt relief. But he would have to give up what he estimated to be close to a million dollars.

His route back down to the last briefcase would lead him onto the open granite shelf that earlier had caused him concern. Standing under a cover of trees; at the edge of the plateau, he surveyed the expanse he would have to navigate before reaching the safety of the trees below. Peering up through the branches Mark looked and listened for any sign of aircraft before attempting the crossing. Hearing nothing, even the hounds, he started out for the wooded area below.

Crouching and running from one boulder to another on the shelf, he successfully managed to transcend the opening. As he entered the stand of pines at the bottom of the shelf, he was caught by surprise by the sound of a helicopter, immediately overhead. He froze, holding his breath. "Damn," he whispered. His injuries disappeared. He was numb with fear. For sure, he had been spotted from above, now he was going to pay the price. He waited. It seemed like an eternity before the chopper lifted and angled off in another direction. The blood rushed to his head, left him dizzy, tingling, terrified.

He worked his way through the cover of the trees toward the stream that would take him down to the last of the cases. Finding the stream, Mark plunged in, using it as a pathway downward, but more to hide his tracks from the dogs that once again became evident from the incessant howling, wailing and yipping. They were nearer than he wanted them to be. At times he fantasized that he could feel their hot breath on the back of his legs.

Trotting at a comfortable pace through the water, he slipped on the submerged rocks, falling into deep unsuspecting holes, submerging him over his ankles in the icy water. Out onto dry ground again shivering uncontrollably, he felt frustration, anxiety, disconnection.

He could hear the choppers, three in all, from his sightings, criss-crossing the terrain, searching for whatever or whoever. To him, they were more of a threat than the dogs. It would be more difficult to run the roads out of the woods with the helicopters zig-zagging back and forth over his escape route.

It was now nine o'clock, the sun was well up into the tree tops. Yet with all the running and darting through the obstacles, he was cold, chilled. Not from exhaustion but from fear. It was accumulating within him. To the point where he wanted to be out of all this. He wanted to be a boy again, back in the mountains, back East. Back home, near his father's farm. Carefree with all the time in the world to explore and come home when he wanted.

His heart was pounding so violently in his chest he was compelled to stop. From his position, he glanced back up the mountain through the trees. A flash of bright light caught his eye. A reflection from a badge or a belt buckle. Now he had their exact location.

They were closer than he realized.

His heart beat slowed. It stopped pounding in his ears. He turned and continued down through the water. With a start he slipped on a rock hidden from sight under the turbulence. Trying to regain his balance his foot found another unstable obstacle. His forward motion thrust him out of control. He threw the briefcase towards the edge of the stream. Again packets of money flew in all directions. The predicament of having to gather up his forbidden treasure repeated itself.

Listening for the animals and trying to avoid detection from the choppers he stuffed the money back into the case.

Then, through the brush he caught a fleeting glance of an image of an animal. It was as if a bolt of lightening had struck him. His imagination went berserk. He thought, the dogs. He mistakenly identified what was a deer crossing his path, running in panic from the sound of the hounds. He stood there shivering in relief. Tingling.

He continued on, the numbness from the apparition of the dogs began to fade. He was within sight of the last hiding place. He rushed to the spot. Quickly brushing aside the pine needles he stabbed at the handle. He jerked it from its nest and sped headlong for his vehicle a short distance away.

Mark continued to use the stream as his best method of eluding the animals and their handlers. The forest canopy overhead protected him from the circling helicopters. The stream widened as it entered the meadow. The sandy bottom and low water level provided good footing.

He listened for the wailing of the animals. It was very mysterious to him that sometimes it seemed that he was outdistancing the dogs and at other times they seemed to be nipping at his heels. It could only be because of the varied terrain making sounds carry in various pitches from one place to another. That was something new to him. In all of his treks into the mountains it was very quiet. Hour after hour of nothing but the whisper of the wilderness. He had never before been chased down a mountain by unrelenting hounds.

The stream meandered out into the open, the tree cover giving way to a bright blue sky. The water's course edged along side the road that Mark would have to travel a short distance to reach his car. Air surveillance now was the biggest threat. The dogs seemed insignificant. He crouched listening for any sign of the choppers. Remembering how sound could be deceiving, he remained in a submissive posture. Knowing that he had to risk exposure, he hesitated to leave his position. He weighed the alternatives, both of which were unpleasant. He had to make a run for the car in the open. It was now or never.

He leaped from the icy waters, cold, wet, exhausted. The leather bags almost glued to his sides. Running as fast as his weary body could manage, he struggled with the briefcases and his will to continue. His luck was holding out. There was no sign of any air traffic.

He scanned the sky as he ran. It gave him encouragement to see nothing more than a flock of Canadian Geese, honking as they migrated south.

He paused under an Aspen to catch his breath. The Aspen leaves in full dress of extraordinary colors, gold, coral, orange and yellow, glistened with the suns light shining upon and through the foliage. It was such a mellow time of the year to be in this kind of predicament, he lamented. From where he stood the area began to look very familiar. His car would be around the next bend in the road, some twenty yards ahead. He broke ranks and darted ahead.

Within minutes he was beside the vehicle. Still there was no sign of the choppers. He pitched one briefcase then the other on the roof of the car. He fumbled for the keys in his pocket, but the inner liner seemed glued together from the moisture he had accumulated while in the water. He pried desperately into his pocket, cursing the stubbornness of the material to cooperate.

Using both hands, one to pull the outer part of the pocket away, the other to lunge down into the gap, he fingered the ring on which the keys were attached and yanked them out into the open. He fumbled for the key on the ring that opened the drivers door. He had meant to organize them but never got around to it. It was never a priority, until now.

Unlocking the door, he reached around the post that separates the front and rear doors and pulled up the locking plunger and opened the rear door. This old buggy wasn't equipped with any modern conveniences or amenities. He was always pleased if it just started in the morning.

He banged the back of his head in his haste backing out of the interior. Cursing again, he grabbed the cases, hastily throwing one then the other onto the rear floor.

Jumping into the familiar pocket behind the wheel. He turned the ignition key. The engine sputtered and faithfully turned over and purred quietly. His chest heaved when he let out a gigantic sigh of relief. The first part of this ordeal was over, thinking to himself.

He sat serenely for a minute planning his next and most important maneuver. He knew if he tried to escape in one fell swoop, he probably would be detected by the helicopters. It would be impossible to hold down all the dust on the road. Then possibly he could wait it out until dark, but it wasn't much past noon and the sun had a long way to travel before nightfall. Inside the vehicle, the haunting of the dogs seemed not to exist at all. At least for the time being he would not have to deal with them. But his reasoning told him that he would have to put some distance between him and the animals. Circumstances were on his side. He had detailed knowledge of the road system in this part of the forest. At one time or another he traveled all of them. He knew where they intersected and their every portal. It was a matter of keeping his cool, using deliberate movements.

He rolled down the drivers window and listened intently. He tuned the radio to the local AM station, turned down the volume so the chatter would not interfere with any faint sign of the choppers. Again, he reflected on the fact that patience would be his best weapon to elude the pursuing authorities.

The engine was warm by now and idling smoothly. He glanced at the instrument panel confirming that all gauges were normal. Confident that the helicopters were not in the area and that the dogs were struggling against their masters plodding somewhere up stream, he slowly backed out from under the snug hiding place and made it for the main highway.

Inching his way along the road, he periodically checked the rear view mirror to make sure dust was being held to a minimum. October's cool nights and days, providing natural moisture, kept the ground damp enough to prohibit the dust from rising.

From time to time along the way he would stop under the cover of trees along side the road, exit the vehicle to look and listen for the helicopters. If it hummed or buzzed he wanted to know where it was and what it was. It occurred to him that Deer Season had ended the week before. That was a stroke of luck. There would be less witnesses in the area. Little things mean a lot, he thought. His confidence was building.

His self assurance led to a momentary feeling of invincibility, when the image of of roadblocks on the highway sprang to mind. "Holy Christ," he said aloud. He pounded the steering wheel in anger and anticipation. It reverberated in his hands. In his mind, flashing red and blue lights atop idling police cars, down below, sent a chill through him.

Again, he pulled up under a stand of Pines along the road. He needed time to think. He was overwhelmed by the visage of roadblocks on the highway. He felt trapped. Ensnared in his own backyard. Every exit from the forest would be watched, he thought. There was no way out. At least not today. Tomorrow maybe. Maybe not for days. Not until they had exhausted all the possibilities that the fugitive was no longer in the area. He could not wait that long. He knew that they would comb every inch of these logging roads before that. I'm having a panic attack, he mused. I've got to get going, he said to himself. Besides, Alexis would be overcome with worry. She would make inquiries. By doing so she would put Mark under suspicion. A thousand scenarios were racing through his mind. He had to make a break for it today. Now. Not tomorrow or anytime in the future. But how?

CHAPTER 4

Sitting and thinking, Mark remembered an old abandoned jeep trail that connected to Granite Springs road, the one he was on. It went over Peavine Ridge meandered down into Stumpy Meadows then out through Georgetown. However, he would have to ford the Rubicon River and it was impassable most of the year. But, this was October, no rain for months and the snow pack gone. It was, in his mind, the only safe way out of his predicament. He had succeeded coursing that route some years before when he owned a four by four. But now, he was driving a Sedan. It would be near impossible under the best of circumstances.

Listening for the choppers, he eased back out onto the road. From his position he estimated it to be about three miles to the entrance of the jeep trail. Three miles at ten miles per hour can seem like fifty miles on the highway doing sixty five. An agonizing time. Wanting to hurry, yet unable to because of the attention the dust would expose him to those above, he crawled. His ears burned with the phantom sounds of helicopter engines, dictating that he look up through the windshield craning his neck for any sign of the machines. He got to thinking about the jeep trail as he inched along. Would it be impossible to get through to Georgetown? He felt sure there would be unexpected and insurmountable obstacles to prohibit his passing. A downed tree across the trail. The river too high. A washed out section from last winters rains. The old buggy would never make it. He would get stuck somewhere and that would be it. Stuck. If he were to abandon the vehicle it would be discovered and the end of this episode. He thought better of the idea. It was just too risky.

He discarded the idea of the jeep trail. He had experienced adventures like that before and they ultimately failed somewhere along the way. Mark learned early on that if there was any doubt, any doubt at all, don't place the bet. "Think, think, think," talking out loud.

He knew these woods, these roads. A road that led down from Sugar Loaf, a youth campground, that exited south of Kyburz on Highway 50, the main route from Sacramento to Lake Tahoe came to mind. His thoughts were racing, flashing ideas.

He reflected back to previous thoughts regarding main roads that would be swarming with police. Also, every well traveled dirt road that led to a surfaced road would be on their list. If only he could find a secluded hiding place until darkness set in. That way he could rid himself of the threat of the choppers and ease out of the woods with his lights off. No, that was not an option either. He could end up in a ditch in the pitch black. It had to be now.

Driving with a watchful eye on the sky above and the road behind, Mark slowly piloted the vehicle towards Sugar Loaf Road. It was just ahead. Once more that feeling of confidence and relief gave him hope. Turning left abruptly on the road down to Kyburz, he discovered it to be seldom used. Overgrown with brush, rutted in places and pock marked with depressions caused his positive expectations to subside somewhat. But it was all downhill. It was a go.

He was pleased to find out that the route the builders took was straight down beside an old stream bed that had carved out this shallow canyon. Obviously, they had diverted the tributary that ran only in early spring after heavy rains and from the snow melt. The old Plymouth bumped and rocked from side to side, barely scraping the bottom. A smile crossed his face more than once on the way down.

Cautiously, he stopped to listen. He had completely forgotten about the hounds. He could only hear the hum of the traffic on the highway below. He knew he was getting close. The anxiety was overwhelming. He wanted to be there, cruising up the highway among the others heading for Tahoe. He visualized the trip in his mind, hoping the reality of it would come true.

The portal onto the highway was covered with brush obscuring even the slightest notion that there was a road there. He eased the nose of his chariot to the edge of the paved highway. He exited the vehicle and scanned up and down the roadway extending in both directions. Nothing. Not a soul. He jumped back in behind the wheel and turned onto the asphalt and headed uphill.

He hadn't traveled five miles when out of his rear view mirror he saw an array of flashing lights atop a fast approaching California Highway Patrolman. As it neared the siren wailed menacingly. Mark slowed, pulled to the side of the road and stopped, thinking he had had it. All for nothing. Just as quickly as it appeared, the black and white passed in a flurry of speed and disappeared around the bend ahead.

His heart was exploding. Sweat trickled from his brow. His hands were shaking on the wheel. How much more of this could he take, he thought. He sat, quietly resting, the engine idling. With his head resting on the steering wheel, he searched for peace. Easing back onto the road, he drove a few hundred yards further up the road and turned into China Flats picnic grounds. It was empty. Clouds had swept over the canyon casting a pall of gray over this beautiful haven beside the American River.

Sitting undetected below and away from the road above, he could hear one police vehicle after another racing up and down the highway, their sirens blaring. Mark realized that getting back to Tahoe on the highway was going to be futile without being interdicted along the way for inspection. He had made it this far on his wits. There was no reason not to continue using his skills to avoid the possibility of apprehension.

The money would be the only thing to incriminate him. If he were traveling the road and stopped by the police without the cash, he would be just another tourist or resident returning to the Lake. He decided to hide the briefcases again, here, on the hillside across the slow running, nearly dry river bed. He would have to risk leaving the money once more. Return in a couple of days and retrieve it when things cooled down. When the police abandoned their roadblocks and the tight security on the highway.

He surveyed the surrounding area to make sure there were no stragglers wandering about. He latched onto the two cases and crossed the slow running river, wading to the other side. The water seemed colder than the stream on the mountain above. His shoes were still damp from his earlier experience in the water, causing discomfort. But not as chilling as the approach of the Highway Patrol minutes before.

He climbed the opposite bank to a rock outcrop above the river. He found a niche between the boulders and carefully secured the money. Heading back down the few yards to the river he glanced back up to the rocks to see if his secret could be detected.

Satisfied that the cases were well concealed, he slid behind the wheel of the Sedan and reentered the highway.

He listened to the radio for news. He was relaxed. His momentary respite was interrupted by the sight of a string of red lights ahead that extended and disappeared over the rise in the road. He realized how wise it was to alleviate himself of the money. After waiting some time in line with the others, he noticed that only one car at a time approached in the opposite direction with long lapses in between. It meant only one thing. A road block ahead. Every car going either way was being stopped and searched. He breathed deeply. He had nothing to hide. It would just be a matter of waiting his turn and then onward.

He eased forward until the roadblock was in view. An armada of black and white Highway Patrol vehicles lined both sides of the road. There was a massive display of flashing red, white and blue lights racing back and forth horizontally on top of the vehicles. The aura of authority was overwhelming.

It seemed as if he were destined to suffer from this anxiety forever. The closer he came the more the beads of sweat poured. He kept reminding himself that he had nothing to worry about. But did they have a profile. He wondered.

His mind turned to the money. Had he overlooked a packet of bills that may have escaped the valise and slid under the front seat. A bone chilling shock screamed through his body. He remembered his impatience when he was gathering it back into the valise. He had no choice but to trust that he did gather up all that was scattered. If he exited the vehicle now and started looking around under the seat the police surely would notice and that would give them cause to scrutinize him more thoroughly.

Three cars from the point of inquiry, there was a flurry of activity surrounding the vehicle being inspected. The driver was hustled from the vehicle and thrown across the hood of the car. It was an awesome display of force. All eyes of those waiting directed their attention to the scene. Mark felt a sense of fear and simultaneously, relief. He knew that if the police were distracted so near his turn that they would likely be more attentive to the current situation than that of his. He waited patiently.

The young man being interrogated on the side of the road was wide eyed with fear. Mark had been there before. He was familiar with grilling suspects from his DEA days.

Eventually he pulled to the head of the line as the officers handcuffed the man and escorted him to the back seat of the patrol car. Two officers, hands on their holsters sauntered up, one to each side of the vehicle, each leaning down peering in with inquisitive eyes.

"Where you headed," the burly one asked of Mark.

"Home," Mark replied.

"Where's home," the officer asked politely.

"I live at the Lake sir," Mark responded.

"Where have you been," again the officer pursuing.

"The Zoo in Sacramento." Mark trying not to tie himself to any place they could easily check.

"The Zoo, I didn't know there was a zoo there."

"In William Land Park, Southwest Sacramento," Mark answered. "A really good one too."

"Hmm." The officer raised his brow.

"Your car's pretty dusty. They got dirt parking lots there," he asked.

"No, they're paved." Mark replied.

"How'd you get all this dust on your vehicle," he inquired.

Mark stuck his head out the window and scanned the side of the Plymouth as if he was unaware that it was dusty.

"Kind of dirty, 1 guess," he said. "I was fishing over in Hope Valley day before yesterday. 1 had to travel about six miles back in, ah, to Lake Burnside. Maybe 1 should give it a bath."

"You have any luck?" the officer asked.

"No sir. I'm too lazy to get up early enough to catch em."

The officer kept his stony expression.

"Pull over there," the officer ordered, pointing to the side of the road.

Mark pulled ahead and eased the car to the requested spot where two more Highway Patrolmen waited.

"Step out sir," the trooper asked.

Mark obliged nervously. Well, I'm either a dead duck or a free man, he thought to himself

"Your drivers license, please, and registration."

Mark handed him the plastic coated drivers license.

The Patrolman disappeared inside the black and white while the other officer searched Mark's car.

Within minutes the officer with Mark's identity returned and handed them back. "OK, you can go now," he said. "Clean that thing up," he said with a wink of an eye.

"Yes sir, this afternoon," Mark replied with a smile.

The balance of the trip home was accomplished with a sense of childish glee. But the money was not secured, still in jeopardy of being found.

"Tomorrow." The radio obscured his utterance.

Mark arrived back at the condo just before five. The sun was down behind the mountains on the western shore. The clouds that had invaded the canyon had advanced to the lake, creating a somber atmosphere. The parking area was bleak. The kind of ambiance that makes shadows dance from out of the corner of your eyes. Not that Mark was seeing things after his ordeal, he just didn't want to. The Plymouth slid smoothly through the opening into his garage. He glanced around, his pseudo-paranoia haunting him. He exited the vehicle and ascended the stairs to what he called his cell. He often referred to his condo as the only place outside of prison that you could come and go without guards, but once you were in, it was like you were not supposed to leave unless you had some meaningful purpose or important reason to go somewhere. He loathed the confinement of apartment living and more than once told Alexis that if he ever hit it big he was going to buy an estate with plenty of grounds so that he could roam about sans the whole world watching.

The phone rang twice before Alexis picked up the receiver. "Hello," her soft voice always excited him.

"Hi honey, it's me."

"Mark, where have you been. I can't seem to keep up with you. Have you been listening to the news," she continued.

Mark excusing his ignorance, "No, what's up."

"The plane crash you mentioned yesterday, I think up around Blue Mountain, the area you like to hike in," she remarked.

"Yeah, what about it, I did Round Top today," he continued, "been out of touch. But, you know, I saw a lot of activity across the canyon in the neighborhood of Pyramid earlier this afternoon. Must have been what that was all about."

'Yes, that's what I'm talking about. They're telling us that it's a big deal," she blurted. "The FBI and your old buddies from the DEA are investigating. Does that mean drugs?"

"If the DEA is there it sure as hell means drugs. Listen, what are we doing for dinner tonight, I'm starved," he said as if he had already been invited.

"Will you take advantage of me if I fix you something special," she said jokingly.

"What do you think," he assured.

"Give me a little time," she begged.

"How much, I'm going to jump in the shower. How about an hour?"

"Perfect, I'll be ready," she finished.

"Look sugar, I'm really pooped, can we just eat and relax on the couch," he pleaded.

"Of course, but I'll still be ready," she chuckled.

"Say, keep the news on and give me an update when I get there, OK," he asked.

"You got it sweetheart, see you in an hour. Bye."

When Mark entered Alexis's fashionable and elegantly decorated condo that hugged the lake shore he detected the goodness of the dinner that she was preparing. He kidded himself by trying to differentiate the distinction between the smell of her good cooking or the aroma from her perfume that attracted him. It was of course, always her. She was the real thing to him. It had been that way ever since their first casual meeting, three years ago. He'd been in love with her, really in love for the first time in his life with anything except his then budding but busted career with the DEA. She was the only woman that could make him squirm and sizzle at the same time. He brooded when she wasn't around and walked on air when they were together. She was the obsession he indulged in except his back country adventuring and even there, she came first.

She unraveled her arms from around his neck. He held her around the waist.

"Now, what's this about the plane crash," he asked.

Without catching her breath, she rattled off all that she had heard on the television.

Mark listened intently. Associating his experience with what she was relating.

"My God, Mark, they had dogs chasing this person down the mountain. Supposedly, there is a lot of money involved. According to the police, he or she got away with a lot of it. They think it's a man because of the rugged terrain and they also believe the person knows the territory well. They had professional search and rescue people with trained hounds going after this person, but somehow he or she got away. Isn't it exciting." She continued, "The plane was stuffed with cocaine and over two million dollars according to the sheriff's office."

Not exactly true, Mark thought to himself. "Three million," he muttered.

"What's that honey, what did you say." She inquired.

"Oh, nothing, just thinking out loud." He said, wishing he had that other million. As of now he didn't even have the two million.

"Well, anyway, this person got away with murder. So far, that is. They're saying that some important people from the entertainment world are involved. All dead at the scene. The pilot and two others. Just imagine. They lost their lives over dope. How stupid," she went on.

"Yeah, I guess," he said. "Big money accelerates the greed in some people. Enough is not enough."

"They haven't released the names of anybody, but I'll bet they hush it up if it's someone big. What do you think?" she asked.

"Probably, just like when high profile politicians are involved. Everybody wants to know who they are, but it's just kept quiet and eventually everyone forgets about it."

Mark wanted to tell her about his last two days, but thought better for now. It would take a lot of explaining. He would let her in on the truth, soon enough.

"Well, what's for dinner, it sure smells good., and I'm starved," he said.

"No kidding," she came back. "You're always starving. Don't you keep anything in that refrigerator of yours," she snickered.

"Beer, that's what I keep in there, Oh yeah, and a chilled bottle of your favorite wine."

"You know, that liquid music you always water down with an ice cube," he chided her, and patted her on the rump. "Let's eat," reminding her of his stomach's condition.

Again, he held her around her waist and close, kissed her on the neck as they headed for the dinette set nestled in the corner of her kitchen. The view from there looked out over the lake with Pyramid Peak partially obscured behind Mt. Tallac. He wondered what might be going on at the crash site as they sat down to dine.

He hadn't eaten since early that day. It was obvious by the way he wolfed down his meal.

"Did you take anything with you today?" she asked.

"No, I had a bowl of cereal before I left. Why."

"You're eating fast," she said.

"I'm sorry. It's just that your cooking is so good. When we get," he stopped short.

"When we what," she asked.

"Guess I was thinking out loud again," he apologized.

"You didn't finish your sentence. At least you can tell me what you were thinking," she demanded anxiously.

"This is not the time Alexis. Please just forget it."

She frowned with disappointment. She knew what he was about to say. She wanted him to ask. They had hinted at the idea of marriage before, but never seriously entertained the prospect because of his lack of employment and meager military retirement income.

Now, he had the money. But he couldn't tell her. And if he did, she would probably demand that he return it. Her practical mind would come into play He knew she would reason that the money would do them no good if they had to stay on the run to avoid arrest. He knew that is exactly what she would say. It was a paradox. Illegal drug money. Who did it belong to. He knew that also. It was up to the Feds or the local authorities to decide whose money it was. And it wasn't his. Not for now. He also knew that if he were caught it would be all over between them. That would be the worst, he thought. Losing her. Frowning, he rolled that idea around in his mind. He couldn't lose her and he wasn't about to give up the money.

"Your ears are smoking Mark," she said.

"I've lost my appetite," he said after eating a little more than half of his dinner. "Guess it's because I'm so doggone tired. Can we hit the couch."

"You go in and relax, I'll clean up here and be in with you in a minute," she said.

"Thanks babe, it was great. I'm sorry I didn't finish. Maybe I can stay for breakfast."

"I'd love it," she said.

At seven o'clock in the evening all the major networks had passed the time for news. It was Hardcopy time, "that sensational grabbing garbage," he called it. He really didn't care at this stage. His aching muscles were just now giving him some relief. The couch swallowed him as he sunk deep into the plush cushions. His pain faded. His eyelids drooped and gradually shut. When Alexis entered he was asleep. She kissed him on the forehead and covered him with the afghan she kept thrown over the end of the sofa. He sighed approval. She turned on the TV, turned the sound down so not to disturb him and quietly snuggled up to his warm lifeless body.

Mark rolled to one side snuggled under the bulky warm comforter. He reached across the bed wanting to touch her silky body. He extended his arm a bit further without success. He realized that she wasn't there. Squinting, he saw the dull gray light through the crack in the drapes. At the same time recognized the yellowish ray of light emanating from the bathroom through the partially opened door. Alexis was preparing to go to work. He had overslept.

Groggy, he debated whether to go back to sleep or make a day of it. The image of the money lying between the rocks along the river brought him to full consciousness. He threw back the covers and hit the floor with both feet all in one continuous motion. He stood and nearly fell back on the bed, dizzy from the sudden drain of blood from the movement.

"That you honey?" her mellow voice asked.

"Yes, its me. How'd I get in here?", he asked not answering her directly.

"You walked in, don't you remember. Like that zombie character you sometimes imitate."

He visualized her smiling as she sat at her vanity putting on her face. The door swung wide, the yellow glow that bathed the room contrasted with the natural light as she pulled back the drapes. The stark light hit him like the flash from a camera. He squinted again and turned away from the window.

"Damn, not so fast," he begged.

"I'm sorry," she apologized.

"Mark, how did you get so cut up, your legs look like they went through a meat grinder. I couldn't help notice when I undressed you last evening."

"I must have really been out," he said.

"Well, let me put it this way. You and Rip Van Winkle have a lot in common. When you hit the couch, you went right to sleep. Finally, about eleven or so, I managed to guide you in here. When 1 slid your trousers off 1 noticed how badly your legs were cut and scratched. Did she have fun?"

"If she did, I missed it," he joked.

Alexis took a soft peach dress with a pleated bottom from the closet and raised it over her head. Wriggling, she pulled it down snugly around her hips. Her lustrous auburn hair bounced randomly as it cascaded across her shoulders. Slipping into her heels she was the vision of something you wished for under the Christmas Tree.

"Oh, 1 got into a little brush with Chaparral yesterday. 1 left the trail briefly, taking a short cut. Before I knew it I was in some heavy stuff. Isn't the first time," he said.

"Yes," shrugging her shoulders, "I know."

"You can stick around if you want, I'm off," she said, "but 1 know you won't," she continued, "Will I see you tonight?" she asked.

"We'll see. I love you. Have a good one," he replied. Continuing, "I'll call you sometime today. Yes, I would like to see you tonight."

Standing in the doorway, she put her finger to her lips and blew him a kiss. "The coffee's on," she said as she parted.

He listened for a minute, heard her start the engine then entered the bathroom and turned on the shower. He mentally mapped out the events for the day as the hot water soothed his muscles but stabbed at the lacerations on his legs. He hopped around under the water until the stinging subsided.

Wanting to give the authorities enough time to clean up their act on the highway, Mark lounged around the town house for three hours, mostly listening and watching the news. Skimpy reports were being broadcast from time to time regarding the incident on the mountain. Especially lacking was any report on the identities of the deceased. He did not think that so strange because whoever was involved must have been pretty important for the media to clam up about who they were.

For sure, he thought, something was being held from the public. He would have liked more information. It would help with his future plans. But, he was in no position to control the situation at this point. He would have to accept things as they were and as they came to him, especially accepting the risk involved.

Finally he dressed and clamored down the stairs to his heap. The air had a crackling sting to it, biting through the light windbreaker he thought would be enough to hold off the cold. The weather channel predicted a cold morning, but damn, fifteen degrees. It was too early in the Fall for this. He cursed the chill seeing his breath blow plumes of steam ahead of him.

The Plymouth turned over on the first try. He patted the icy steering wheel that endured the overnight freeze. Mark nodded his approval and checked the gauges. He wasn't going very far without petrol. The adventure today would require a bit more than he was used to putting in. Pulling into the first discount station on the boulevard he reflected on his near empty wallet. Ten bucks ought to do it he murmured to himself, that is, if he had that much on him. He'd have to dip into his mad five dollar bill. The one he kept out of sight and mind behind his drivers license. He laughed out loud comparing his present financial condition with what lie hidden in two briefcases down in the canyon. "Never more," he whispered.

After checking his wallet, he pumped in ten gallons and was satisfied that that would be enough to accomplish his goal. Traffic was moderate with the noon time lunch crowd. He eased along with the others and headed west up the mountain over Echo Summit, then down the American River Canyon to the picnic area where his prize awaited.

His anxiety was relieved when he discovered that the police blockades had been lifted. His patience ebbed with what seemed to be an endless strip of asphalt to his destination. He had driven a good distance when he began to doubt just where he was on the highway. Had he gone too far, he wondered. Did he inadvertently pass the entrance to China Flat picnic area. He was tempted to turn around to make sure. He was about to pull over when he recognized the familiar turnoff ahead. This section of the highway had always confused him, even though he had driven it many times.

There was again no activity in the picnic grounds. An eerie absence of life. It was ghostly. He nosed the car into the same slot he chose yesterday and came to a stop. He sat for a time examining the surroundings. It appeared safe to continue with the recovery. The river was trickling. The hot summer had sucked all the moisture from above leaving little for the stream bed to bathe in. Somehow the river looked different than it did yesterday. Was the river really a mile wide? No, it was his imagination. The more he looked around the more it confused him. Where were the rocks that hid the treasure? Baffled by the difference in the position of the sun he stood motionless at the edge of the water looking in every direction in order to determine his position in relation to where the briefcases lay. He wanted to scream, where are the rocks? Were they up the hill farther? No, they were down the hill, closer to the steam. Could it be that he was at the wrong place. His imagination ran a muck. Wild, like the river in spring. He was in the first stage of panic. He shivered. The money that was his, now, suddenly was not.

He turned one hundred and eighty degrees looking back up toward the parking lot thinking he saw someone. There was no one in sight.

Where was the money? He desperately wanted to get to it and leave the area. He listened to cars passing on the road above. The sounds disappeared into the distance, interrupted by the approach of another. Was it the police, still searching? The aspect frightened him. "Where's the damn money," he said out loud. He crossed the stream and climbed up the hillside in one direction then the other. He continued up the steep incline to a rocky outcrop, but that was not the spot. Back down to the rivers edge. Breathing hard, gasping, he stopped to orient himself. He knew he was in the right place. He couldn't mistake it. He looked back across the river. His car was in the same place as yesterday. He was sure. Looking down at the stream he recognized the stones he'd used to cross the stream the day before. Turning from the river he looked up the hillside again. He knew this was right. The confusion began to evaporate when he realized that he was here late yesterday. It was earlier this day. The sun had completely transformed any familiarity from that time until now.

Slowly and deliberately he ran his eyes across the rise in front of him. About twenty yards away, behind a clump of California Holly, he spotted the rock outcrop. He had overlooked the Holly yesterday. As he climbed, he chided himself for his lack of recognition. He reached the hiding place and rapidly uncovered the cases. He sighed, acknowledging that this was the last segment of an adventure that commenced three days before.

Balancing like a high wire artist, he worked his way across the river on the unstable stones. He climbed the short grade to his car. Upon reaching his vehicle he placed the cases on the back floor.

Safely arriving back at the condo, sitting in the garage for a minute in silence, he felt a sense of invincibility and power again. A puffing of the ego, if you will. He was elated, even to the point of laughing out loud in the privacy of his own company. It dawned on him what he had gotten away with, so far. He rested his head on the back of the front seat staring at the ragged, water stained headliner. Not for long would he have to endure this bony existence.

He rushed up the outside staircase to his condo. He immediately went to the hall closet, rummaged for an old blue navy wool blanket he kept for nostalgia, never imagining he would now use it for the purpose he had in mind. He folded it carefully in a neat square, tucked it under his arm and returned to the Plymouth.

Spreading the blanket across the back seat he busied himself in wrapping both briefcases.

It made a clumsy package partially exposing portions of the cases. The back seat was too small to do the job right. He placed the blanket on the ground, beside the vehicle, bringing the cases out of the car and re-wrapped them.

"What you got there, Mark." A voice rang out from the balcony above.

It was Mark's neighbor, Yates, who always seemed to be in the wrong place at the wrong time. This was one of them. Stymied for a second, Mark was bereft for an answer.

He hesitated, then said, "A gift for Alexis. It came apart and I didn't want to scatter it all over the lot."

"What is it," Yates asked.

"A puzzle," Mark answered aloud. "Son of a bitch," Mark whispered. "Get out of here." Mark disliked the man and took every opportunity to shun him.

Yates was a pasty faced, skinny, bespectacled nerd. That's how Mark described him to Alexis. Had his nose into everybody's business most of the time. Didn't have a job and was always touting the "Big Inheritance" he was about to come into, but no one ever witnessed its happening.

"A puzzle, what the heck kind of puzzle could be that big?" Yates inquired.

"Look, it's a surprise for her and I don't want anyone to know about it. Is that OK with you," Mark put him off.

"Need any help?" Yates offered.

"No thanks," Mark said as he closed the back door and leaned over to pick up the bulky bundle.

"Let me get your door for you then," he insisted.

"It's open," Mark snapped. He was getting irritated.

"No, it's not," he persisted.

"Check it then, see for yourself," Mark said as he climbed the stairs cradling the package in front of him. He tripped, catching his toe on one of the steps and nearly fell forward.

"Look Jim, just let me get this thing inside."

"Can 1 see it?" he asked, "I can't imagine a puzzle being that large. What kind is it?" continuing to pursue.

"Not right now," Mark said as he entered the room kicking the door behind him with his heel, slamming it, leaving Yates's nose two inches from its exterior.

Mark went straight to the bedroom, gently laying the blanketed cases down on the bed as if a child was cuddled inside. He returned to the living room and peeked sideways through the window to make sure Yates had gone. Then he rushed back to the bedroom. He pulled the drapes together and turned on the night stand lamp. The soft yellow light bathed the room. For the first time since he entered the aircraft and spotted the briefcases was he able to comfortably play his eyes on the hoard and bask in the fantasy.

He sat on the edge of the bed, opened one case and ran his hands through the packets, imagining how much it amounted to. He gathered up several bundles and threw them into the air. They fell haphazardly across the bed and onto the floor. He stood at the foot of the bed and raised his arms above his head in a display of triumph. All of his desires were within reach.

He dwelled in the euphoria for a long time, it seemed, playing mind games with himself, getting the most out of it. He walked in and out of the room five or more times, he lost count, staring at the dough, sometimes snickering at the idea of what was lying about and what he had succeeded in doing. He remembered what a friend had said that kind of money represented. "Screw You Money". He liked that.

It was approaching five o'clock. Time to call Alexis. The thought of her and how he would divulge his secret brought the specter of cold stark reality into focus. What have I done? He wasn't free. Not free to do just anything he wanted. Not yet. He was a wanted person. He would be at the center of a massive manhunt. The money belonged to others. It wasn't his. How would he tell Alexis? How could he suppress his immediate desires to spend the money before the heat was off? If it ever would be. For now, he was going to enjoy his bounty and indulge in the daydreaming.

Mark gathered the unbroken packets and loose bills and placed them into the cases and slipped both under the bed. He realized that his body needed a cleansing. Feeling sweaty, grimy he headed for his second shower of the day.

After refreshing and before calling Alexis, he turned on the television for the five thirty news. To his surprise, the top story was about the disaster in the Sierra Nevada. The anchor referred to a reporter on the scene, who was standing in front of the wreckage talking with the local sheriff.

"Yesterday," he began, "we reported the crash of a small unidentified aircraft here above Lake Tahoe. What makes this occurrence significant is that it involves two or more prominent individuals from the entertainment industry and their pilot. Their names will not be released until the next of kin have been notified." He continued. "A substantial cache of cocaine was found on the craft, intact. A large sum of money that was supposed to be on the airplane, is missing. According to our sources approximately three million dollars. How we know this is that a portion of the money was government funds being used by the FBI in a sting operation. They are concerned as to its whereabouts. The local sheriff's search and rescue team have picked up a set of footprints leading away from the crash site. It appears that either one of the passengers survived and made off with the money, or that by coincidence, someone happened upon the disaster before the sheriff's people arrived. In any event we have three confirmed fatalities and possibly a fugitive on the run with a lot of ill gotten money. More later."

Mark flushed. "Jesus Christ," he muttered.

Distracted by the commentary and not paying attention to the continuing report by the sheriff, Mark vaguely overheard something about not being able to disclose any further information until confirmed and cleared by the Federal Bureau of Investigation.

Mark turned and went for the bedroom. He could barely discern what the sheriff was saying about the details of the wreckage. Something about the rugged terrain, the kind of plane involved and other superfluous chatter.

He immediately began examining samples of the currency from each case but could not determine if the money he possessed was marked. Here he had all this dough and now it was practically worthless. If he became impatient, careless and started squandering any of the money, which he was seriously tempted to do, it would leave a paper trail wide enough to drive a semi through. All of his efforts for naught, he cringed.

Maybe, just maybe, the briefcase he left behind contained the marked bills. But the reporter did not say a thing about the authorities finding that case. Maybe too, they were hushing that up. That would make sense, he thought. If the thief refused to think of himself as a thief, but more as an opportunist, thought that the money he possessed was marked, he would not spend it so quickly, or at least, hold off spending it. That would give the feds time to track the culprit and recover all their money. They were buying time he said to himself.

Yes, that was it, Mark amused himself. They did not mention the third briefcase he left behind for that reason. And he was sure they had found it. But, he was not positive. Not at all. He was speculating. He continued examining the hundred dollar bills, holding them up to the ceiling light, looking for any unusual markings. He knew altered bills. He and his DEA associates had used it many times in the past. But the feds had their ways. Maybe they changed their methods of branding the bills.

Mark was determined. He spent the next hour and a half examining the bills randomly from each packet. He could not distinguish any unusual effects. The threads were intact. The ink was not smeared or distorted. All the numerals and letters were consistent. The presidents picture was not winking at him. He was beginning to think that his theory about them keeping quiet about the third briefcase was right. But since the third case was missing from the craft, the feds knew that the perpetrator would know about it and would conclude that the branded money was in it. Would it make any difference?, he thought. The only thing he had to worry about was whether he left any fingerprints on the case. He was positive he had wiped it clean and rubbed dirt over the entire surface before he laid it to rest.

CHAPTER 5

On the mountain, at the crash site, Sam Weston, investigating the circumstances of the tragedy, was the embodiment of the consummate detective. This was his fifteenth year on the force. Sam, at one time or another had been involved in the solution or part of the solution of every major crime that ever been committed at Lake Tahoe. His reputation of deduction had won him accolades and honors befitting any super sleuth. He had been offered positions in cities far more populated and notorious than South Lake Tahoe. Not that this town didn't have it's share of bizarre crimes and numerous ones. And not that those in charge were not capable of handling them. They certainly were and did solve many of the infamous occurrences that occurs in a popular gambling and tourist haven. But, Sam's abilities were sought after because his techniques were unique. He was dogged on a case. Putting more effort into the foray than almost anyone else. To sum it up, he was a fast paced, quick thinking problem solver. From a glance, Sam could tell you what kind of car you drove, what color it was likely to be, if you owned or rented your residence, educated or not, if you were married or single, what brand of cloths you were likely to buy, and what you had for lunch. Yes, he was good. His superiors loved it.

His shortcoming was that he loathed paperwork and the fear of being put behind a desk and in charge of others. He refused promotions. He was obsessed with the criminal mind and the challenges it presented. He worked alone. Sam was well aware that he'd reached his level of competency as a detective and wanted to go no further. He was very satisfied with his position.

Sam was in his early forties, muscular, a ruddy complexion, deep set penetrating green eyes, spaced evenly above a well proportioned nose and below that a heavy dark neatly trimmed mustache. His square chin dimpled in the center gave him the air of a rugged individual. He had many admirers, but none that stole his heart. He was single. Whenever he was questioned about that particular status he would shrug it off with aplomb, saying that when "she" came along she would know it. He wasn't the nattiest dresser preferring casuals to a suit. When he wasn't driving an official vehicle, he got around in a dented, dinged up cadaver that needed a paint job.

It was about three in the afternoon. He had spent the greater portion of the day going over every piece of evidence he could lay his hands and eyes on. He had come to the conclusion that the aircraft had experienced a violent explosion while in the air. He was not sure whether the explosion was from some internal malfunction or whether a bomb had been planted on the craft. But he had his suspicions that it was an intentional attempt to down the craft with the idea of killing all those aboard.

For one thing the trauma to the airplane appeared to occur in the aft section of the fuselage. Not an area where an explosion would normally happen. He found bits and pieces of metal that could have been a timing device. But nothing was conclusive. He knew he would have to cooperate with the feds. The NTSB, the DEA and the FBI. Which, to him, was interference. The late afternoon turned frigid, so he decided to get off the mountain and return to his office. Besides, the aircraft was to be brought down to the Tahoe airport and reassembled, piece by piece. He decided to complete the task there.

At the station he was called into Captain Dickson's office, his commander. A hard nosed individual that demanded, what Sam referred to as, the ultimate sacrifice, from his people.

"What's it look like up there Sam."

"A mess," Sam answered.

"Got any ideas," Dickson asked.

"A couple captain. For one, I think we've got a homicide on our hands."

"How's that."

"I think it was blown out of the sky. The plane was splintered before it hit the ground."

"What makes you think so," he asked.

"Well, there are burn marks where the fuselage split apart and the frame shows signs of fragmentation with the metal bent outward from the center. It looks like a classic bomb explosion."

"When do you think you'll know anything for sure. The feds are arriving. Including the NTSB, FBI, DEA and the ATF. We are going to be engulfed." Dickson said.

Here comes that ultimate sacrifice stuff, Sam thought.

"Well sir, as soon as they get the remains down here and reassemble it. There's not much we can do up there on the mountain." Sam replied. "I've sifted through everything. We know there was some money involved, lots of money from what I gather. The sheriffs people chased somebody down the mountain with their dogs and ran across a briefcase, loaded. On down further the tracks led to a vehicle. They're trying to put a make on it. When we get the plane put back together we'll dust it again to see if we can identify anyone. Right now I'll work with the Sheriff and also a few other things until then. By the way, what's with the feds?"

"Like I said Sam, I'm anxious because the FBI are involved due to a sting operation in this situation. They've inquired as to our progress. They are always difficult to work with and I want them off our backs before they step in and confuse the situation. This is in our jurisdiction and by damn I want the credit for the conclusion. Understand?"

"Yes sir, I'm thinking the same. I'll do all I can to get in the cracks before they do. I've already got some ideas. I just have to look into them more carefully."

"Listen, I'm going to put you down in the basement for this. Keep it out of sight. Take the office at the end of the hallway. Set it up with what you need and keep it to yourself except whoever you choose for your gopher. I want a briefing everyday before four in the afternoon on your progress. I'll keep you informed as to what the FBI is up to. If needed. Let me repeat Sam. This is going to be a back breaker. There's some real stinking implications going on. We're going to be under the microscope from the commissioners office. They are going to want results, so I don't think I have to pound on you about that."

"Yes sir," Sam replied. "I know what you're saying. Let me get started. I'll put some time in today getting organized."

"Oh, by the way," Dickson said as Sam started out the door, "this things got a code name," "Gold Mine."

"Gold Mine, ha, that's a good one," Sam retorted "Gold Mine it is then." Sam shut the door behind him and headed for the basement to look over his office in the "Dungeon," as it was called.

Walking toward the stairway leading down to the basement Sam noticed Officer Ron Blamebridge talking to an individual in a three piece suit. No doubt it's an agent Sam thought.

"Hi Ron, can I see you when you get a minute, I've got a favor to ask you," Sam said.

"Sure Sam, but first let me introduce you to Phil, our contact with the FBI." He continued. "Phil is on Gold Mine."

"How did you find out so fast." Sam inquired.

"Phil let me in on the skinny." Ron said matter of fact.

Sam took Phil's hand, "Nice meeting you."

"Same here Sam, I guess we'll be working cooperatively on the case."

Sam grimaced, inwardly.

"Yes I just heard that you fellows would be involved. Am ready to help in whatever way you need." Sam said.

"Have you been to the sight?" Sam asked.

"Yeah, and I didn't come up with much. We're waiting on the NTSB. Their boys are going to bring it down in pieces and reassemble it at the airport."

"Got any idea when?" Sam asked.

"It'll take them a couple of days, it's rough up there. Til then we'll have to cool our heels. Maybe we'll get a make on the vehicle before then. We can work on that. Pretty cut and dried regarding the people and the crash. Was a typical drug operation. We'll put some substance on the parties involved. What we want is that money. I guess you know we were involved in planting the money on the craft."

"No, I didn't know that, Thanks." Sam offered. "I've got some work to do right now. I would like to get together with you day after tomorrow to go over some items. How about eight am then." Sam asked.

"Fine with me," Phil responded. "Say eight o'clock, here."

"See you then," Sam said.

Ron Blamebridge was a good officer. Young, eager, aggressive. Fresh out of the academy. He was anxious to please Sam.

"Ron, come on, we've got work to do. I've just volunteered you to assist me on this thing. Dickinson recommended you." Sam lied.

"But ..."

"But nothing," Sam said, "I've got the OK."

"But, I'm right in the middle of something." Ron said.

"Yeah, and so am I. Let's get downstairs and get organized."

On the way down the thirteen or fourteen steps Sam explained the situation to Ron and swore him to secrecy as to his role and their lair.

"But, Sam," he continued.

Sam just kept ignoring Rons's pleading while taking two step at a time going down.

The hallway at the bottom of the stairs seemed to extend into a pitch black abyss. The only thing that illuminated the passage was a 25 watt bulb at the bottom of the stairs.

"Christ, it's dark down here," Ron said.

"Austerity my man, austerity." Sam replied.

Several closed windowless doors, evenly spaced, each with a label, "Records A through F," lined the hallway. Nothing had gone on down here for a long time.

"Ever been in solitary," Sam Asked.

Ron followed quietly nipping at Sam's heels. "We get the one at the end. I think its got a desk and a typewriter."

Ron didn't respond to Sam's sarcastic humor about solitary.

Reaching the office at the end of the darkened hall, Sam turned the knob. The door was stuck. He put his shoulder to the wooden frame and pushed. The door sprung open with a groan and a high pitched squeal. "Hinges need oil," Sam grunted. A stale musty odor rushed to greet them.

"Whew," Ron uttered.

"Get the light," Sam asked. "It's right there beside you on the wall."

Ron fumbled in the dark, running his hand along the cold face of the interior. "Can't find the damn switch Sam."

"Here, I got it" Sam said. "Aint it great to be familiar with the crypt," Sam uttered, reaching across Ron's shoulder. "It's a gift Ron, not everyone's got it."

Two overhead fluorescent fixtures flickered then glared on, bathing the starkly furnished room with a ghostly luminescence.

The room was small, nine by twelve at the most and his recollection was right. One desk, one well used manual Royal typewriter, an ebony dial telephone and one arm-less cane back swivel chair.

"We'll make do Ron," Sam said looking at Ron who had already taken possession of the chair.

"Pretty cool Sam, I didn't know such a thing existed," Ron quipped twisting semi circle in the unforgiving seat.

"The first thing I want you to do is contact Deputy Parch over at the sheriff's office. They had a dog team chasing someone down the mountain yesterday. Get all the info, and I mean everything they know. And, by the way, get another desk and a new phone in here this afternoon. The phone jack is over there," Sam said pointing to the corner baseboard. "I'll be in Reno, at the airport first thing in the morning."

"Why, you leaving town?" Ron asked.

"No, the pilots log indicated that that is where the flight originated. The plane was registered to a charter outfit. I'll call you from there to find out what you got from Parch. He should have an earful. Just to let you know, the sheriffs people did a good job. They've got foot and tire prints but no fingers, yet. Shoe size indicates it's a male. Probably so unless we got some healthy broad with a heavy leg. We're assuming it's a guy at this point. Shouldn't be too difficult to get a handle on this."

Sam continued, "Whoever it is has a lot of bucks on them. It'll be hard for them to hold onto the dough before they start spending it. Contact all the car dealers, jewelry stores, fur shops, department stores and Realtors to be looking out for large purchases with cash. Yeah and the casinos. They know who their high rollers are. Anybody new with big bucks, we want to know about."

"It looks like this guy spends a lot of time in the woods, the high country, else he wouldn't have been able to get out as fast as he did. He's probably into quality backpacking gear. Check with the sporting goods stores for anybody outfitting themselves. Like I said, I figure he will lay low for about a week or two. When the media cools down, temptation will get the best of him and he'll start spending."

"What about travel agents, boat dealers Sam," Ron asked.

"Good, good, put anybody on your list. If we can solve this thing fast, it'll put a feather in our caps and you'll probably get a promotion, eh, you like that," Sam teased.

"A couple more bucks in my jeans wouldn't hurt." Ron quipped.

"O.K., then, let's get hopping." Sam looked Ron straight in the eyes. "Listen, Ron, if you think you'll need any help on this, let me know and I'll get all you need."

"No sir, I can handle it," Ron said assuredly, throwing his shoulders back.

"I'm serious." Sam said. 'We want to put this one in the box as fast as we can."

Ron closed the door behind him. Sam sat there for a minute thinking about his next move.

As Ron Blamebridge approached his desk on the floor above, Captain Dickson stepped out of his office.

"Blamebridge," the Captains voice always demanded attention. "I saw you talking to Weston. You working with him on the Gold Mine thing, right?"

"Yes Sir."

"I want you to give him all you got, you hear."

"Yes sir," he heard himself repeat. Here comes the ultimate sacrifice speech, he thought.

"Good man, 1 know you will."

Ron waited. The captain continued on down the aisle through the ten or so desks that dotted the office.

"Whew," Ron whispered softly, out of earshot of the boss.

He had escaped the usual ten or so minutes the speech always took on loyalty and dedication to the cause. He didn't need it this time. He was primed and eager to help Sam.

"Banks," Ron said to himself. "Sam didn't mention banks. Got to put them on my list."

"Talking to yourself again Ron." Came a voice from across the room.

Ron sat quietly working with his yellow legal pad listing those he planned on contacting leaving space for any entries he would think of later. Then he called Bill Parch at the Sheriff's office and introduced himself. Deputy Parch had an accommodating and receptive attitude over the phone and Ron liked him immediately. He requested a meeting for the next morning and Parch agreed. The sheriff's office had a stake in this case and wanted to solve it just as badly as the police department.

Ron checked the "Regulator" clock on the wall. There was still time to make one visit from the names on his list.

Blamebridge entered Borg Neillsons's Merecedes Benz dealership and five pairs of eyes greeted him. In plain clothes he looked like just another customer.

"Hi fellas, I'm here to see the boss, is he in?"

"Yeah," he's upstairs," one of the salesmen said, looking away disappointed. "In his office."

"Thanks," he replied. Ron was familiar with Neillson's office. Located on the second floor behind a huge one-way mirror that allowed Borg to oversee his empire in privacy. From that vantage point he could overview his entire inventory and the dealings of all the sales people down on the showroom floor.

Ron climbed the stairs to the private office greeting Neillson's blond, blue-eyed knockout Danish daughter carrying a bundle of papers nestled against her large breasts.

"Hello," she cooed. "Can I help you."

"I'm Ron Blamebridge, Police, here to see, I think, your dad," pretending he didn't know. He knew from the many photos in the local newspaper.

"Is he in trouble?" she asked. A concerned frown wrinkled her unlined brow, temporarily ruining her image.

"Naw, just routine police business. We like him," Ron said, kidding.

"O.K., you can go up, please knock first."

"Sure, I'll do that, softly." He was thinking of her.

The door was ajar. Borg overheard the conversation that took place on the stairway.

"Come on in," his voice resonated off the bare walls.

Sitting behind a dark mahogany desk in a plush brown leather high back chair sat this imposing figure of a man. Borg Neillson grinned broadly from behind a deeply lined leather face. He appeared to be one with the chair. His eyes sparkled when he spoke.

With a head crowned full of white wavy hair, Ron wondered if this could be the real Santa Claus.

Ron introduced himself and identified his reason for being here, at this time in history.

"Oh, for christs sake, I thought you were from the bank and was here to determine how far behind I was on the flooring." He roared a bellowing laughter. Ron thought surely he had been Santa Claus at one time or another.

"You have heard about the plane crash," he said.

"Hell yes, who hasn't," he said.

Ron nodded, "Well, it seems there was a lot of money on board. It is missing."

"What the hell, you think I got it," Borg responded, laughing boisterously. "I'd have to have a mule train just to get up there" He laughed again. Ron went along with a smile.

"How much did they get?" Borg asked.

"We're not sure, yet, but in the neighborhood of two to three million," Ron answered.

"Two million, two goddamned million," he repeated "Christ, that would handle my flooring," Borg retorted.

"Well sir, we want your people to be on the lookout for anybody making large purchases with cash." Ron was still trying to figure out what flooring was.

"What's flooring sir?"

"That's what I owe on all that iron down there," he answered.

"Oh, Ron muttered, You mean the cars?" he asked.

"That's what I mean, son. The goddamned inventory."

"Can you let your people know?" Ron asked.

"Yes sir, I sure as hell will. Tomorrow's Friday. I'll bring it up at the sales meeting."

"That's all I have, Ron said, If you have any questions, here's my card. Give me a call if you suspicion anything."

Ron started out the door when he turned and said. "We don't have anything substantial on the suspects at this time. We're waiting for some things to come back from the lab."

"When we do, we'll supply you with descriptions. We'd like for you to pass that information around also. Will that be all right?"

"Sure, sure, you let me know what you guys need, and we'll comply. By the way, when you need a car, come see me." Borg was always in his selling suit.

"I don't think I could afford it," Ron said.

"We'll finance it son," Borg replied, still selling.

Next morning while Ron was making his rounds checking off the businesses on his list, Sam was arriving at the airport administration office with the registration numbers from the aircraft's wing.

Inside, Sam bellied up to a wooden counter that prevented any further progress. Uninhabited metal desks arranged haphazardly, silently greeted him. Must be on break, he said to himself. He was not a patient man. He reached across a metal file basket and tapped the service bell that beckoned anyone absent from their post.

A plump middle aged woman, wearing what looked like something she'd slept in, approached from an ante office. Peering over her Ben Franklin glasses, looking as if she had been disturbed and didn't care to be, asked if she could help.

Sam identified himself orally at the same time flashed his badge, which got her immediate attention. She dropped the bundle of papers she was carrying on the desk beside her. Plop, she turned to see if they had landed safely.

"Yes officer, how can I help you?"

"Point me in the right direction," he said, handing her the registration numbers.

"Just a minute, I'll have to check."

She disappeared into the office she had just exited.

Sam killed time by studying the aerial photo of the airport, a blow-up glossy the size of the wall. He was fascinated by some of the aircraft depicted in paintings scattered around. Especially the P-51 Mustang in an apparent aggressive wartime posture, firing it's weapon. When she reappeared, her ashen face, indicated to Sam that she had discovered which aircraft Sam was inquiring about.

"Isn't it a shame," she said, as if Sam would agree with her.

Sam knew what she meant, but went along as if he didn't.

"Shame about what?" Sam didn't like her or the perfume she bathed in.

"About Mr. Hancock," She said.

The name didn't mean a thing to Sam until he asked.

"Who's Hancock?" he asked, knowing she would come clean.

"Bruce Hancock, the pilot," she divulged voluntarily. "He was such a nice man, we all loved him. He was so funny and jovial. Always had a nice word. Outgoing. He was just getting his charter service off the ground when this awful thing happened. His wife is just devastated by it all."

"His wife, Sam asked. What's her name?"

"Rosanna," she said. Sam was taking notes.

"How long had he been here at the airport, with his charter business?" Sam asked.

"Oh, I'd say about a year. He just bought a new Cessna. He was so proud of it. He told her that one day he would own the airport, laughing about it. We were all for him. We thought that if anybody deserved success, he surely was that person."

"Uh huh," Sam nodded in an affirmative manner.

Her mouth was running faster than Sam could muster up the questions. He had a real chatter box by the tail and wanted to keep her talking. He figured he could get as much information as possible before talking to anyone directly associated with the charter business. If he could put up with her odor.

"Did he have anybody working for him, like a mechanic, office people?" Sam asked.

"Well, Rosanna runs, or rather ran the office. I just don't know if there will still be a business over there," pointing across the airport to a group of hangars. "He also had, yes, a mechanic. His name, I think is Bill Crenshaw, or something, like that."

"Do you know if there's anyone around now?"

"Rosanna hasn't been there since the accident. But I did see Bill this morning. I think he's trying to wind things up. He is in kind of a quandary, you know, a dilemma."

"Yeah, I can understand," Sam said.

"What's his name again?" Sam asked.

"Bill Crenshaw, he's a talkative one," she warned.

"Listen, thanks for your help. Oh, I forgot, where are they located?"

"Across the field, in hangar ten. You'll have to drive around the airport to get over there. Here, I'll show you." She led Sam around the counter to a window that had an uninterrupted view of the area.

"See, over there, those facilities are for the small operators."

Sam could see fifteen or so low buildings lined neatly on the far side of the airport. Each building had a large number painted above the hangar door. He spotted number ten and pointed to it to let her know he was tuned into the location.

"Thanks again," he said, excusing himself.

It took Sam two attempts to reach the area. The road leading around intersected and split into "Y's" several times without signage, leaving him to guess which road to take.

He pulled in back of the hangar in a parking space identified as Bruce's personal slot. He took it.

"You can't park there," a voice from just inside the gaping entry said. "That's the owners space."

"Pardon me," Sam said, sarcastically, exiting his vehicle, ignoring the order to not park in that location.

"Is the owner around?" he asked as if he didn't know.

Sam was sure he was talking to the mechanic. He caught a glimpse of the individual that warned him. A faint image of a very tall, lean individual. A man attired in light blue grease spotted overalls, who disappeared behind a stand of metal lockers.

Sam stood in the hangars double doorway, looked around for the mystery voice. There was no one in sight.

"Hello." He got no response. "Hello," he said louder and more authoritatively.

"What do you want?" Came the response from behind the lockers.

"I'm Sam Weston, police. I'd like to ask you a couple of questions.

"The police have already been here," he shot back. "I gave them all the information I know."

Sam knew it must have been the feds.

"The FBI?" Sam asked.

"Yeah, the FBI and somebody from the Drug Enforcement Agency or something like that."

Sam was still talking to the face of the metal lockers.

"You mind coming out here so I can see you?" Sam asked. "These lockers got no personality," Sam continued.

"Just a minute, I'm washing up."

"When were the FBI and the DEA here,?" he asked staring at the names on the lockers.

"Yesterday, all day yesterday. I didn't get a damned thing done. Got a lot to do shutting this place down. And I gotta look for work now that this business aint here no more," he said as he came around from behind the lockers wiping his hands with a blue rag.

Sam was disappointed. He wanted to get there before anyone. Why, he wasn't sure.

Bill Crenshaw was a wiry looking fellow. Tall, thin, sunken cheeks with deep set dark eyes. He looked like he worked hard in a tough business. His overalls were smudged with oil and grease that many washings over a long period of time couldn't erase.

Sam extended his hand. The mechanic responded with a firm grip.

"I'm Bill Crenshaw. 1 am, er, was Bruce's mechanic. Helluva nice guy he was."

He continued, "Listen, 1 aint got all day to talk to you. Yesterday was a waste. Unless you're paying me 1 gotta finish up here and look for work like 1 said."

"1 understand," Sam said. "What if I buy you dinner. Could we talk then?"

Bill looked at Sam with a puzzled expression. Nobody had bought him dinner in a long time. The feds sure as hell didn't offer, he thought, not even Bruce in the full year he had worked there.

"Yeah, you can do that. That'll work for me."

"You name it," Sam said. "A nice place. Maybe downtown at one of the casinos."

"Naw, I know a great place off the beaten path, except for the truckers. They got the best rib eye steak in all Nevada, Steve's," Bill said, "Near here, Off 395,"

Sam knew about Steve's. "About six then, that OK with you," Sam wasn't sure that he was letting the bird in the hand get away.

"I'll meet you there," Bill said, enthusiastically, smiling.

Sam had the impression that this guy didn't get out much. From Bill's response, Sam thought that it was almost as if Bill was dating someone. Sam wasn't worried about this bird.

"You mind if I nose around while you work?" Sam asked.

"No, he said, shrugging his shoulders, aint much here to see, now that the planes gone. Damn, she sure was a beauty. We just got her you know. Slick, easy to work on, not that there was much to do. Cause she was brand new. 1 just kept her clean. She purred like a kitten warming up for flight. I'd watch Bruce take her down the runway. She glided like liquid music. She had a low silhouette. When she became airborne, she looked like a graceful swan taking flight. 1 got goose bumps just watching her."

Sam nodded, feeling the emotion. "I can imagine, Bill," he said.

"Well, 1 guess I'll see you at six then."

Bill was right. There wasn't much to see. The typical hangar. Tools, benches, an A frame, just the ordinary stuff. One wall with shelves holding spare parts, a fifty five gallon drum, empty, except for oily rags. Everything in its place, clean, orderly. Even the floor shined like a mirror, throwing a reflection from the sealant. Sam could never figure out why mechanics with the greasiest and dirties attire always had the cleanest workplaces. Those that worked in offices', that looked like they just stepped out of the shower often worked in pig sties.

Sam checked in with the watch commander at the lake. Then he asked for Ron Blamebridge.

Ron, he found out was in the field informing local business establishments about looking out for individuals making large purchases with cash, just like he was supposed to be doing.

Atta boy, he said to himself.

"I'll be in touch sometime this afternoon. Until then, you'll have to get me on the radio." He hung up.

Sam spent the next three hours visiting other charter outfits at the airport. The same information came forth from all those he encountered. Bruce

Hancock was a good pilot. Kept clean and busy. Nothing out of the ordinary.

Sam hadn't been in a casino, even the ones at the lake, for over a year. He hadn't been in Reno for the same amount of time. The casino scene to him was as foreign as the local movie theaters. Sam was a loner, who spent most of his time on the job, or at home.

He had few hobbies and no companionship with the ladies. Not that he wouldn't like the company of a beautiful woman once in a while, he just never made the attempt.

He spent the last hours before meeting Crenshaw whiling the time away reacquainting himself with the Biggest Little City in the World. It still was.

At a quarter to six Sam had no problem finding a parking space at Steve's Steak Stop, as it was known. When Steve Bocchi negotiated for the property ten years ago he acquired fifteen acres. Enough to put up a truck stop with twenty rows of gas pumps all under a metal canopy, a motel, showers and parking for fifty or so big rigs. One pound Rib Eye Steaks was the specialty of the house. It was a success from the day it opened.

Sam sidled through the double doors and stood momentarily at the glass counter in the entry. Looking around he spotted a waving arm in the rear of the restaurant. Bill Crenshaw's grin spread ear to ear. He had taken up residence out of traffic, away from earshot, at least for the time being. Sam appreciated Bill's concern for privacy.

Sam worked his way down a row of sparsely occupied red vinyl booths. It was early on a Monday evening. In between lunch and dinner. Bill stood to greet him, holding a cup of coffee in his left hand.

"Thanks for coming," Sam said.

"No problem, you mind if I call you Sam?" Bill asked.

"Not if I can call you by your first name." Sam smiled returning Bill's courtesy.

"You hungry?," Bill asked. "The Rib Eye here is something to behold."

"Why not," Sam returned.

"They got big doggie bags here," Bill chuckled.

Sam hardly had time to lay his leather jacket down before a waitress approached.

"What can I get for you boys?" she asked smiling.

"Coffee for me for starters and a warm up for my friend here," Sam glancing at Bill's cup.

"Nice che che's, pretty face and a lot of hip" Bill commented, raising his eyebrows as she walked away. "We used to be sweethearts. Name's Jeannette. We broke up two years ago. Now she treats me like a stranger. We had some good times. Real hot in the sack." Bill paused for a second then said, "and in other ways too. Couldn't live together though, she had her ways, I had mine. Fought too much, but damn she sure could please me with her lovin."

Sam turned, "Yeah, uh huh," he agreed.

"I always did like women in pink. How about you?" Bill commented.

"Never thought about it," Sam answered. "But, you got a point."

"I don't know where he gets em, but he sure does have a talent for good looking well built waitresses," Bill said.

"You mean, Steve?"

"Yeah, I've been coming here since this place opened and every one of them have been knockouts. They don't fool around though, most of them are married. Look for the rings."

Sam went along with the small talk, making friends and not wanting to get into any serious discussion until their food arrived. He wanted Bill to feel comfortable when it came time for meaningful questions and answers.

The steak spilled over the edge of the hot aluminum oval dish, accompanied by a pile of french fries that would feed three people. Sam was impressed.

"How long did you know Bruce?" Sam asked.

"On and off about ten years, 1 guess."

Sam cut into the steak. The juices oozed out sizzling on the hot plate. A few French fries spilled onto the table.

"How the hell you supposed to keep all this on the plate," he complained.

"Ha, you aint," Bill replied, chewing on a chunk of beef. He could hardly mouth the words.

"I remember you told me how long you had worked for Bruce, but I forgot," Sam said.

"About a year," he responded.

"Where'd you work before you started at Special Charters? And before that?" Sam asked.

'Which one you want first? Bill asked, still savoring the first bite. "Damn this is a good steak," he volunteered.

"I don't care. Start with the first one." Sam said.

"I worked around at different places. Mostly here in Reno. I was in the Air Force before that. That's where I learned my trade. Aircraft mechanic. Too much pressure in the service. So, I got out. Wish now that I'd stayed in for the full twenty. Would have a nice retirement coming in. But, when you're young, you don't think of those things. Ah, what was the other part of that question?"

"You answered both," Sam responded. "But here's another. Where did Bruce come up with that name? Special Charters."

"Oh that, well, he wanted to get the message across that he'd take on most anything. You know, thinking that if the company name were something like, say, Western Charters or Sierra Charters, it wouldn't have a zing to it. He said he wanted to catch the attention of anybody that wanted to ship something special or unusual or out of the ordinary. If they thought otherwise they might go elsewhere. Made sense to me."

"1 see. Did you know what was on board at the time of the crash?"

"Not until yesterday. The FBI and those other guys told me it was drugs, cocaine. I guess Bruce's idea of special cargo worked, huh."

"What else do you know about the lading?" Sam asked.

"There were two passengers aboard."

"Anything else you can think of?"

"Nope. That's about all, 1 guess. Let me take another bite here, OK, Sam."

"Yeah, sure."

Bill sliced off another thick slab of steak and opened wide. His eyes shone with delight.

Sam's food was getting cold. His interest had been diverted. Bill noticed.

Jeannette came by with the coffee pot. "You boys need anything?" She asked.

Bill didn't respond. Sam held up his cup. Jeanette responded then walked away. Both watched her movement.

"Did you know about the cargo before departure?" Sam asked.

"You just asked me that," Bill said with a frown. "I told you that 1 learned about it from those other guys. 1 was off on the day it was loaded, Saturday. When 1 came in Sunday, Bruce was taxiing out on the tarmac. He left me a note saying he'd be back around six that evening. I just went to work on a spare engine that he bought the week before."

"You ever know Bruce to contract for illegal contraband before?"

"No sir, Bruce was straight arrow. At least as far as I know, he only hauled people."

"These people that were on board. You know their names? Was there a list? I mean, did Bruce leave any indication who the passengers were? Or how he came in contact with them?"

'No."

"Tell me about Bruce's wife, Rosanne, isn't it?" Sam asked.

"Yeah, Rosy," Bill said.

"What part did she play in the business?"

"1 tell you the truth Sam, I think she was the power behind the whole thing. She ran the show. Strong, domineering woman. I stayed out of her way. I got into it just once with her and from that time on I tried to ignore her. All my business was with Bruce. They fought like cats and dogs. If she knew how to fly, I think she would have ran the whole show. It wouldn't surprise me if she wasn't the one that made the deal for the cocaine. She kept the records and the check book. I didn't like her like I said. She was always jumpin my back about something. Once, I threatened to quit, but she fired me on the spot. Bruce stepped in and told her to back off. Then they went into the office and screamed at each other. It was a helluva match. Went on for ten minutes or so. Finally, he came out and winked at me and told me to forget it. I think the only reason they stayed together is because they needed each other to keep the business running."

Sam took the opportunity during Bill's dissertation to take a bite of beef

"You are right Bill, this is a damn good steak."

Bill started to cut into the steak when he stopped and laid down his utensils. His face grew pale.

Sam noticed. "What's the matter, Bill?"

Bill was fixed on somebody that had just walked through the door.

"Jesus Christ, it's her," he said.

"Who?" Sam turned to see.

"Rosy. What the hell she doing here?" he continued. "I never saw her in this place before."

Sam turned around towards the door. He recognized an extraordinarily beautiful woman. Tall, blond, large breasts being held in check by a red sweater. Her gray slacks looked as if they had been shrunk, to fit around her shapely rear and thighs. She moved gracefully toward another part of the restaurant and seated herself, still visible with her back to the admiring pair.

Bill pushed his half finished plate to the side.

"Come on pal, you can't let her upset you," Sam said.

"She pisses me off. When I see her I get the heebies. Christ, Bruce isn't even in the ground yet, and she's out here on the prowl."

"I doubt that," Sam returned.

"Let's stick around and see what happens, Come on, finish you meal," Sam pleaded.

"Besides, she needs you right now," Sam continued. "You probably don't realize it, but you're her most important asset. Who else has she got to wind things down at the shop?"

Bill pulled the plate back under his chin and continued. "You're right Sam, why should I let her do that to me. But she still ticks me off. It's something about her demeanor."

"Relax, she doesn't know you are here," Sam said.

"You ever check the flight logs, Bill?"

"Sure, all the time. Got to. I have to know when maintenance has to be done. At ten thousand feet up you can't just pull over and call Triple A when you got a problem."

"Can you get your hands on the logs?"

"I could, but the federal agents have them."

"Damn," Sam muttered.

"Tell me, you ever see the two individuals that were on the flight come into the business. Ever notice the same two faces all at once or separately at different times?"

"What, Bill said, I don't understand?"

"Yes, that was a clumsy way of putting it. Let me rephrase it. Ever notice the same faces at different times?"

"No, I told you I was off on Saturday. I don't have any knowledge about who they were. And their identities haven't been released yet. But, if I had seen them, I probably wouldn't know because I don't pay any attention to who comes in. There are so many. Bruce had a lot of friends that just dropped by to visit. I kept busy in the back."

"Can I ask you a question, Sam?"

"Sure, go ahead."

"Rumor has it that there was a bomb on board. Is that true?"

Sam hesitated.

"Well, we're not sure. I can't talk about that right now."

Bill was about to ask another question, when he reached over and tapped Sam on the forearm.

"Look," he said, pointing with his eyes. He was directing Sam's attention to the area where Rosy was sitting.

A handsome, rugged looking individual was standing over Rosy talking to her. She gestured for him to join her.

"See, 1 told you. She's up to something," Bill said.

"You ever see him before?" Sam asked.

"He looks kinda familiar," Bill said.

"Yeah, he continued, 1 saw him talking to Bruce a couple of weeks ago, but I don't know his name."

Bill continued. "1 think they're arguing."

Sam turned slowly and peered over his shoulder. The stranger had an angry expression on his face and was shaking his finger in her face. Neither Sam nor Bill could hear what was being said, but by the stranger's manner they could tell that the discussion was heated. Almost as quickly as he had engaged her, he stood, and continued, as if trying to make a point with her.

"What'd he say?" Bill asked.

"I think he said, he'd be in touch."

From the window, Sam watched the stranger walk across the parking lot and enter his vehicle. Sam got only a portion of the license plate and jotted it down on his napkin. He couldn't quite make out the model of the car as it drove away. He thought it looked like a Chrysler product.

"If that guy shows up before you move on to another job, give me a call. Get his name first. And do me a favor, see if you can find out who he is, tomorrow," Sam requested.

"Just how am 1 supposed to do that?" Bill asked.

"Hell, I don't know. Use your imagination. Think of something. Use some old records as a pretense to inquire."

Rosy got up and started for the cashiers counter. Bill turned away in an obvious attempt to conceal his presence.

"Bill, do me another favor. Don't tell her that I talked to you. I want to chat with her sometime tomorrow and I don't want her to know that we've been in touch. That's important, you understand?"

"Yeah, sure. I'll keep mum,"

Rosy disappeared through the double doors without recognizing Bill's presence.

"What's her hours?" Sam asked.

"She usually comes in around eight."

"OK, I'll be there sometime after that, about nine. See if you can find out about the stranger before I get there. All right with you?" Sam asked.

"Damn Sam, I wish you could give me some idea how to go about it."

"1 just did my man, use the old logs."

Sam paid the tab and left a hefty tip. He checked into the truck stops motel. Made one phone call to Blamebridge. He was in.

"Ron, how you doin?"

"Fine sir, I've hit just about everyone on my list."

"Come up with anything?" Sam asked.

"No, but all those I contacted are aware of the situation."

"OK listen, I've got a partial license plate for you to check" Sam read it off. "It's on an older Chrysler product. I couldn't tell whether it was a Dodge or a Plymouth. An early seventies model. You know, those damn things all looked alike then."

"I wouldn't know sir, I was too young. Gimmie a color."

"Tan or light brown, I'm staying here tonight," he continued. "I want to talk to some others before I return." Sam gave Ron the telephone number. "If you get anything on the wire call me immediately."

"OK sir." They disconnected.

CHAPTER 6

At nine 0' clock, despite the fact that he was addressing a newly acquired head cold, he sauntered up to the office of Special Charters. The morning air possessed a discomforting chill. Just about what he expected from the mistress of the air charter.

Was he surprised when he entered the small room with a desk and other office paraphernalia, including one of the most beautiful women he'd ever laid his eyes on? He received a warm smile coupled with a generous handshake.

"I heard you were coming," she said.

Bill, he thought, but didn't care after seeing her up close with that sincere greeting.

"The FBI said you would be here this morning. I just got off the phone with them."

Sam silently apologized for accusing Bill.

"You're Sam Weston, aren't you?" She asked. "I've heard good things about you. I hope you can get to the bottom of this terrible thing. Bruce was such a good man. I don't know how he ever got mixed up with those horrible men and their drugs. Bruce never before did such a thing. That was our agreement when we started this business. Everything was to be within the law, not that we ever engaged in anything other than that."

Sam was wondering if she was going to catch her breath. He was enjoying watching her. Animated in a way, waving her arms around as she spoke. She seemed programmed with answers to questions Sam would have asked.

"Bruce was either forced into doing the flight, she continued, or he saw a way to get out of debt quickly with the illegal cargo. I didn't know that he had contracted for the business. If I had, he wouldn't have taken the assignment and he would still be here today."

"You're Rosanne, am I right." Sam said.

"Why yes, who did you think 1 was?"

"Well, I just wanted to make sure, we didn't formally introduce ourselves."

"Oh, I'm so sorry," she said. "I guess I just assumed that you knew who I was."

"I guessed as much. You know, we have to be sure who we're talking to," Sam said with tongue in cheek.

It went over her head.

Sam decided that this was as good a time as any to get in a couple of questions lest she get him involved in conversation that wasn't pertinent.

"Tell me, Mrs. Hancock."

"Oh please, call me Rosy, everybody else does."

"OK, ah, Rosy then, is there anybody else involved in the business, say like an investor or other silent partners?"

"No, just Bruce and I. We started this thing. We scraped together every penny we could lay our hands on. We did borrow a little, but we've made the payments every month. Not always on time, but the blood suckers got their money before the month was out."

Sam detected a little feistiness in her voice. He liked that.

"How about the aircraft, I understand that Bruce, ah, you and Bruce just bought the ship."

"Yes, it was brand new. We financed it. But it was fully insured. And we were current on the premiums. Just two months old."

"I suppose it was fully equipped. I mean, it had all the gear for all weather flight. You know what I mean?" Sam asked.

"Yes, it was very expensive. Radar, VHR. It could fly in any weather, at night, long range. It was a super airplane. Bruce was so proud of it. Everybody around here came to see it. He took several of the other charter owners and just about anybody else that wanted to go on a short flight. I flew it myself. Of course, with Bruce in the captains chair."

Sam couldn't help but notice that in all the conversation, she didn't once sound a note of sorrow about Bruce's passing. It appeared to him that his death wasn't of great importance to her. Maybe he was wrong, he thought, but it just didn't seem that she was concerned about her ex-husband. More so that the business and the airplane were gone and of greater importance. But on the other hand, maybe she was right in talking about the loss of the plane and subsequently, the business. He was there for answers, not a eulogy.

Bill Crenshaw peeked into the office window. Sam ignored him.

Rosanne motioned for him to come in.

"Bill, this is Mr. Weston. From up at the lake. He's that policeman that I told you was coming."

Bill, going along with Sam's prearranged plan of denial pretended that this was their first meeting.

"Pleased to meet you, Mr. Weston," he said.

Both shook hands to confirm their mutual understanding.

Sam started in again. Looking directly at Rosy, he said, "Just by chance, 1 was having dinner last evening at a place called Steves. Ah, I could have sworn 1 saw you there. Am I mistaken or is that so?" He paused.

She flushed, then hesitatingly she responded, "Why yes I was, I didn't see you there."

"Well, you wouldn't have recognized me in any event since we hadn't met up to then,"

"1 guess you're right," she said.

Bill seemed to enjoy watching her squirm. The smirk on his face was obvious.

She glanced over at him and frowned.

"You were joined by a guest," Sam continued, shortly after you sat down. Can you tell me who he was?" Sam quickly inserted.

"You must be mistaken," she said. "I met with no one."

Bill shifted from one leg to the other.

Sam did not acknowledge Bill's apparent dis-belief.

"1 see," Sam said, "Well. 1 could have been mistaken."

"Tell me," he continued, "about what time where you there?"

It became apparent that she didn't like the direction of the questioning when she said, 'What's this got to do with what happened to Bruce?'

"Probably nothing," he said. "1 was just curious. You know, we have to find out everything there is about a case. You never know when the most insignificant thing will turn out to be important."

"Case, what case?" she asked. "The plane crashed, Bruce is dead. My God, Mr. Weston, I'm in mourning here and you are acting like I had something to do with it."

"No, not at all, Mrs. Hancock, I'm just trying to get to the bottom of this, like you said earlier, remember?"

Bill's grin widened.

Sam continued. "On the day of the crash, you were here at the office, yes?"

"Yes, why?"

"Did you see who boarded?"

"No," she emphasized boldly.

"How could it be that you didn't see anyone hanging around waiting for the plane to load passengers?"

"I was busy with the office work," she said.

"Did you see the cargo being loaded?"

"No she said again. Mr. Weston, I think it's time you left. If you don't mind. I've got a lot of work to do and you're taking up too much of my time."

Bill said, "Nice meeting you Mr. Weston," turning as if to leave.

"Mr. Crenshaw, that's right isn't it? I would like to chat with you for a bit. You got some time?"

"You can leave now Bill," she interrupted.

Bill, not wanting to jeopardize his short time left at making income, did just as she directed. He left without answering Sam's request.

"You needn't bother asking him any questions Mr. Weston, he doesn't know anything about this thing."

"I'll be the judge of that Rosy," Sam said, "Thanks for your time. There may be some other items I'll want to go over with you. I'll let you know." Reaching into his shirt pocket, he pulled out a card. "If anything comes up that you think will be helpful in getting to the bottom of this, give me a call." Sam backed away slowly.

"You confuse me Mr. Weston. Why do you keep referring to getting to the bottom of this?"

"We think that a bomb may have been placed aboard. Did'nt the FBI mention that."

"What?" she said. As if she did not know.

"Yes Mrs. Hancock. I know that you knew that. Why are you acting surprised?" Sam walked into the maintenance area and said to Bill, "You're right Bill, she's difficult."

CHAPTER 7

A week had passed since Mark came down off the mountain with the money, secured in two briefcases, lying under his bed. The allure of what it represented kept beckoning to him. However, the event was still making news. Every time there was any piece of new information, the media went at the story as if it had just broken, airing the entire scenario from the start to the moment.

Outside of his pleasure of being with Alexis, he spent the majority of his time hanging around his condo dreaming about all the things he would do when things cooled off. Watching television, reading the newspaper, staying close to the money was becoming an obsession. He was, he felt, a prisoner, held captive, fearful of leaving the condo. Alexis was beginning to notice the change in him and wondered why.

At dinner, at his table, she goaded him into a conversation about his elusiveness.

"Mark darling, I think you're going into one of your shells again. You've been so distant lately. Is there something bothering you?" she asked.

She continued, "You have not touched me and you've been snippy. Cutting me off whenever I say anything. I'm afraid to start any conversation. What's wrong honey?"

"Nothing," I don't feel any different. Why do you always have to nag at me about my moods?" Mark knew exactly what she was feeling. He could sense it in himself, but was afraid to admit it. He knew why too. It was the money and the fact that he had to keep it's existence from her. Mark knew he was feeling guilt. It was becoming a bother.

"Listen, let's get off the hill today," he said. "Take a ride somewhere. I feel like getting out and exploring a bit."

"Where would you like to go?" she asked.

"I don't care, just get the hell out of here for a while. Go see something. This place is getting to me. The walls are closing in."

"I don't know why you don't get some sort of hobby started," she said. "It's not like you have a regular job to go to. You could occupy your time with something until Spring. I know that the winters are confining for you."

"It's getting so that I despise the coming of winter and the snow. That shut in feeling. No freedom to get out into the woods and roam."

That's exactly what I'm talking about," she said. "If you had something to occupy your time, winter would fly by and before you know it you would have your precious freedom."

They had been riding for an hour when he decided that he had to get the deed out into the open and off his conscious. He couldn't keep it from her any longer. It was eating away at him. It would only get worse the longer he secreted it, go deeper into despair. He felt guilty yet deserving of the loot. He struggled for an easy way of approaching her on the subject. It escaped him. Struggling in thought, seeminly caught in a fathomless abyss of illlegality, he fumbled for a way to explain it, logically.

He started by saying that he had something extremely important to tell her. "I was at the crash site. I am involved in the disappearance of the money". It came out hesitatingly and clumsily.

She knew even before he said it. She had been putting two and two together because of the way he had been acting recently. His demeanor completely out of character.

Alexis's complexion turned ashen. Her mouth slightly parted. Her eyes widened as he went on about how he happened onto the wreckage. Deep furrows crossed her brow. He tried to explain that all the passengers were dead, including the pilot. He would have done whatever was necessary had there been any life left in anyone of them. He saw the cocaine, then discovered the money. He weighed the morality of taking the money. He thought of his situation, and knew that the money would solve all his financial problems.

"I decided to take the money and get the hell out of there," he said. "That's it. I've got it at the condo. It's been driving me nuts."

At first she did not say a word, but stared straight ahead through the windshield as if in shock.

"Say something, dammit," he said.

"I don't know what to say. I'm astonished that you would do such a thing."

"What do you mean, do such a thing?" I just happened to be there. I didn't kill those people. They got what they deserved. They were in the bull ring. They fooled with the bull and got the horns."

"Oh, that's not what I mean. With your background I would think that taking the money would not have entered your mind. The first thing you would have done would be to report it and walk away from any part of it. Your sense of honor is the one thing I love most about you. Of course, there's a lot more about you that appeals to me, but you've always displayed a strong sense of right and wrong."

"Look at me Alexis. I'm in my mid forties. I don't have a damn thing. I don't own a home, a nice car, anything. No savings and worse, no marketable skills. The lousy piddling pension I get from the government isn't paying the bills. The goddamn wolves are always just three feet from my front door. It was an opportunity to get out from under the burden. Able to buy you things, travel. Damn, it just made sense at the time. But now I'm having second thoughts. Trouble is, I'm in it up to my neck.

Even if I turned the money in, they would shaft me, right where the sun doesn't shine."

'Well, you're not going to get the shaft, But, you are going to turn the money in. We can live without it. What do you want to do, run for the rest of your life? Is the money worth having to look over your shoulder everyday? Jump at every little sound in the middle of the night? Be suspicious of everybody that casually looks at you? See things out of the comer of your eyes? No Mark, that's not the way we're going to live. Your occasional moods are enough to live with. I can just imagine how long we would be together if you were depressed all of the time."

Mark listened and could reason with the principles she brought to light. But, he wasn't ready to give up, yet. The money and the allure were overpowering. If he couldn't convince Alexis just how important the money was to him, he would have to make other arrangements.

Alexis went into a long, tedious dissertation about the importance of turning in the money and how important it was for his own good and the well being of their relationship. He could see that by the way she went on that he would probably not be able to persuade her to come along with him to a better future. Mark pretended to listen attentively, but his thoughts were targeted at planning ahead with the money, without her, at least for now. The money had become dominant.

The fog that veiled his rational caused his mind to ignore that this was the first challenge of many to come. Mark's awareness had become lazy since leaving the DEA. He hadn't made any decision more important than what to cook for dinner or what to wear upon arising. He confided in Alexis that when he got up in the morning he would perhaps decide what to do, then decide if he wanted to do it. Retirement wasn't much of a challenge. He needed something to put some pizazz back into his life. It seemed that the adventure of eluding the authorities, holding onto the money was what he needed. What did he have to lose. He was already in deep. Stretching it out might prove to be very interesting.

Sam Weston hopped into his tan, stripped down taxpayer owned chevy that had seen too many miles. The six cylinder heap struggled to maintain fifty five miles per hour climbing the winding four lane ribbon of asphalt cut into the side of the mountain that would eventually bring him back to the Tahoe Basin. He had stayed in Reno much longer than anticipated.

He inhaled deeply when he reached the summit, sensing the cool crisp thin air at seven thousand feet. He loved it up here at the top, wondering how anybody could live anywhere else on the planet.

The Chevrolet performed beautifully coasting back down to six thousand feet, running quietly along the lake shore. The deep blue water of Lake Tahoe and the seemingly endless expanse that it covered always brought a sense of insignificance to his existence.

The partial license plate number he had provided was hindering the Department of Motor Vehicle's ability to conclude the owner's identity. With what they had to go on, there were three possibilities and all three were registered in the Los Angeles area. Sam was counting on at least one of them being local, or at least in the vicinity of the county. It wasn't to be. And he wasn't having any luck with fingerprint identification either. All the prints taken at the scene of the wreckage turned out to be either investigators, the pilots or the passengers. So far. The lab was almost positive.

In follow up encounters with local business people and the casinos, nobody had made any large purchases with cash nor had there been any new high rollers at the tables. It looked like a dead end.

After examining the wreckage which had been carted off the mountain and laid out on the floor of a hangar at the airport, Sam's speculation that an explosion had brought the aircraft down was right on target. Bits and pieces of plastic explosives were found embedded on the inside of the fuselage. The FBI lab in Washington was working on the type of detonator used and the origin of its purchase. The results would be skimpy and would leave little to go on.

The briefcase that was left on the mountain was devoid of prints. All the police had as hard evidence were some plaster casts of the suspect's footprints and a cast of the tire tread. The tires were Goodyear's All Weather brand which sold in the millions and marketed throughout the world. The boot prints were of the Colorado brand, also sold in the thousands at every shoe store in the USA and elsewhere. The only sure thing about the boots was that they were worn by a man, The size of the shoe prints and their deep indentation in the ground could have been made only by a healthy male.

Sam's frustration was evident by his attitude, as he groped in sullen quietness. However, his approach to the situation was what any experienced detective would do at this juncture, Take a deep breath, step back, rely on his patience, and start from square one, Re-examine the evidence from the beginning. Look for any thing that might have been missed on the first go around. It had been his experience that there was always something over looked in the heat, excitement and confusion of the initial investigation. Throughout the following week, Sam was either at the airport going through the pieces of wreckage, interviewing anybody that he thought could shed some light on the case or back up on the mountain, retracing the suspects path of retreat from the crash site to his car. Nothing. Not one new shred of evidence turned up.

The entire week produced one dead end after another. One frustration on top of another. Sam was sure that whoever had the money would turn his hand sooner or later. It was now a matter of waiting for his man to make that miscalculation. The only consolation for Sam was that the feds hadn't been able to garner any new information either. In a way he felt that he was in a race to beat the FBI and the DEA to the punch. Captain Dickson, as a result of the commissioners, began pressuring Sam for progress. Everybody wanted this thing concluded, but no one more than Sam.

Yes, there was a positive in that endless week. The media quieted down. Since their man assigned to the task had nothing to give them, the daily news casts were devoid of any utterances of the incident. Besides, the police were getting damned tired of hearing about their lack of movement in the case. Another positive was that Sam was counting on the void of news coverage to encourage the suspect into making that mistake he was sure would take place.

Mark noted the absence of reports which dangerously put him in the frame of mind that he could relax somewhat.

The roads in and out of the basin were scrutinized by the Highway Patrol and were alert to any suspicious person or persons. The local airport was covered as was the bus terminal. There was still a sense of urgency of covering their bases and a sense of awareness of the situation. No one was letting their guard down.

Still, not much was happening. It was as if a lethargy had set in. Except for the commissioners office that kept up the pressure. In turn, Captain Dickson's carpet was beginning to show signs of wear where Sam stood, shuffling from side to side, trying to explain why there had been no progress in the case. Sam was developing a stutter. That afternoon, Ron Blamebridge came rushing downstairs, taking two steps at a time, clutching a glossy sheet of paper, bent for the temporary office he and Sam had set up earlier.

"Sam," he shouted excitedly as he entered the small room, "This fax just came in from the DMV. I think we've got something here. A make on the vehicle"

Sam looked up from the paperwork scattered across his desk.

"The DMV put together another possibility on that plate number," he said trying to catch his breath. "It's an address here at the lake."

Sam's eyes widened as he read. He had a gut feeling that this was the break he was looking for.

"Nineteen Seventy Two Plymouth, tan, License number OMB 555."

"That's good enough for me," Sam said with enthusiasm. "Here Ron, handing the paper back, read off the address," Sam reached for his coat and hat, that had been thrown over the empty chair along side the desk. Ron rattled off a street address and apartment number followed by, "1 think this guy lives over on the east shore, in Nevada. His name is Mark Baxter."

"Yeah, I recognize that address. It's in those condos just past Round Hill," Sam said. "Damn Ron, we needed this. It may not pan out to be anything, but it's the best thing that's happened in an eon."

Sam's excitement rubbed off on the young officer. He was dancing back and forth on his toes as Sam slipped into his parka.

"You stick close here Ron, I'll call in just as soon as I get anything. If this guy is who we're looking for we're going to have to keep in close proximity of each other."

"How's chances of going along with you?" Ron asked.

"Not just yet, Sam said. "I don't want to get this guy excited by showing up with a uniformed officer."

Sam pulled into a space marked for visitors. The six inch rectangular sign perched on top of a four by four post was barely visible, partially hidden, by last nights snowfall.

Sam glanced up through his windshield. Through the wrought iron railing he spotted the number he was looking for affixed to a door on the second floor. Turning in his seat he searched around the parking area looking for the Plymouth. He was disappointed. Perhaps around in the back he thought.

He exited his vehicle and stood along side for a second patting the side of his waist to make sure his nine millimeter was tucked snugly in it's holster. He wasn't anticipating to use it, but just in case.

He climbed the ice encrusted stairs carefully. At the top he turned to his right on the walkway and made his way two doors distant, to the address. He rapped on the door and waited. Getting no response, he tapped again. Still there was no answer. Out of the corner of his eye he spotted a head leaning out of the adjacent doorway.

"Can I do something for you?" Sam overheard the stranger to say.

"Is there anyone home here?" Sam asked.

"Nope. He's gone. Packed up lock stock and barrel about two days ago. Haven't seen him since," Mark's neighbor said.

"Crap," Sam said aloud.

"Got a minute?" Sam asked. "I'm with the police." He reached to show his badge.

"1 know," the neighbor said. "Spotted your car."

"How the hell would you know I'm with the police by that?" Sam inquired."

"For one thing you got an official license plate and another who'd drive anything like that except the cops?"

"You're right," Sam said, raising his eyebrow in agreement.

Sam did not like this individual. He guessed that not many people did. His manner was effusive, as he was soon to find out.

"Did Mr. Baxter say where he was going?"

"I have no idea, he never talked to me much," Yates said.

"Did he have any friends that, say dropped in to visit him?"

"Only his girlfriend," he said.

"Do you know who she might be?"

"Only that he called her Alexis."

"Do you know her last name?"

"Nope. Just Alexis. A real knockout of a woman."

'Has she been around since Mr. Baxter left?"

"You mean Mark?"

"Yeah, Mark." Sam was perturbed.

"Nope," Yates replied.

"Can you tell me anything unusual about Mr. Baxter, I mean Mark?"

"Ordinary guy. Quiet. Kept to himself, most of the time. We never socialized. I think he was kinda retired. I don't think he worked. At least I never saw him come and go on a regular basis. I can't say there was anything unusual about him, I mean he wasn't weird or anything like that."

"How long has he lived here?" Sam asked.

"You mean, did he live here, don't you?"

'Why, doesn't he live here anymore?"

"I would say that's a fair assumption." Yates answered.

"Why?"

"Cause, he took all his possessions. Several suitcases. All his clothes. It's a furnished unit. So all he had in there were a few personal things and his clothes."

'Were you ever inside?" Sam asked.

"Once, for a minute or two. Borrowed some oregano."

"Notice anything unusual?" Sam figured that if anything were offbeat inside Yates would have picked up on it.

"Nope. Say this guy do anything wrong?" Yates inquired.

"We're not sure, just a routine inquiry," Sam said.

"He have anything to do with that plane crash?" he asked out of the blue.

Sam thought for a second, then said, "Why do you ask?"

"Oh, no particular reason. Just thought, uh. He did a lot of hiking. He always carried a day pack around with him. I asked him once what he carried in it. He told me not much, just some hiking gear. You know, a compass, first aid, little flashlight, stuff like that. He wasn't talkative."

"You ever meet this Alexis?" Sam asked.

"Nope. But I've seen her come and go."

"Describe her to me."

Sam made mental notes as Yates told him in minute detail how Alexis appeared to him right down to the way she walked.

"What kind of a car does she drive?"

"A Camaro. A late model. Red," he informed Sam. "Her license plate reads, 'Spicy 1'."

"Bingo," Sam said to himself. "Is there a manager on the premises?" Sam asked.

"Yes, Mrs. Buckwall, downstairs in number one."

Sam handed him a card with a request to call him if he could think of anything that might be of help. He knew Yates would comply. He seemed the type.

Mrs. Buckwall answered the door displaying a puzzled expression.

Mrs. Buckwall was a pleasant looking elderly lady in her late sixties, Sam guessed. An apron snugly tied to her waist and looking every bit like everyone's grandmother preparing dinner for the evening, she inquired as to the strangers identification.

Sam politely produced his badge for her review, and introduced himself.

"I'll bet you want to know about Mr. Baxter," she said aptly. "I saw you go upstairs and knock on his door. He left us. Such a nice man. Always paid his rent on time. Never gave anybody cause to complain. No noisy parties. Wish everyone could be like him. As tenants, I mean?"

Sam let her ramble on figuring she would give him all the information he needed without having to ask any questions. He was thinking that she would continue, when abruptly she stopped and for a second, stared at him. Then before he could open his mouth she started again. "Well," she said, "what do you want with him? I can't imagine the police wanting him for anything."

"Uh, er, not just yet, maam," Sam said. "We just want to question him." Sam had this boyish charm about him that he used when trying to disarm someone or distract them from their intentions.

"Would it be possible to get into the apartment?" Sam asked.

"It's a condominium, not an apartment, there is a difference, you know."

"Yes maam," Sam half apologizing. "Would it be OK if some of our people visited the condo?"

She stopped him in mid sentence. "Condominium." She corrected.

"Yes maam," Sam said.

"Besides, Mr. Baxter left some belongings, and I'm sure bound to protect them until he returns to get them. I got into trouble once before by letting someone into an abandoned condominium and I am never going to let that happen again."

"Yes maam, I'll secure a search warrant so hopefully that'll make you feel more comfortable."

Once again, Sam furnished his business card with the usual request and a promise to return shortly.

He wanted into the unit as quickly as possible. Returning to the station he acquired a search warrant. At the same time asked Ron to get Alexis's address from the DMV. Within an hour he was back standing before Mrs. Buckwall with the authority in hand.

"My, young man, that was quick. I didn't expect you back for at least a couple of days. How's come you can get a warrant and get back here in an hour, when it takes two or three hours to respond to an emergency?"

"Now, now Mrs. Buckwall, you know that's not the case."

"Well, let me tell you about my daughter ..."

"Not just now maam, maybe later. I'm being pressed for time. I don't mean to be rude, but I've got to get on with this. Please, will you get the key for me? I'd be grateful."

"Of course," she said.

When Sam returned with the warrant, he was hoping to find something, anything that would link Baxter with the crime. He wasn't sure, but he felt that somehow Baxter was involved. Maybe just as an innocent bystander, somebody that happened to be in the area at the time of the crash. Then again, who knows, perhaps he was solely responsible for the tragedy. And maybe he wasn't the one they were looking for at all.

Inside, Sam couldn't help but notice that Baxter was neat about himself. The few things that he left behind were orderly. Not like he left in a hurry and scattered things about in disarray. Newspapers, personal effects, some clothing, and especially the kitchen looked as if a maid had just left after a routine cleaning. Sam was careful not to place his fingers on every item he came across. He wanted some good prints. While Sam snooped in and around every comer, his fingerprint man, who had accompanied him, dusted for prints.

Mrs. Buckwall followed in Sam's footsteps. Continually babbling about the intrusion into ones private affairs. She couldn't understand how the police would even think that Mr. Baxter was involved in anything unscrupulous.

Sam kept apologizing telling her that Mr. Baxter wasn't a suspect. They were there to make sure that the person they wanted wasn't, in fact, Mr. Baxter. But, contrary, Sam was hoping to find something. It would make his job a lot easier. It would mean that he could start pursuing the culprit, rather than having to continue looking for a prime suspect.

In the bedroom on the dresser, Sam gazed upon a photograph of whom he thought had to be Alexis. He held the frame at arms length and changed its position trying to find a way that would put her beauty in a different perspective. Much to his admiration, she was beautiful at any angle. He envied Baxter.

On the wall beside the chest of drawers Sam looked over a group of photos, one which was obviously a portrait of Mark. The same individual was in another photo with Alexis. It appeared that he would be in his late thirties early fourties. He removed the picture from the frame and secured it under his coat, assuring Mrs. Buckwall who was behind him that it would be returned. Sam thought that he's seen this person before, somewhere. At the moment he couldn't bring it to mind.

Sam turned to ask Mrs. Buckwall, who was standing nearly on his heels, if Mr. Baxter said any thing about returning. Mark had left behind a majority of his clothing and what seemed like valuable personal items. There were rings and an expensive looking watch in a jewelry case on the chest of drawers. Why would anybody leave valuables behind if they didn't intend to return. Or on the other hand, if they were running from something, then leaving in a rush, abandoning valuables would be understandable.

"No," she said. "Mr. Baxter said that Miss Cottier would be over to pick them up."

"Uh huh," Sam muttered.

Sam finished his business and asked the fingerprint expert if he needed anymore time.

"Negative," he said. "I've got all I need to make an ID."

Sam was anxious to talk to this Miss Alexis Cottier. For more than one reason. He had to see if she was as beautiful in person or was she just photogenic.

He thanked Mrs. Buckwall for her cooperation and understanding leaving the door open to her for possible future inquiry.

When he returned to the station, Ron had Alexis's address and phone number neatly written on a note pad.

It had been a long day, he was tiring and decided to call it quits for now. He asked Ron to do him one big favor before leaving. "Ron, my man, this guy Baxter. What do we know about him?, except that he's a neatnick and lives here at the lake."

"Not much yet Sam, but I'm working on it. One thing he doesn't have a rap sheet. No evidence of any criminal activity in his past. I'm looking into his former occupations. Right now, I've not come up with anything about what he does or did for a living."

"Thanks Ron, stay on it. I'm still not sure if he's our man. I'm anxious to see if his prints match any that we found at the crash. If they do, we're on our way. If not, it's back to square one. Tomorrow I'm going to check out the beauty that he shares a relationship with. Have you seen her picture?"

"No, why?"

"She's a beaut. It'll be an experience just meeting her even if it is a dead end."

"That good, huh?" Ron asked.

"Yeah, she'd make you rise to the occasion." Sam emphasized the word rise.

"Maybe we could interview her together," Ron blurted. Hoping for a positive response.

"We'll see," Sam said, winking.

Sam stepped inside the door of his apartment, in the Bijou district, when the telephone sounded. It was Ron.

"Sam," his voice was electric with excitement, "we've got a match. They finally found some prints on the plane that match our guy Baxter."

"All right," Sam said. "That's great. Now all we gotta do is find him. Before the feds."

Ron broke in. "Listen to this Sam. The background on Baxter came in right after you left. This guy's got some credentials. He's a vet. In the Navy back in the sixties, during the Vietnam War. You ever heard of the Navy Seals. A commando bunch. Did all kinds of T type personality stuff. You know, no fear of death. He was decorated for bravery. Purple Heart, The DSC. Then after that he went with the DEA, a narc. He was with them for something like eighteen years. Got shuffled out because of some misunderstanding with his superiors. But he had a distinguished career with them. Was a field supervisor. He spent a lot of his time in Mexico and Columbia. What do you think?"

"I'm impressed."

"Other than that, Ron continued, "he's been kind of retired. About the last five years he has lived here at the lake. He's clean Sam, real clean."

"I wonder how much the feds know about this guy."

"Probably as much as we do." Ron replied.

"This guy is going to be a tough nut. My guess is that he'll head for familiar territory. Probably back to Mexico. At least until the heats off"

Sam continued. "Put out an APB on him and the car. We've got to locate the car first. That will give us an idea as to where he might be headed."

"I've already done it," Ron said.

"OK, the first thing in the morning I'll call on Miss Cottier. See just how much she knows or is involved. Put a surveillance on her apartment immediately. And let's get a bug on her phone pronto."

"I've done that too." Ron said.

Is this guy buckin for a promotion or what, Sam said to himself.

The sun was just now rising over the Nevada mountains as Sam lounged under a hot shower. The phone was ringing but he didn't hear it.

On the way to the station his cellular beeped.

"It's me, Ron"

"Yeah, I know, what's up?"

"We got the car located." In the same breath he said, "it's at SFO. In long term parking."

"I knew it," Sam said. "The bird has flown. OK, I'll be right there. I'm only a block away."

Sam came through the door barking orders. "Ron, get the car impounded. We'll need it for evidence later. Get in touch with the airport authorities. Get the portrait of Baxter duplicated and fax them a copy. Have them pass it around, see if somebody can identify him and what airline he's on. Yeah, and get in touch with the authorities in Mexico City. Fax them a photo too. Do the same in Bogota. Make sure they know it's urgent. Tell them to hold him and we'll pick him up. Any questions? And by the way, that was Baxter I saw with Rosy last week. If I don't get time to get back down there, you do so and confront her with the picture and get her reaction."

Without waiting for an answer, he asked, "You ever did any of this before."

"No."

"Well you were trained at the academy. Nows the time to use it. OK!. Get in touch with Parch at the sheriff's, if you need help. I'm off to see the fairy princess, Lady Cottier. Page me if you get anything."

Captain Dickson interrupted just as Sam was heading out.

"I hear you have a lead on this Mr. Baxter," he said.

"Yes sir, it's a start," Sam said.

"Good, you know how badly we want him. That is, before the FBI gets their hands on him"

"Yes sir, I'm aware," Sam said.

"Whatever you need Sam, just ask." Dickson played right into Sam's pocket.

"Well sir, I'm going to need some travel authority."

"Anything Sam, like I said, just ask."

"I'm on my way to talk to his girl friend. I shouldn't be long. When I get back later this morning, I figure I'm headed for the airport and probably Mexico City. Unless I find out he's headed somewhere else."

"You have a blank check, Sam."

"Good, I'll see you then." Sam excused himself and departed.

It was fifteen minutes before eight when Sam pulled up in front of the address given him by Ron. The red Camaro was sitting idly in its assigned space. Good, he thought, she hasn't left for work yet. That is, if she does.

He rapped firmly on the sculptured oak door.

"Who is it?" he heard from inside.

"Police, Sam Weston, I would like to ask you a few questions."

The door opened as far as the three inch security chain would allow. Only her face was visible through the small opening. He wasn't disappointed. The image was better than her portrait that he'd seen at Baxter's condo.

"I'd like to come in and ask you about Mr. Baxter." His ID held for her to see. "You do know Mark Baxter, don't you?"

"Why yes," she said, as she released the chain.

"Thanks," Sam said as he stepped inside.

She was wearing a pale green bathrobe. Bathrobes on beautiful women is like pouring ice over Creme de Menthe. It ruins it. But in this case she looked like divinity oozing out of a cocktail glass. Like mist flowing over a levee on a warm summer morning.

Sam got right to it. "We're looking for Mr. Baxter. When did you see him last?"

"Why ah, just last evening. Why, what do you want with him?" She was playing a con.

"Did he stay here last night," Sam asked. He knew that Mark wasn't in his condo last evening.

"He was here for a while, then he left. We're supposed to have dinner this evening. Why, is anything wrong? Has Mark been in an accident?"

"No, not exactly, but I don't think you'll be having dinner with him this evening. That is, unless you're catching a plane to meet him."

"What," she said with anxiety. "What do you mean by that?"

"1 mean that Mr. Baxter has left the lake. You're not telling me the truth. We know Mr Baxter left the area two days ago."

"We have his car impounded at the San Francisco airport."

Her eyes widened below a pained furrowed brow. It threw her looks out of kilter. It disturbed him.

"Come clean with me Miss Cottier. You know as well as I that Mark has absconded with the money from the plane crash." It was a jab she wasn't expecting and he threw it intentionally.

"Why, I don't know what you're talking about."

She didn't bite.

He was getting nowhere fast. His ploy to intimidate her into opening up failed. He knew that if he pursued, she would hold fast to her innocence. Besides, he had a flight to catch and couldn't afford to waste any more time.

"Well, thanks Miss Cottier, I think we'll let it rest there for the time being. I'm sure you are as concerned as we are. I don't want anything unfortunate to happen to him."

"What do you mean by that?" she asked with a tad of scorn.

"I mean that if Mark turns himself in, soon, before we have to go after him, it will go a lot easier on him. Do I make myself clear? If he communicates with you, lay it on him square."

"Yes, but, I don't understand."

"Anything you can do to help will be appreciated." With that Sam pretended a salute with his index finger to his forehead and left.

Sam returned to the station for a meeting with the Captain and Blamebridge. He related his conversation with Miss Cottier indicating he left an impression with her, but other than that came up with no substantial information regarding Baxter's whereabouts. Ron reported that he had nothing to report on which airline Baxter might have taken nor his destination. But, an Aero Mexico airline desk clerk indicated that he recognized the photo. In addition, the airlines and the authorities in Mexico and Columbia had Baxters photograph and all of their people were aware of his possible arrival and would be on the lookout.

Captain Dickson handed Sam an envelope containing sufficient money to see him through to south of the border. Arrangements had been made with Aero Mexico for a flight when Sam was ready if in fact that's where he would go. As Sam reached for the envelope, the Captain warned, "Let's not take it for granted that Mr. Baxter has taken a commercial airline. He could have chartered a private plane. Maybe he parked the car at the airport as a decoy, then, he could have rented a cab, gone to the bus station or the train station or even rented or bought another car and is humming down the damned freeway right now. Remember who we're dealing with here. He's going to stay one jump ahead of us. He's in the drivers seat right now, literally. Furthermore, the FBI has been awfully quiet these past few days. They've not been communicative. My guess is that they're on to something and don't want us to know about it."

"I'm not taking anything for granted sir. My options are open with this guy." Sam said.

"We're building a profile on this person," the captain continued, "From his background I can tell you that he has a lot of connections in the southern hemisphere. There's a lot of people that owe him favors down there. I'm with you that he's probably in Mexico, Mexico City. We'll run every possibility on that assumption from here. I wouldn't fool around with any other theory than that one for now. So, my advice is to get on to Mexico City now. We'll work out other probabilities from here and keep you informed. I want a report every third day by four in the afternoon. Watch the time differences down there. I believe they're one hour behind. Any questions?"

"I'm packing sir."

As they, he and Ron left the Captain' office, Ron whispered, "Sure wish I was going with you."

"You're more important here. I will be reporting to Dickson through you. That way you'll know everything I know. And I expect you to lay everything you know on me. OK amigo?"

"You keep close tabs with Miss Cottier. You are in charge here while I'm gone. Put someone on watching her movements. Monitor her phone calls. You know what to do." Sam left.

CHAPTER 8

Mark had a gut feeling that the police were getting close. He had no proof, but his intuitions told him that he could not have left the mountain void of evidence. He knew also that the amount of money involved would put pressure on the local authorities to find out who has it and where is it.

He certainly wasn't aware that Sam Weston existed or that he, Weston, was certain that Mark was his man. How could he? From the news accounts that Mark watched, Weston was not mentioned. However, the news gave him impetus to do something. That something was to get away.

Agonizingly, and without confiding in Alexis, Mark packed one medium suitcase with a few belongings. He secured his passport, another medium size suitcase with the money, removing a packet of one hundred dollar bills for expenses. The denomination worried him. Nobody pays any attention to a twenty, but everyone glares at a hundred dollar bill, lustfully. He would have to be discreet when and where he cashed them. He'd have to risk that because he needed that money to travel.

In an almost panic state and hurry to flee, Mark decided not to notify Alexis of his plan. He knew he was risking a rift in their relationship. But, to accomplish the better part of secrecy and not leave any evidence to his whereabouts, he knew he had to leave in this manner. He would contact her later and read her response. He expected she would be angry, at first, and insist on her desire to end their relationship. It definitely would be a test of their love.

Mark drove to the San Francisco airport in South San Francisco arriving at nine o'clock in the evening. He chose SFO because it would be nearly impossible to be recognized at this huge facility. Better than at the Reno or Sacramento airports which are smaller and used extensively by locals.

Although he knew that his vehicle would be discovered eventually, he counted on being long gone before that. He needed at least a couple of days before the authorities would pick up on his trail.

Mark booked a flight on Aero Mexico which departed at eleven thirty that same evening. His carry on containing the money fit tightly in the overhead.

Mark's knowledge of the Mexican authorities was one from experience. They were lax and exceedingly partial to corruption. In his dealings with them in the past it was one of frustration and constant follow up to accomplish the most minute effort on their behalf. He felt confident that his arrival and stay there would go unnoticed for as long as he wanted. He would be proven wrong in that judgement.

Upon arriving in Mexico City, he circumvented customs using his knowledge from past experience. Their system permitted loopholes if one knew them. And Mark did. Standing among hundreds of new arrivals outside the airport, who were filling busses, vans and other assorted means of transportation, Mark waved down a cab.

"Buenos Dias, Senor, Se habla Espanola, por favor" was the greeting from inside the taxi.

"Not very well, Senor, Se habla Englesia," Mark replied.

"Si Senor, where to."

During the conversation with the cab driver, Mark divulged that he was on a business trip with a small US firm.

"This is my first visit to Mexico City." He lied. "In addition to my business here, I would like to see and learn of the Mexican customs and culture of your country. Would it be possible to stay at an out of the way hotel used by predominately Mexican businessmen and visitors, say where they speak a little English."

"Si, Senor, I can fix you up." Is it important to be close to anything?"

"No, not necessarily."

"Very well then, I know where to take you. To a nice hotel in old Mexico City, Good food, hombres muy friendly. Maybe you will learn about Mexican ways. Perhaps not like you hear about from gringos up north."

"Thanks." Mark introduced himself, using his alias. Miles Bradford.

"My name is Carlos, nice to meet you Senor."

Mark knew it beforehand, from the picture and ID on the windshield visor. He accepted the courtesy of his announcing it, graciously.

The driver maneuvered his taxi through Mexico City's confusing traffic patterns, weaving and dodging what appeared to be uncontrolled chaos. Mark was familiar with it and began recognizing land marks as Carlos drove to his destination. He kept his knowledge to himself.

The Avenue of the Revolution, the Palace of Art, the Basilica of Guadalupe, down the Paseo de la Reforma, a beautiful tree- line boulevard with many colonial period buildings and monument adorned traffic circles. Off in the distance Mark recognized the pyramids at San Juan Teotihuacan.

The fewer people that he came into personal contact, the better, Mark surmised. "Carlos, do you think it possible that I could count on you to chaperone me while here. I mean, if I were to call you, could you escort me during my visit?"

"Si, Senor, it will be my pleasure. If I am available." Carlos responded.

After driving for some time along wide boulevards lined with the lush, beautiful trees, the route and the scenery changed to narrow tree lined avenues, giving the impression that they were surrounded with a local atmosphere, with fewer automobiles, less so than the inner city where the traffic was extremely hectic. Here was a calm. Small compressed alley ways. Small shops. Clean, warm ambiance. Small store fronts mixed with residences with well manicured lawns.

Carlo's taxi pulled up to a courtly building of obvious Spanish architecture mirroring a Moorish motif. The circular driveway passed under a massive arch way covered with a rose colored flowering vine. On one of the archway columns a sign in gold lettering read, The Ascension.

The surrounding grounds were heavily vegetated with lush plants, trees and flowering gardens. A broad set of steps covered with red carpeting led to a spacious opening to the interior. On each side of the stairs were ceramic urns housing fully matured Kentia Palms. No sooner had the taxi come to a halt, a uniformed doorman descended the stairs to assist Mark. His brilliant burgundy uniform adorned with epaulets of gold fringe and gold buttons and cap topping his handsome face made Mark feel important and at ease.

"Buenos dias, Senor. Como esta usted."

"Thank you sir, I'm just fine and you?"

"Muy bien, Senor, gracias."

"1 speak very little Spanish," Mark replied. "1 hope you speak English."

"Si, I speak enough to get by."

"Good." Mark replied

The doorman proceeded to gather Mark's suitcase containing his personal belongings from the taxi's trunk. Mark held onto the case with the money throughout.

Entering the spacious lobby, Mark couldn't help admire the interior. Palms and ferns made for a tropical paradise. A brilliant, shiny black and white checkered tile floor mirrored the high ceiling constructed of stained glass windows allowing rays of vibrant colors to brighten the room. Clusters of deep cushioned furniture, meticulously placed throughout, provided for private meeting and conversational niches.

Carlos escorted Mark and the doorman inside. Standing beside Mark as he registered, he asked if there was anything further that Mark needed. Mark responded that there was not but to stand by until he finished his business of securing a room.

When finished; Mark took Carlos aside and paid him for the fare and tipped him with a ten dollar bill. Carlos responded as if it were unexpected and gave thanks by bowing slightly toward Mark.

"Carlos, let me get settled here. Perhaps tomorrow, or sometime soon after, I would like to call you, and if you are available I would like to do a little touring. I will call in plenty of time to give you notice so as not to interfere with, say maybe a good fare you have going at the time. Will that be ok?"

"Anything for you Senor, please call. I will pick out some good sights for us."

"Great Carlos, and thanks for your help. This is a wonderful hotel you have brought me to. I am very pleased. "Give me your telephone number and thanks again." Mark said.

Carlos responded with the number and "Por nada, Adious Senor."

Marks suite was elegant and fulfilled exactly what the exterior promised. It was spacious. It looked out onto a vine covered terrace, through white French Doors. The pink and red bougainvillea languished gracefully over the railing. He placed his suitcase on the bed and began sorting out what few clothes he had carried, hanging them neatly in the spacious walk in closet. When he had finished, he opened up the suitcase containing the money and gloated over it again.

Looking into the bathroom mirror rubbing the scruff on his face; he was pleased that the stubble began to represent a beard. A disguise he needed but reluctantly agreed to, since he had never grown one before. It looked and felt strange to him. It would have to mature much more before he would feel secure in this disguise.

He called down to the front desk to inquire if the hotel provided a vault or safe to store personal belongings while a guest at the hotel. He received an affirmative answer.

"May I see it, please," he asked.

"Si Senor, at your pleasure."

Leaving his room and descending on the elevator, the clerk escorted Mark down another flight of stairs situated behind the front desk. The granite walled hallway in the subterranean area was once used as a hideout for refugees from the revolution. It exuded a musty odor from the dampness that seeped through the walls. It was well lit and led to a dead end at the extreme. An iron door protected the vault therein. After the attendant manipulated a combination, the door swung wide exposing an enormous room lined with metal drawers along the interior walls.

"Fine," Mark said. "When can I have access? Will I be alone to place my contents?"

"Si Senor, we do not interfere with our guests business. I will be outside when you are conducting your affairs in here."

"Good, I will return in an hour or so. But first I'll call the desk."

"Muy bien, Senor."

Mark returned to his suite and began removing packets of bills counting out enough to last him several days, or weeks, if necessary. While doing so, Alexis weighed heavily on his mind. He had not contacted her since departing the lake two days ago and knew that she must either be worried senseless or as angry as he more rationally could expect. Perhaps both. He closed the suitcase with the money, locked it. Her image, in is mind, sickened him with the thought of losing her. He knew he would have to contact her as soon as possible. Or else.

Escorted by the desk clerk once again to the vault, Mark secured the suitcase in a large vault box.

The clerk handed Mark the only key that would open the box and both ascended the stairs to the lobby.

The hot Mexican sun surrendered it's penetrating rays as it disappeared below the distant mountains. The evening was warm and gentle. Mark's day had come to an end as he retired to his bed contemplating communicating with Alexis first thing in the morning.

From a phone booth some blocks away from the hotel, the phone rang on Alexis's night stand. It was seven AM on a bright fall morning. Nine o'clock in Mexico City.

"Hello," she said drowsily.

"It's me, Mark."

There was silence. A long excruciating time to him. This was going to be difficult and he was unprepared for it. Even though he anticipated it.

'Where are you?" she asked.

"I can't tell you at this time. And we can't make this long. You're phone is probably tapped." He said. Continuing, "I just wanted to get in touch with you to let you know I'm OK."

"Come back, please Mark." They are after you. The police. I've talked to them. It will be a lot better for you if you return immediately and return the money."

"Are you all right, Alexis?"

"Yes, I'm OK, but I'm seriously distressed over this whole thing."

"I understand, but I'm not coming back just yet. I've got to think things through. Coming back won't make any difference, not now. I'm in too deep. Coming back today or next year, the results will be the same. I've got to get off now. I'll contact you later. We'll have to work out a way to talk, but not at your place. 1 love you. Please give me some time."

He didn't wait for her response. He hung up hoping there was not enough time to trace the call.

Putting the receiver down, he felt a wrenching loneliness. A despair unknown to him until now. He was alone, running, the subject of a massive manhunt. The money took on a different aura. It was the utopia he'd dreamed of for years, at the same time, the money was the perpetrator, representing the demise of his existence.

After returning to the hotel, he sat on the edge of the bed, his eyes dreamy. His eyelids dropping as if in a deep depression.

It was time for a warm shower to extinguish the lethargy. His feelings were something that he would have to suppress with activity and adventure.

At eleven o'clock, feeling somewhat better, he prepared for the day. He called the cab dispatcher to summon Carlos' services. Mark requested Carlos presence at the hotel at twelve noon, if that were possible. The dispatcher assured him that his man would be there on time.

Mark left his room and descended the elevator to the lobby and into the cafe that was situated adjacent to the front desk and accessed through a set of double doors trimmed in brass. The room had a pleasant atmosphere, painted in a soft green, adorned with a multitude of plants and flowers. It was warm, comfortable and the aroma from the kitchen stimulated his appetite.

Finishing his breakfast some fifteen minutes before noon, Mark strolled through the interior of the hotel, visiting briefly, a few small gift shops, a floral business, thinking of Alexis, then scanned the magazines and newspapers at a news stand. He purchased a pack of gum then proceeded to the main entrance, waiting at the cab stand.

It had been fifteen years since Mark last visited Mexico City. He was eager to curtail, overshadow, his current feelings of guilt and heartache. He knew the only way to do that would be to get involved in activity.

Mark recognized the cab and the driver as it pulled up alongside the waiting area. It was Carlos.

"Buenos dias Senor," Carlos greeted Mark.

"Good afternoon Carlos."

"Did you get a good nights sleep?"

"Yes, I did, thank you."

"Where to?" Carlos asked.

"Let's just drive around for a while. I would like to get acquainted with the city," Mark said.

"OK, then, we will find out what you like." Carlos responded.

CHAPTER 9

When Sam approached the Aero Mexico airline counter to check in, he handed Mark Baxter's photo to an olive skinned beauty in a dark blue uniform crowned with a bright red hat.

He introduced himself in order to relieve her as to who he was and why a photo of a different person was shoved in her face.

"You recognize this man?" Sam asked.

"This is the photo that has been passed around for two days. I think I recognize him, but I can't be sure. He checked in a couple of days ago. I remember because I was assisting that day and was not too busy. He is a handsome man, that's what I remembered. But he did not check in under the name you have supplied. Here, we wrote it down and stapled it to the desk. Let's see. He used the name Miles Bradford." She said.

Sam called Dickson and informed him that an airline employee recognized Baxter and that he did in fact book a flight to Mexico City under an alias, Miles Bradford.

"Captain, listen up. Notify the police in Mexico City that I'm on my way. Have someone at the airport meet me. I should be there within a couple of hours. My flight number in 712. I leave at one this afternoon."

Dickson agreed. "Our contact man there is Alfonso Enrico Jesus Menendez. Can you swallow that? Either he or an assistant will be there Sam."

Sam was encouraged by the information the attendant had given him. It was the best he had so far. And if right, his trip to Mexico City would be justified back at headquarters. He was concerned about that.

Sam's direct flight and landing went smoothly. He hated flying. The indentations on the armrests attested to that. His philosophy was that he didn't want to die in an oversized tooth paste tube. He did not like the feeling that he had no control over his fate. Besides, it was a long way down. You would have time to think about your destiny. In an automobile, it's quick. Happens instantly. No time to consider what's about to occur.

Upon arriving he hauled his carry-on up the ramp to the inner confines of the terminal. Among the confusion, he spotted a small, slim dark skinned individual holding a sign emblazoned with his name on it. "Sam." His broad white toothed grin under a pencil thin black mustache welcomed Sam. Sam raised his arm high over his head to signal his contact person. The man bore down on Sam, pushing and shoving his way through the crowd.

"Mr. Weston, over here. Senor Weston, over here." Sam was aware of his presence. He assumed it was Menendez. His grin, exposed the whitest teeth Sam had ever seen, except for the one gold tooth in front which seemed to reflect a twinkle of light back in his direction. Menendez exuded warmth in his welcoming manner. It eased Sam. As they neared, Sam returned the greeting with a broad smile and extended his hand, which Menendez grasped firmly and confirmed that he was indeed Menendez.

"How are you senor?"

"Fine, just fine. Thanks for meeting me here. I'm afraid I would have wasted a lot of time getting oriented without you."

"My pleasure sir. We have been anxious to see you." He spoke fluent English. "Yes, this is a big airport and even bigger city. Most people who come here for the first time have a hard time of it. Before getting their bearings."

"Have you got anything new on Baxter?" Sam asked.

"We're working on it, but no, not just yet. Come let us get through customs. We can talk business after that."

During the check through process, Sam exposed Mark's picture to each officer. All responded that they hadn't seen the man in the picture.

Together Menendez and Sam proceeded to the outside.

"Give me a minute," Sam requested of his host. "I want to make a couple of inquiries."

In front of the terminal, Sam saw a line of cabs stretching along the curb to infinity. He wondered how they could make a living with so much competition. He walked the line of cabs, shoving Mark's photo in through the passenger window, not missing a beat. He wasn't learning any Spanish from the responses. "No Senor."

"Come senor, let's get into my transportation and get you settled. We can talk on the way. We have selected a nice motel for you near our headquarters."

As Menendez danced through traffic with the ease of a ballerina, Sam asked again, "Have you anything new on Baxter?"

"Mr. Baxter is not going anywhere. He will be here when the time comes to capture him."

"What makes you think that?"

"I know. We have a complete dossier on Mr. Baxter. He spent much time here and has many friends. That is why he came to Mexico. He has returned to his old stomping grounds. He will make contact with some of them. We have our eyes out on them now. When he slips up, we will be there. Trust me on this."

Sam liked his confidant, matter of fact, attitude. The way that Menendez talked it looked like just a routine matter of playing the waiting game. Have patience until the criminal made the mistake of taking things for granted. Sam was in their hands. He would, to some degree, have to play the game by their rules. Something he was not used to doing.

"You are aware that he is using an alias." Sam said.

"Yes, he will probably use many more before his arrest."

Accommodations were not on top of Sam's priority list. Because he wanted to spare the city too much expense. Menendez sped through traffic into a mixed commercial and residential area. He pulled up in front of a modest but clean and well manicured motel.

"This it," Sam asked looking over at his host. It was a pleasant looking motel. The surrounding structures appeared to be freshly painted with neatly trimmed grounds. The streets were spotless and the inhabitants were dressed in what appeared to be business suits along with blue collar types.

"OK, Senor. This motel I think you will like. They are personal friends of mine and they will take good care of you during your stay."

Sam checked in and was in his room within ten minutes. The room was comfortable, clean, located on the back side of the complex. The motel was built in a square configuration with an atrium in the center. It provided a sense of privacy and quiet. His window allowed a view that looked out into the atrium, planted with an array of colorful flower gardens, a few palms and assorted flowering shrubs.

Menendez escorted Sam to his room. Noting that Sam looked exhausted he excused himself, with, "Why don't you get some rest. We will pursue our prey in the morning."

It was late afternoon. Sam agreed and decided to retire for the balance of the day. The sun was boiling down on the motel. The air conditioners were taxed to their limit. The only sound Sam noticed was their persistent humming.

Using the in-room telephone, Sam contacted Ron Blamebridge, communicating his address and phone number.

Blamebridge indicated that the Mexican police had sighted who they thought was their man, Baxter, but lost him and now, were not aware of his whereabouts. He continued.

"They've got a make on him, Sam." Blamebridge said. "Had a tail on him yesterday, but he eluded them and the trail is cold."

"OK, Ron. Thanks, you're doing a good job. I'll call first thing in the morning to see if you have anything further. Right now I'm bushed. I'm going to rest for the remainder of the day. If you want to contact me, just ring. Tomorrow I'm going straight to the main precinct and see our contact here, Alfonso Menendez. Then I'm going to spend a lot of time at the airport showing Baxter's picture. I'm positive I'll run into somebody that saw him. Any questions?"

"Nope, good luck Sam." Ron placed the receiver in its' cradle.

After unpacking, Sam wanted a nightcap. He made for the bar he spotted when entering the motel. Sitting at the bar he stared into an ornate mirror, contemplating his haggard expression. With a scotch on the rocks cupped in his hand, he ignored the discomfort of the cold glass, mulling over the days events.

He felt a tap on his shoulder. He turned to see Menendez standing behind him with that ear to ear gleaming grin.

"Hey, what are you doing here. 1 thought you were going back to the station."

"I wanted to drop by to see how you were settling in. I hoped I would catch you before you retired. Guess I'm in luck, eh."

"What time is it anyway?" Sam wore a watch, but seldom looked at it. He had this thing about time. It went by too fast for him, so he tried to ignore it. A watch was for emergencies only.

"Nine thirty Senor."

"No wonder I'm so tired. I've been up since six this morning. Been a long day, Alfonso."

"May I join you Sam? I will stay but a few minutes."

"Be my guest. My glass is full." Glancing down into the amber liquid. "Let me buy you a drink."

"No thanks, senor, I don't drink. Perhaps a Perrier."

"A Perrier it is."

"I told you this morning," Menendez started, "that we have a complete dossier on Mr. Baxter. You remember that? Well, you should know that as I said, Mr. Baxter spent several years in Mexico City. He made a lot of contacts here during that time. He will be able to conceal his whereabouts by using his friends for that purpose. You understand what I'm saying?"

"You mean that it's going to be tougher than you thought to nab him."

"Exactly."

"I'll tell you frankly, Alfonso, I knew it was going to be difficult without you spilling it."

"I think we both can agree that Baxter is no dummy. So far he's stayed one jump ahead of us. I can't figure out how he got out of the airport without customs or a rental agency or a cab driver not spotting him. Nobody recognized his photograph. Maybe I haven't got to all of them yet, but tomorrow, I'm starting from scratch. Go back and interview anybody I can lay my sights on. Somebody has got to have seen him. It's just a matter of a little luck."

"In the morning senor, I would like for you to come to headquarters. I will send someone to pick you up. We would like to go over some strategy with you and furnish you with a vehicle while you are here. We have contacted your Captain Dickson, and we were informed how you like to work, alone. He says you work best that way. We want to cooperate with your wishes. But, we need to organize our efforts. Just so we know what the other is doing. Will that be all right with you."

"OK So long as you know how I operate, I'll work with you. I expected to."

Menendez smiled. "What time do you wish to start?"

"Eight is fine with me," Sam said.

"Eight O'clock then, we will have a man here at the motel at eight. His name is Raul Montoya. He will be in uniform so that you will recognize him."

"Raul," Sam repeated, after emptying his glass and setting it down on the bar.

"By the way, can I see the dossier?"

"You needn't ask, Menendez said, that is one of the things we want to go over with you tomorrow."

"OK then, I'm going to turn in. See you tomorrow, and thanks for your help."

"Hasta Manana," Menendez bid him farewell.

Sam was reading an American newspaper while waiting in what could be described as a small sitting area in the foyer, when an impeccably dressed officer with the sharpest creases in a uniform Sam had ever seen, appeared standing under the doorway arch. He looked in Sam's direction and Sam acknowledged him. Sam laid the paper down and motioned for him to approach.

"Good morning young man."

"Good morning," the officer replied in perfect English. "Did you sleep well?"

"Yes I did, thank you, even though it was not my mattress."

"Did you have breakfast?"

"Yes, and what a plate of food. Do you people eat that way all the time?"

"Look at our women, Senor. That will tell you, eh. Muy grande. Not all of them, of course, but our Senoras are great cooks. We fry everything." He laughed.

Raul Montoya was a very handsome man in his twenties or thereabouts. Tall and muscular. Olive skinned with deep brown eyes and a heavy downward curving mustache. He smiled through pearl white evenly spaced teeth. His immaculate uniform emphasized his broad shoulders. Was this Pancho Villa's grandson, Sam thought.

"Are you ready then sir?" Raul asked politely.

"Let's go," Sam said.

On the way, Raul and Sam made small talk. Mostly answering Sam's questions about the city and how polluted the air seemed.

"Automobiles, Raul said, we live in a bowl here. Mountains surround us. It is hard for the smog to escape. Much like your Los Angeles."

Sam entered the police precinct with his escort. He couldn't help notice that all the officers in their tan and khaki uniforms appeared to be more military like than civilian police.

Raul excused himself with a smile. "1 hope we get the chance to work together, senor."

"Thanks Raul. Thanks for the guided tour. Maybe we will, I'll put in a good word for you." Sam winked and smiled in return.

"Menendez at your service. Did you get a good nights rest?" he said in his deep resonant voice.

Sam turned, "Ah you startled me,"

"Please excuse me, I had no choice." His slicked back hair and thin black mustache seemed to shine as he moved under the light.

"Yes I did, thanks," Sam wasted no time on small talk. "I'm anxious to get down to business. My people tell me you had him in sight and then lost him. I'm not surprised. He's very adept at subterfuge. A slick, alert individual."

"We had him at the airport yes, but lost him in traffic, We have a general idea where he may be. Also we have a general description of the taxi he took. But, we are sorry to say that we never got close enough to distinguish the taxi's license plate or the cab number that all taxi's must display boldly on their vehicles. There are so many different companies that it is always difficult to get an exact make on them. In the heavy traffic he got away. Come, let's go into my office, we can talk in private in there."

Entering Menendez's office Sam was impressed with the position Menendez held. A grand room with an outside view of a large park adorned with palms, flowers and huge ornamental fountains. That would have been enough but the interior was furnished with elegant furniture. A large teak desk accompanied with a plush leather high back chair. Behind, the flags of Mexico and the state gracefully hung in folds on highly polished mahogany poles. A conference area for ten or more people who could lounge on plush sofas surrounding a round oak table with claw feet. On it neatly arranged were hand cut crystal ashtrays and drinking vessels. All this sitting on thick red carpeting. Sam felt a bit intimidated.

Menendez sensed Sam's suffering. "Relax Sam. This is all show. I'm just a regular policeman doing police work. They gave me this office and a title when I received my last promotion. But, you know, I'm still working as hard as I did when I started years ago."

He continued, "I hear you have an honorable reputation. You work hard and smart. Stay at it until the job is finished. Me too. I like that. But, it doesn't make any difference what your title is, police work is the same at the top and the bottom. Am I right about this?"

"Not much to look forward to then," Sam commented wryly.

"Ha, you make a joke, I see," Menendez said.

"One damn thing for sure Alfonso, it keeps us hopping. Seems like I eat, drink and sleep this work. Interesting."

'Well, let's take a look at our Mr. Baxter", Mendendez said, reaching for a folder on the comer of his desk, entitled 'Mark Baxter.?'

Sam noticed the size of the yellow manila folder. It was bulky. He sensed that Baxter must have compiled some kind of record while with the DEA in Mexico.

Menendez started. "Mr. Baxter is quite a character. It seems he is a very respectable and scrupulous individual. It's hard to see him as a man on the run involved in a criminal escapade. From our records he exemplifies the kind of person we would strive to secure for our purposes. I wonder where he went wrong?"

"It's hard to say," Sam said. "When things aren't going right after a time, well, maybe you'll do things that aren't in character. Life's short. Maybe he saw it all coming to a close too fast. Decided this was his chance to make it better. Perhaps he weighed the benefits against the risk and said what the hell. I'm not sure that I might not have made the same choice. Three million dollars had to be a helluva temptation. Well, he left a million behind, even two million would be something to have to consider."

"The money then, was the reason for his decision. Is that what you think, Sam?"

'What else. He obviously didn't have any interest in the cocaine on board. He might have considered it, but how was he to carry it out of the mountains? The money was neatly packaged. All he had to do was grab it and run. If he's into drugs, he can buy all he wants. No, I think it was the money for sure. Nevertheless, he's got it and we have to get it and him."

The two men talked for some time. Discussing details in the dossier and strategies. The one thing that kept coming up seemed to be to start from square one. Get back to the airport and expose Baxter's photo to every cab driver until one of them recognizes him and go from there.

"Other than that, Menendez said, everyone will keep their eyes and ears open. Maybe our man will make that one fatal error."

Sam agreed. "I'll spend the balance of today doing just that. I'm off to the airport,"

"It will be tiresome my friend. But until we have more it is the best we can do. Our people have been interviewing taxi drivers, but we've had no success."

Sam departed. He indicated that he would check in later in the day. He asked if Menendez had his telephone number at the motel. He got an affirmative.

CHAPTER 10

Up to this time neither the South Lake Tahoe police nor Mark Baxter knew that another entity had their eye on the prize.

Jack Bates an ex-DEA agent, who had fooled with the rules at the agency, that soured some supervisors, who questioned his continued existence, had him summarily discharged and put on the street. Jack wandered for a time before he made a renewed acquaintance with some old friends in the Mafia. Jack got too cozy with the mob during his tenure at the DEA. It was one of the reasons he was terminated from the agency. Skimming moneys from the hauls they made in their drug bust ended up in Mafia coffers and his own. Jack kept in touch with almost all of his contacts during his DEA days. At least the ones he thought he could benefit from in the future. Jack Bates was a shrewd one. Short, stocky always with a stubble of beard on his face. His clothes had the appearance that he'd slept in them, rumpled with creases where creases didn't belong. Jack also had a reputation for ruthlessness. You might call it excessive force. That, among other things mentioned earlier is what got him thrown out of the DEA.

Jack Bates was in a bit of a predicament. He was beholden to the mob because they had enough on him to send him to the slammer for the rest of his natural life. It was kind of like a mutual need. They needed him to get their money back. Jack's need, of course, was for the mob to keep their mouths shut. He also needed their money to fuel his pursuit of Baxter.

What also interested the mob was that Jack and Mark were arms-length acquaintances from years back. The mob by this time knew that Baxter had their money but did not know exactly where he was. Interestingly, Mark was only aware that some of the money was FBI sting money, from media reports. And he wasn't sure if in fact he had the FBIs dough with him. He, Mark, did not know that two million dollars out of the three million on the downed aircraft was purchase money for cocaine to be bought in San Francisco. They, the mob, had just made a large buy and sale in Reno and were on their way for the second purchase when the plane went down.

Reno and San Francisco were now the hot spots for making drug deals since the DEA and the Alcohol, Tobacco and Firearms agency, (ATF) had thrown a net over LA and San Diego. For that matter over the entire southern border of the US. Reno and San Francisco were now terminal and distribution points for most of the drugs coming into the West Coast.

A second meeting took place between Jack Bates, now a runner for the Mafia and one of the honchos in charge of West Coast operations, four days after the crash. Jack needed the money and he knew it would pay well if he were successful in recovering the mobs outlay. In a plush suite of rooms high above Las Vegas' skyline, Jack was receiving instructions, better described as a dressing down from the number two man on the coast.

"Bates, my boy, you let this baby slip through your fingers. You had a handle on it right up to the time the plane went down. What happened? You said it was in the bag. We want that money and we want it right now. We put a lot of time and effort into completing the deal. Now no one knows for sure where the money is, to say nothing of our stash. The boys are getting nervous and that makes me very nervous. You get my point?"

Jack wasn't too keen about his attitude. "Let's get one point straight Fritz, I'm not your boy. but you have my permission to call me Jack." Fritz smiled. Jack continued. "You think I'm happy about this situation?" The cigarette hanging from his mouth bobbed up and down as he talked. "I'm the one that put in the time, not you guys, or your boys, if you get my drift. Don't push me, and tell your boys to cool their heels, I'm their only hope of recovering the money. You people better get that through your skulls. You press me and I disappear. I'm not going to be bullied by a bunch of punk assholes who do nothing but sit on their butts and give orders. You keep forgetting that I'm the one that introduced you to the opportunity. Without me you don't have dick. You want to send them around, I'll talk to them. Your sleeze bags don't scare me one damn bit. Besides, I know most of them and some are my friends."

"Cool down Jack. I just wanted to emphasize the urgency. We know you've got a tough situation on your hands. It's just that they get anxious when they don't know what's happening. You know we're talking a lot of money here. And I'm responsible."

"Don't worry, I'll keep everyone advised as soon as I have anything and I've already got a lead."

The meeting was brief. Jack was in the drivers seat and he knew it. They knew it too. Without him they were dead in the water in so far as recovering the money.

Jack had another contact, a very good one. It was one within the local police department. The police knew that someone in their organization was spilling information, but an ongoing investigation up to now failed to reveal who the culprit was. Through his source, Jack had knowledge of Sam Weston's involvement in the case and his departure to Mexico City. He was familiar with Mexico City. True to his principles of keeping contact with old friends, Jack had a ton of source information in Mexico.

Another ironic factor in this crazy quilt was that Bruce, the deceased pilot, and Jack Bates had been a team when both were employed by the DEA. Mark Baxter entered the picture at the DEA sometime later. Mark, Jack and Bruce had crossed paths, briefly, on a couple of occasions but for all intents and purposes really did not have intimate knowledge of one another. However, Mark and Bruce later became loose friends as a result of working together on a couple of investigations. Their relationship, if you will, continued after leaving the DEA because of the proximity of their existence. Reno and Tahoe are geographically close. However, they didn't socialize.

Jack Bates visited Rosanne in Reno to pay his respects and condolences.

Rosanne was surprised when she looked up from her desk to see someone she didn't like very well.

"Jack Bates," she said with a frowned expression, "What on earth are you doing here? I thought by this time someone would have done you in."

"Ha." Jack looked at her with disdain. "Sweetheart, nobody is fast or good enough to do that. I just dropped by to pay my respects. I'm really sorry about Bruce. Bruce was a great guy. We had some good times before you. I mean when he was still single. We raised some hell together south of the border."

She was not comfortable. "What do you want Jack? You can see I'm busy. He left me with a mess."

"Tell me Rose, do you have any idea what happened? You know, about the crash. It looks suspicious. An explosion, they tell me. Is that right?"

"I don't know. I'm as much in the dark as you. All I know is that I lost a husband, my future, my security. Jack, you won't get anything out of me. The FBI and a detective from the police department up at the lake have been here. They haven't told me anything that I can say for sure what happened. Nobody knows what really happened. They're still investigating. I was told that they would let me know when they knew more."

"By the way, an old friend of yours, Mark Baxter was here. The only thing that Jack was interested in from her conversation was that Mark Baxter was here."

"Well by and bye." He said. "We did some business in Mexico City once. A long time ago. I remember Bruce and he had something going at the time. I ended up in the bust after they had almost completed it. Baxter, I think was stationed in Columbia at the time. He was on temporary assignment because the connections in the Cali Cartel were using Mexico City as a hub for the movement of kilos to the US."

"He was here," he continued. "That's very interesting. When?"

"I thought you might be." Rosy said. "About a week ago."

"Is he still at the lake?"

"As far as I know."

"Rose if there's anything I can do, I wish you would let me know."

"Why Jack, that's so unlike you. Are you mellowing?"

"Rose, I'm really not like I pretend to be. I've got some soft spots, just like everybody else. But, nobody wants to think of me as a nice guy. So, I play the asshole. It works."

"Jack, you can't fool me. I've known you since you were a kid. You grew up looking for a fight. You were always in trouble. You were the school bully, remember. I can't imagine you turning over a new leaf"

"Well, if that's the way you feel, then so be it. I can't change your mind over night. My fighting days are over, unless, he hesitated, unless someone does something stupid and pushes me to the edge."

"I'll bet that wouldn't take much," she said.

"Sometimes," he shrugged his shoulders. "Anyway if you need anything, buzz me."

"Good luck Jack, in a way it was nice seeing you again."

"Same here."

Jack landed in Mexico City some six days after Mark and Sam.

After securing his luggage, he headed for the nearest telephone. The concourses were teeming with people. P A systems blaring departures and arrivals in five different languages consuming any tranquility that might possibly exist. The hordes of travelers, dragging their assortment of tattered suitcases, cardboard boxes and reluctant screaming children trying to make connections set an atmosphere of pure pandemonium. Somewhere secluded in the distance he could hear the rhythmic strains of a Mariachi band welcoming all arrivals to Mexico.

Eyeing a bank of telephones along a brightly multi-colored tile wall, Jack made for one of the empty booths. The phone on the other end rang twice.

"Buenos Dias," a soothing pleasant voice announced.

"Yes, this is Jack Bates, an old friend of Jimmys, is he there?"

"One moment please."

Jack could hear the muffled conversation on the other end. "A senor Jack Bates" ... she was interrupted abruptly. "Momma Sita, Jack Bates, tell him I'll be right there."

"Jack, you old buzzard, how you been?" His English was perfect and should have been. Jimmy was educated at UCLA, his mother Anglo and his father a Mexican, lived in the US for a time.

"Hey Jimmy, I'm fine, and you?"

"Great Jack, what the hell you doin down this way? You still up in the states?"

"Hell yes, why leave a good thing." He continued, "Jimmy I need your help. Are any of the old guys still around?"

"Some of them. They've scattered. Ceasar Gonzales, remember him?, he stayed on after we left the agency. Sometime later somebody with the Medillian Cartel wasted him, about a year ago. He got in the way of a bullet. Where are you?"

"At the airport. Came in on Aero Mexico."

"Hang there. I'll pick you up. Gimme a half hour. OK?" His voice was full of excitement. "How long has it been?"

"I can't remember partner. A while. I'll wait. I'll be outside on the concourse."

In anticipation of Jimmy's arrival Jack fidgeted on the sidewalk outside the airport under the Aero Mexico sign. Jimmy pulled up in the same 1982 Pontiac Trans Am, that he drove when Jack left Mexico. The paint faded and peeling, and a few more dents. Each recognized the other immediately. Jack's slouch and disheveled appearance hadn't changed. Even if he had transformed the cigarette butt hanging from his mouth would have been enough to place him. Jack never got the message from the Surgeon General.

The two men embraced warmly. They held onto each other, patting and talking with exuberant chatter.

"Jack, you haven't changed a damn bit," Jimmy said, stepping back slightly to confirm.

"I see you're still driving America's scrap."

"Hey, what the hell, it runs good, just like me." He laughed.

"What are you doing down here?"

"Looking for one of our compatriots." Jack said.

"Who?"

"Mark Baxter."

"Who?" Jimmy asked again. Confused. "I don't recognize that name."

"Maybe not, as a team, you and me, we never worked with him, but you might remember the guy that headed the southern sector, ah, sometime around eighty two, eighty three. His people got into some kind of trouble and he took the rap. He was canned. They hushed it up quick so not to taint the overall operation."

"Well, vaguely, but I'm still not tuned in. Anyway, what you want him for?"

"He's running with a lot of dough. He flew in here a couple of days ago. Last week, I believe."

"How much?" Jimmy asked.

"I'm not sure, Jimmy but its substantial."

"Like how substantial?" Jimmy asked.

"A couple of mil."

"Geees. You with the feds?"

"No, hell no. I'm representing some friends that want to get their hands on it."

"What kind of scratch is it? I mean, legit or no?"

Jack smiled. "You ask too many questions. Actually it is legitimately my clients money, but what they do with it is questionable. Enough said?"

"Not exactly," Jimmy responded. "I would like to know who the money belongs to before I get involved."

"As far as I know it is or was mob money. And from what I can gather, some of it belongs to the feds. I'm not quite sure who owns what or how much or how it came down, but I do know it was purchase money. The plane's destination was San Francisco, but it turned into a tragedy when it crashed. Both the feds and my clients want the dough back. It's kinda like a chase to see who can get to it first. Naturally the feds want all of it. Weston, a Lake Tahoe cop in the jurisdiction where the theft took place wants it for the glory and the prestige. More likely, for self gratification, because he's got a reputation of being a goddamn hound dog that won't let up. Me, I really don't give a shit. If I come across some of it, all the better. I'm being paid to see if can win the race. It's no skin off my nose if I don't succeed. Does that ease your mind?"

"Sure, I'm real relaxed. I don't know which is worse. Screwing with the Mafia or your government. Those bastards can be more brutal than any mob goon."

"If you feel that way, you can back out now. I'll work it on my own."

"No way. It's squirmy, but what the hell, look at me. What have I got to lose? Except stay on the run for the rest of my life." He laughed. "Anything in it for me? I mean, if I'm instrumental in getting it back. I sure could use the bucks."

"I can't say for sure. Like I said, I'm being paid, but I'm not guaranteed."

"My time's got to be worth something." Jimmy said.

"I'll see that you get taken care of if there's any profit for me. You know that."

Jimmy seemed satisfied with Jack's response.

Jimmy was living over a bar in a run down section of the old city. One room upstairs, overlooking a tree dotted park filled with down and outers lying on and under weathered benches resembling piles of rags in a landfill.

Climbing the rickety stairs, stepping over pieces of plaster that had fallen from the graffiti scared walls and ceiling, Jack commented, "Surely, you can do better than this, James. Why the hell you living in a trap like this?"

"Listen Jack, our government discards us when they're finished with you. I worked my ass off for the bastards and look where I end up. No pension, no nothin. I told you I needed the bucks. Now you see.'

The room was in disarray. Litter strewn everywhere. It smelled of pungent spices. His bed unmade, newspapers scattered throughout. Uneaten food on several plates in the chipped and stained porcelain sink. Jack was nauseated.

"I gotta clean this place up, sometime."

"It needs some TLC, my boy."

"Yeah, I know. Let's get down to facts. Where do we start?"

Jack bulldozed a stack of papers aside and sat on the edge of the bed. It sank almost throwing him to the floor. "I thought you might tell me." Jack played him using his penetrating stare to elicit a response. Jimmy remembered that look. "Any of the people we used to know? Anyone at all, think. Maybe one or two that have kept tabs on what's happening."

"I'll tell you Jack, I've lost contact with most of them, but I can make a few calls and find out."

"What about Pedro Cortez and that other mope that used to pick fights with me, until I knocked him on his ass, ah, Hector Ruiz, is he still around?"

"Ha, yeah, I remember him, and that stupid expression he carried on his face, like he was always sleepy. He was a turd. But I think he got shoved upstairs and they moved him to Columbia. He's somebody else's problem now."

"Find out where Cortez is. I've got to get a handle on this pronto. Where's a phone?"

"Downstairs, in the bar."

The bar was not much of a beauty. It could have duplicated Jimmy's room. It was easy to see how it rubbed off on him. The phone was hanging by a thread on a wall in the rear, next to the heads, which made themselves obvious by their smell. Jack stood by while Jimmy flipped through the tattered pages. Most of them were missing.

"There's a million Pedro Cortezs' here Jack. This ain't going to be easy."

Jimmy dialed away and Jack kept feeding him Pesos, ten at a time. One futile call followed another.

"This is a waste of time Jack. I got a better idea. We'd have better luck at the station. I know some people there. They'll know if Cortez is still around."

As Jack and Jimmy approached the station house, Jack said, "Jim, you go in alone. Just act like you're looking up some old friends. It would look kind of awkward if I'm standing around. Besides, I don't necessarily want them to even know of my existence. That be OK?"

"Sure Jack, no problem."

Jack waited patiently in Jimmy's car. A half hour passed before he returned. Entering the vehicle, Jimmy smiled. Jack wasn't sure how to take his demeanor.

"Goddammit Jimmy, what'd you do, interrogate the entire force."

"At first I wasn't getting anywhere. Practically nobody in there that I knew. I had to nose around. I thought they were going to throw me out, but I hung in and got some real good info."

"Let's have it."

"You're going to love this. You ever heard of a Sam Weston? He's a detective from up your way."

"Yeah, I mentioned him a while ago. He's down here for the same reason as me."

"You got that right," Jimmy said. "Weston pulled in here two days ago. He's working with the big boys inside. A honcho by the name of Menendez. They're hot on his tail."

"Baxter is still here in the city. I got some skinny as to where Weston is holed up. So I think if we tail him we will get our man."

"Sounds plausible. Where?"

"A motel just a couple of blocks from here. The 'Ensanada.'" They've furnished him with transportation too. A Toyota Corolla. Tan."

"Did you by chance see him? Weston I mean, we've got to know what he looks like."

"No, but it shouldn't be too difficult to spot him, he'll be the only gringo staying at the motel. From what I understand he's at the airport passing Baxter's photo around. Trying to find the cabby that took Baxter to wherever he's dropped his shorts."

"Then, that's it. Let's check out the Ensanada. Find a good spot to observe from. Gonna be a long day Jim."

CHAPTER 11

Mark felt uneasy being out and about. Especially from exposing himself in such open public locales. He hadn't been in the Palace of Art but a short time when he thought better of his situation. Carlos had left the Palace on Mark's insistence that he should be trying to make as many fares as possible the remainder of that day. He told Carlos that he would catch another taxi back to his hotel. Carlos agreed. Carlos had visited the Palace many times before and wasn't interested in going through it again.

Mark arrived back at The Ascension and went straight to his suite without so much as stopping to pick up a newspaper. Lying on his bed he began to reminisce about Alexis and the past weeks events. It brought on a mixed bag of good and bad feelings. The good were ecstatic. The bad were worrisome. And there was more bad than good. It felt debilitating. He began to sweat. He forced the ill feelings from his mind. The bad he could do nothing about for now. It would pass he hoped. Alexis. What to do about Alexis. He thought about her constantly. She was in his dreams. He would see her face in other women. He felt as if it was beginning to effect his sanity. He had all this money, but no Alexis to share it with. The money was again taking on a hollow victory. He was deep in thought about her when his room telephone rang.

"Senor Bradford?"

He kept forgetting he was using the name Bradford. It didn't ring at first. Mark was edgy. "Yes."

"Senor Bradford, there is a gentleman asking for you."

Mark sat upright and lost his voice momentarily. "Do you know who it is? Did he give his name?"

"No Senor, but he says it is important."

"Ask him to wait. Try to stall him. Don't tell him I'm here. Ah" he hesitated, "Never mind, I'll be right down."

"Yes sir, I'll keep him occupied."

Mark anticipating the worst prepared himself for the circumstances. The perspiration that had evaporated from minutes before again moistened his brow. He felt once more as he did when on the mountain with the dogs pursuing. Who could it be? He thought. Carlos was working the line at the airport. No one else knew of his whereabouts except Alexis. Surely she wouldn't have turned him in. Besides, she only knew that he was in Mexico City, but not exactly where. The museum, he mused. He had been spotted. It could only be the police. His mind was racing. He cringed in fear, thinking that this was the beginning of a long and tortuous trip.

In a trot, he hustled down the hallway to the stairway that exited into the lobby. He did not take the elevator knowing it would open directly into the lobby exposing him to whoever was waiting. At the bottom of the stairway he cracked the door leading into the foyer. He could not recognize any familiar faces. Carefully he opened the door and proceeded hugging the wall down the hallway to the corner where he could see into the entire lobby. He continued looking over the individuals milling about, but still no recall of anyone of them. Hesitatingly he stepped into full view at, the expense of being apprehended.

In the far comer standing beside a large marble column, stood a man with his back to Mark. It appeared to be Carlos. Mark wasn't sure. He chanced an approach. As he neared who he thought was Carlos, he glanced over at the desk. The clerk nodded toward the man he thought was Carlos, indicating that he was the individual looking for Mark. Sure that the person was Carlos, Mark felt a heavy weight disappear, Mark tapped him on the shoulder. He turned.

"Carlos, this is a surprise, What brings you here?"

He reached into his shirt pocket and extracted a photograph. He held it up for Mark to see. "Is this you Senor?"

Mark remained expressionless. He examined the photo without comment. Mark knew it was him but refrained from confessing.

"Why, where did you get this?" he asked nonchalantly.

"Look on the back Senor."

Turning the photograph over, he saw emblazoned in large letters "Mark Baxter."

"1 was confused when I received this photo Mr. Bradford, because it is not your name, but it looks exactly like you. I thought I might be mistaken, because the name did not make sense."

"Tell me Carlos, where did you get this picture?"

"At the airport. They are passing them out to all the cab drivers," he said with his Spanish accent.

"Who's passing them out?" Mark knew, but wanted a confirmation.

"The police. They started yesterday and are there again today asking for any information about this man. Is it you Senor? Carlos continued, I was off duty last evening when they first passed them out. My amigos said so. This afternoon when I left you at the Arts Palace and returned to the airport, I was, how you say, approached by the police and asked about this person, Mr. Baxter. I have been busy all day with fares, and this is the first chance I have had to come to find out if I am mistaken."

"No, it's not me, Carlos, but is sure does look like me, eh."

"Well anyway, I thought that you should know, just in case. It has been bothering me all day. I am sorry to have disturbed you with this thing Senor. Can you forgive me? I hope that this man they are looking for has not done something evil. I feel sorry for him if he did. It frightens me," he said in his child like manner.

Mark reached into his wallet and handed Carlos a ten dollar bill.

"That is not necessary Senor."

"Take it Carlos, you've probably lost a fare to come here."

He accepted with a bow and Adious. "If you need me Senor, contact the dispatcher. Here's the number." Carlos handed Mark a business card and parted.

"Thanks again, Carlos. Don't worry, it's not me in the photo. Somebody else obviously."

Even though Mark's beard somewhat obscured his clean shaven face in the photo, from Carlos, it meant he could be recognized. An alarm sounded. It rang loud and clear. Just as if it were a fire in the lobby. He knew instantly the authorities were closing in. It was time to depart Mexico City for the time being. But first he had to find out how the desk clerk knew to call him if Carlos had asked for a person named Baxter.

He approached the desk. Several patrons were being attended to. Mark was biting at the bit, nervously. He squirmed. When the clerk was free Mark asked, "Tell me, how did you know to ask for me, when Carlos asked for a guy named Baxter?"

"From the photo, it looked exactly like you sir. I don't care what name you register under. Your dollars are good here no matter who you are."

"That's admirable of you." But it wasn't me. I don't know who the person is. Ah, by the way I will be departing soon. My employer has asked me to return to the office. But I'm sure I'll be coming back very soon. Will the contents of the vault be safe in my absence?"

"Yes sir. The contents of the vault is privileged. Besides, you have the only key. If we are asked we disavow any knowledge of anything stored. Under any circumstances. Will you be staying with us when you return? I hope your short stay has been a pleasant one."

"Yes, most pleasant. Thanks."

Mark returned to his suite, made some brief mental notes while packing his belongings. He jotted down Carlos' taxi number and tucked it in his wallet.

Mark returned to the desk, his suitcase and overnight bag containing a bunch of cash in hand. Reaching into his wallet he pulled out five twenty dollar bills and handed them to the clerk.

"Do me a favor, will you?" Mark asked.

"Surely," the clerk said, holding the money, "anything Senor."

"Take my name off the register. I've never been here. You never heard of me, period. Can you handle that?"

"Done sir."

Mark left the hotel with plenty of cash. He refused the assistance of the doorman to hail a taxi. He walked ten blocks or so before the pain in his shoulders begged relief from the suitcase. At a bus stop he noted the times of arrival and departures. It was difficult in Spanish, but numerals are numerals in any language. While studying the schedule a bus belching smoke, pulled along side, screeching and squealing to a halt seemingly against the drivers wishes. It was crowded, filthy and bathed in graffiti. The windows were coated with a haze of bluish gray. Passengers had etched their names and initials onto the windows as one might inside a steamed window. Mark struggled with his luggage trying to find a seat. Standing room only. Frustrated, he grabbed onto a strap and cradled the suitcase between his feet. He choked on the pungent exhaust fumes that whirled in through the open windows. There were more fans waving back and forth than in a mosque. The brakes continuously ground and squealed to a stop at the end of every block. Then, the over laden behemoth would buck and lurch forward as the driver changed gears in his attempt to get the vehicle up to speed. The jerking back and forth created a stinging, aching agitation as the leather strap dug into the palm of his hand. Hanging on to avoid falling, he wondered where this contraption was taking him. But, it didn't matter for the time being. It was taking him out of harms way.

Leaning down, looking out through the haze on the window, in an attempt to determine his location, he recognized the Shrine of Guadeloupe, on the Avenue of the Revolucion. He realized that the motor coach was heading in the direction of the airport. Exactly where he wanted to go, but not in this vehicle. It would take a week to get there at the rate of stops. He exited, tripping on the ragged rubber mat from an overly worn stairwell. Regaining his composure, he stood on the curb. Both he and his baggage were awash in diesel smoke as the bus pulled away, groaning.

Sam in the meantime was not having much luck flashing Mark's photograph in the face of every cab driver. The line of taxis was long, at least fifty or so, all waiting for that ultimate fare. He heard, "No Senor," so many times he began to acquire a rejection complex. Even though he was working under a protective canopy, the intrusive heat from the sun overhead caused him to sweat profusely. He was about to take a break when he struck pay dirt. His luck was about to change.

"You ever see this man?" Sam asked, his arm extended halfway into the cab through the open passenger window. His badge dangled under the photo.

Carlos had seen the photo the day before when the police had presented him with it. At that introduction he asked for a copy pretending not to know Baxter.

Carlos first looked at the image then the badge. "Si Senor, I know of him."

Sam smiled. "Was he in your cab? Did you take him from here?"

"Let me think." Carlos responded.

Sam opened the door and sat down next to Carlos. "Let's go, he said, you can think on the way."

Carlos pulled away from the line and passed the others waiting.

"Ah, he started again, I think it was The Acenscion."

Carlos was very fond of Mark Baxter. He knew at the time when he presented the photo to Mark yesterday that it was Mark, not Miles Bradford, even though Mark denied it. And he also knew that Mark would vacate the hotel from his reaction to the photograph. At least he hoped so. Carlos, in order to cover his knowledge, went along with Sam. Pretending that he'd never known such an individual by the alias. It made no difference and it would make him look like he was cooperating with the police.

"Are you sure?" Sam asked.

"Si Senor, I am sure. It was several days ago."

"Where is this hotel?, The Acension."

"On the edge of the city. I mean it used to be on the edge. Now it is very much inside the city."

Confused, Sam asked, "What do you mean on the edge, maybe used to be? That doesn't make any sense."

"It does to me," he said, his mustache widened as he smiled. "Don't worry, Senor, it is but a short ride there. Maybe fifteen minutes, maybe twenty. It all depends on traffic. Are you in a hurry?"

"Mucho Pronto." Sam shot back sarcastically.

Carlos chuckled, thinking Sam's Spanish sounded foolish.

"My name is Carlos," he volunteered, extending his hand across the front seat.

"Sam Weston, Carlos, nice to meet you."

"Nice to meet you senor," he said politely, nodding his head.

"What do you want with this Mr. Bradford?"

"Bradford, Sam asked, is that the name he used?"

"A very nice man, Senor Bradford."

"Are you sure we're on the right track here, Carlos?"

"Let me see his picture again," Carlos asked. He knew it was Baxter.

Sam handed the photo to Carlos with an inquisitive look.

Carlos held the photo up in front of him, glancing at it then at the road, then back again to the image.

"Yes, that is him. Maybe just a little difference in the eyes, but I could not mistake the rest of the face. He is a very handsome man. Large, strong looking. He said he was visiting on business. Something to do with the art business. Why do you want him? Did he steal some art?"

"You might say that, pre-printed art."

It was Carlos' turn to look confused.

Carlos' artful act in traffic was world class. His bobbing and weaving through unimaginable and uninhibited chaos startled Sam but not a sign of stress or anxiety could be seen in Carlo's demeanor. Converging lines of hurtling metal seemed to be coming together all at once with complete disregard for spacing. Arms waiving, signals being ignored, horns blaring, astonished Sam. All this being accomplished under a shroud of yellow and gray haze. Not a traffic cop in sight. It was hot.

When the cab pulled up in front of the elegant old hotel the doorman rushed down the carpeted steps to open the door, but Sam beat him to it.

"Thanks anyway," he said.

The doorman bowed his usual curtsy.

"Wait here," Sam ordered. Carlos nodded.

The hotel lobby was empty. Sam went straight to the reception desk. The clerk sitting had his head down reading a girlie magazine. Sam's attention was distracted by the beautiful nude centerfold. Does sex sell, he thought instantly.

The clerk looked up. "Como esta usted, senor. Can I help you?"

Sam flashed his ID. "Yeah, You have a Mark Bax ... er, a Miles Bradford registered."

The clerk flipped pages in the registration book back and forth.

"No sir, I do not see that name here."

"May I see it?" Sam asked.

"Si." He swirled the book around for Sam to see straight on.

Sam carefully scanned each page as if he were memorizing each guests name. Nothing. Not in the past five days. No Miles Bradford, no Mark Baxter or anything resembling either name.

Sam pulled out Mark's photo and shoved it towards the clerk. "Ever see this man?"

The clerk studied the photo, viewing it from one angle then another. He held the image at arms length then up close as if being sincere.

"No sir, I've never seen this man," lying.

"I'll be right back," Sam said, "Hold on." He rudely snatched the photo from the clerks hand and headed out the front entrance.

Carlos had pulled the cab over to the curb away from incoming traffic.

Jack and Jimmy who had followed, waited across the street from the entrance.

Sam was upset when he jumped in beside Carlos. "Dammit Carlos, they've never seen or heard of this guy."

Carlos turned off the radio and the raucous music he'd been listening to.

"Are you sure you brought him here, to this hotel."

"I'm sure senor." Confessing. "I talked to him yesterday in the lobby. It has to be the same man."

Sam thought for sure that Carlos must be mistaken. That it had to be somebody that looked like Baxter.

Sam went back into the lobby. again ordering Carlos to stick by.

Jack and Jimmy sat waiting. "This could take some time. I'm getting thirsty." Jimmy said.

"Pain in the butt, I know James, but I love it when someone else does the grunt work."

Approaching the desk, the clerk looked up again from his magazine with disdain. He didn't like having the twitching in his shorts disturbed.

"Who else can I talk to that occupies this position? How many shifts are there?"

"There are only three of us, senor. I would be glad to pass the photograph around for you, if you like."

"When's the next shift change?"

"In an hour, sir. Would you like to wait?"

"I can't" he said, "I'll be back."

Sam returned to the cab. The music blaring again. Rhythmic mariachi. "Carlos, 1 don't know if you are right or wrong about this guy Bradford, but it's the only lead I've got. We're going back to the airport. Let's get hopping."

Carlos revved the engine and eased into traffic, maneuvering into the fast lane. Moving against oncoming traffic made the going easier. The stream of dented, sun bleached and faded vehicular mass flowed smoothly even though the streets were busy with the rumbling horde. Traveling at forty sometimes fifty miles per hour, Carlos displayed his expertise, out foxing everything in his path. Patience paid off for Jack. Aware that Sam had come up with something important by the way he hustled into Carlos' cab, the two followed close behind.

"Hustle, damn it Jim. They're getting away."

"For crying out loud, get off my butt. I've got them in sight. Keep cool my friend, remember 1 live here. Besides they're headed for the airport."

"How the hell you know that?" Jack asked.

Carlos was nearing the airport when suddenly out of nowhere on his blind side a delivery van ran a stop sign and slammed broadside into the taxi, near the front door opening. The cab spun around throwing the vehicle and its occupants in a complete three hundred and sixty degree circle. Sam, in the rear seat was thrown across the interior, smashing his forehead into the window handle, opening up a large gash. Bleeding profusely, dazed from the confusion, he arose from the floor to see and hear more turmoil outside. The ringing in his ear wasn't from the crash but from the pulsating of a siren approaching in the distance.

Carlos, instinctively hung onto the steering wheel and escaped injury.

Nearby, Jack and Jimmy witnessed the accident. Jimmy parked the Trans Am to the side, out of the way of traffic. They waited.

The taxi was completely incapacitated, lying dead in the intersection, steam swirling in the air, emanating from the radiator. Air escaping from the rear tire hissed and evaporated. Then, out from the deafening noise that had just preceded a silence blanketed the scene. Sam's thoughts went immediately to the futility of the chase.

He stumbled out the opposite side into the crowd that had gathered at the scene. A police car was inching its way through the tumult to reach the wreckage, its siren now silent. Over a loudspeaker, the crowd was chastened to disperse. Few, if any, obeyed, then reluctantly.

Sam recognized a sharp thumping in his left shoulder. He tried to raise his arm. The pain stung. With his right hand he reached into his rear pocket for his handkerchief. Pressing it against the wound on his forehead he managed to stop the bleeding. He was about to succumb to the discomfort when he heard a reassuring voice tell him that an ambulance was on its way. It was the officer.

When the ambulance pulled along side the accident, Sam was in serious pain. More than he could tolerate. His shoulder was bleating with sharp, stinging pangs. He had managed to halt the flow of blood with the handkerchief, but when he let up the blood spilled as before.

The paramedics kneeling beside Sam determined his condition before moving him. Recognizing him a gringo, they spoke in English. Carefully they moved him to a stretcher, securing his neck with a brace. Before he realized he was inside the red and white van, the siren sounding its warning, heading to the nearest emergency room. Laying quietly inside the van, over the muffled wailing of the siren, he cursed his bad luck.

Jack and Jimmy followed the ambulance using the path that the ambulance's siren cleared for anyone close behind.

Sometimes luck comes in waves. Good and bad. He was in and out of the emergency room within an hour. His head wound was stitched and patched securely. He called for a cab. With his left arm in a sling he struggled to stow away the bottle of pain killers the doctor gave him.

The cab delivered him to his motel where he called Menendez to inform him of his situation. The pain killers worked their wonders. He felt fit and wanted to proceed. It was just after two 0'clock in the afternoon. Resting somewhat on his bed he felt compelled to get going. He couldn't let the opportunity pass and let Baxter escape. If there was any chance of getting his man, he had to work through the pain.

Jack and Jimmy patiently waited, not saying a word to one another. Jack dozed off.

Sam summoned a cab. It wasn't until that moment that he thought of Carlos. If he was all right. The thought of catching Baxter had completely occupied his mind overshadowing all else.

The taxi pulled up in front of the airport. At the Aero Mexico airlines counter, the one he assumed that Baxter would use, if in fact Mark had departed, he exposed Mark's photo to a pretty thing that smiled at him in sympathy.

"Rough day, Senor." As if making a statement.

The scowl on Sam's face wasn't a friendly response. It even hurt to do that.

"No just a friendly soccer game." He knew that would throw her off, more importantly, shut off her next question. "Ever see this guy?" his eyes pointing to the photo.

She studied it for a couple of seconds. "Yes, he was here this morning. About ten o'clock. He's in Columbia by now. Why? Do you want," she stopped in mid sentence, recognizing Sam's ID.

"Anybody with him?"

"No, he was alone."

"Columbia. Where, Bogota?" Sam surmised.

"Yes, Bogota. It would have arrived about an hour ago."

"Thanks, you've been more than kind," he winced. Why he hung that courtesy on the end he couldn't figure. Unless it was the way she appealed to him.

Sam looked around for the nearest phone bank. "Phones, were are they?"

"Behind you sir."

On the opposite wall there were five empty booths. Reaching around his waist with his good arm to get to his wallet was not only awkward but irritating. He let out a groan. The slick leather wallet kept escaping his grasp, each time sliding back down into his pocket. "Damn," he said aloud, catching the attention of some passerby.

"Poor fellow." He heard one say. Insult to injury, he thought.

Pinching the wallet between his index and middle finger, he slowly and carefully lifted it out of the pocket. It dropped to the floor. Leaning over to pick it up his shoulder reminded him that he wasn't a well person. Sharp undulating pain riveted down his left side and pounded at the wound site on his head. Again he cursed, looking around to see if anyone heard him.

"Menendez, this is Sam."

"I know. how are you feeling?"

"OK, I guess. Listen, our man has fled to Columbia."

"We know. However we have no authority in Columbia. Something about their extradition policy. A problem the bureaucrats haven't worked out yet." The emphasis was on yet. "We can't go after him legally. They won't allow us to enter their space to apprehend fugitives. We were afraid this would happen. We didn't bring it up since we were hoping that it wouldn't happen."

"Suppose he knew that?" Sam said.

"What do you think." Menendez answered.

"I've learned that he just arrived there. Maybe he'll hang around there for some reason. Do you have any way of stalling him at the airport in Bogota until I can get there?"

"We can try, but no guarantee. Their people get into trouble with the higher ups if they are suspected of helping the Mexicans. So, they let criminals come and go without so much as an inquiry. I'm afraid it's up to you. You should stay in touch with us in case he comes back here."

"I'm hurting," Sam said.

"I know that too, sorry."

"How come you people are so quick on info, but you let this guy get out of here without detection."

"Because maybe he's a little quicker than we are. You ever think of that possibility?"

"Never occurred to me," Sam said.

"1 think we have got, how you say, one smart cookie on our hands." He continued. "After all, you let him get out of your country before we even knew of his existence. You agree?"

Sam grunted. "Well then, looks like I'm off to South, south of the border."

"Sam, we will do whatever is necessary to assist you on this thing, but right now our hands are strapped. 1 remind you to keep in touch with us. You never know, he might, or should 1 say, will be thinking of his next move. It could be back here. One thing is sure, he is going to do whatever makes him feel comfortable. He knows Columbia and Mexico City in particular very well. It is safe to say that he knows he is being stalked and his wits are going to be working overtime to stay ahead of us."

CHAPTER 12

Taking Mendendez's advice about not being able to stall Baxter, along with the pain, Sam decided to return to his motel. The aching was unbearable, the medicine was wearing off. He reasoned that getting to Columbia several hours or even a day or two later wouldn't make that much difference.

Setting off for the motel again, this time in the Toyota, Sam was followed by Jack and Jimmy. Both men had witnessed the after math of the accident, followed the ambulance to the hospital, waited, then proceeded to follow Sam to the airport. And now back to the motel once more. And waited.

Sam succumbed to sleep. Some four hours had passed. The pain over his eye and in his shoulder awakened him to a crescendo of throbs. He reached for the pain medicine and the glass of water on the night stand. Falling back onto the bed, he waited for the pain to subside.

After a time he reached for the telephone. It seemed like he had to talk to half of the operators in Mexico before getting through to Dickson.

"Captain, this is Sam. I've got a bit of troubling news."

"We've heard. How are you Sam?"

"Ah, a bit under the weather. But it will pass. You know about the accident then?"

"Yes, we're worried about you. Do you think you can continue?"

"Of course. But what I wanted to tell you, is that our man has fled Mexico. We think he might have gone to Columbia. I want to rest for the balance of the day and then get on with it. I almost, I think, had him. I was right on his tail. Maybe missed him by an hour or two. He's real quick to pick up on our moves. Got to respect him. He's living up to his reputation."

"Sam, I talked to Menendez a while ago. He briefed me. I get the opinion that Columbia, if that's where he is, won't cooperate with them and I know that they will not work with us either. The Colombian authorities can't seem to want do anything for anybody but the DEA. They have some sort of reciprocal agreement. Even then they chew at the edges of the paperwork before they sign anything. It's bureaucratic crap. So, if you're up to it, when and if you want to, get on to Bogota as soon as possible. But, for God's sake get well and take care of yourself You need anything, and I mean anything, call."

"Do you suppose if we called the DEA."

The Captain interrupted. "You want to talk about bureaucratic nonsense or get some rest."

"1 suppose you're right." He put down the receiver and fell back on the bed once more.

Sam knew as he waited for boarding that this was going to be a day of hurting. His shoulder had stiffened over night and the stinging over his eye would not let up. He needed a stronger pill. The sights and sounds from the multitude of passengers milling around temporarily distracted him from the pain. It was an easing. He appreciated it.

Sitting in the waiting area, it seemed to take forever for the boarding to commence. He looked up at the clock. Time was passing, he was itching to get going. After what seemed to be a dispassionate delay on the part of the airline employees, an announcement of apology came forth on the P A system. The flight was going to be delayed for the want of a crew. They were on their way but it would be fifteen to twenty minutes before their arrival. Sam calculated that to mean at least another hour. He was right.

"Damn, at least they could offer us a drink," he mumbled out loud. The man in the next seat nodded agreement.

Finally the word came. Walking down the long entry tube to the waiting aircraft the line stalled every other second. He wondered why it always took so long for the passengers ahead to stow their belongings and sit down. Get on with it he grumbled. He wanted to remind those that appeared to have excess baggage that they didn't need to drag their entire household along.

Lost in thought, the thrust of the engines threw him back into his seat. The ground fell away beneath the craft. He tensed. Go baby go, he mumbled to himself. Looking down he thought that Mexico City was much more interesting from the air than on the ground. The myriad of interconnecting streets and freeways with the yellow gray haze in the background, again reminded him of Los Angeles.

The flight was smooth, without incident. Arriving he went for his baggage. Here too, it seemed one was on another planet. He was taken aback by all the strange looking dark skinned people running in all directions. Each staring intently at every passerby. Each adorned with a colorful woven shawl. It was warm here, why the hell were they bundled up so. The scene puzzled him. He wondered about the derby like hats on some. Incas, he thought. Weren't they supposed to be in Peru? A constant prate of chatter in Spanish blared over the PA system adding agonizing noise, polluting the air. No one seemed to notice but him. What were they thinking?

He continued on to the baggage claim area following the suitcase icons on the overhead signs. Upon arriving he noticed that the system was as modern as any in the US. To one side and unattended sat several suitcases. Must be one hell of an honor system here, he thought.

While watching and listening to the still empty stainless steel merry go round that-would bring his one small bag to his person, he glanced again at the ten or so bags sitting off in the corner. He couldn't reason with the fact that they just sat there. In the states, he thought, they wouldn't last five minutes before somebody lifted them. His curiosity got the better of him. He strolled the few feet away to inspect the cases. On one he noticed the initials, MB etched on a gold plated medallion. Without so much as a thought, he returned to the carousel.

"MB," it struck him like a hammer blow to the head. "Geez, could it be," he said. Ignoring his suitcase that was approaching he hustled back to the deserted bags. Thinking that if it was Baxter's suitcase he would come to redeem it. The mistake he was hoping Baxter would make. Wham. The arrest. He would have his man and be on his way back to Lake Tahoe with Baxter in cuffs. He felt such an elation that he forgot his suitcase that was bumping along on the carousel alone. He glanced back to see it disappear into the tunnel at the far end of the treadmill. Patience.

His immediate yearning was to go to the lost baggage office to see if Baxter had inquired about it. He hesitated thinking of Murphy's Law. If he did, surely Baxter would show up in his absence, grab the suitcase and be gone.

Again he ceded to patience.

Sitting off in a corner within sight of the suitcases but obscured from traffic by a pillar, he waited on a well worn wooden bench. An hour and a half passed. All of the bags were claimed except two. One of them marked "MB" sat waiting. The one that interested him. He continued reading the Time Magazine he had bought in the terminal in Mexico City. The minutes turned into hours. Three had passed. His butt ached along with his back, shoulder and forehead. He paced, he read, he watched. No claimant.

Then the dawn lighted the day. His waiting, he knew, was for naught. Baxter, if it was Baxter's bag, was not going to claim it. Why should he. The bag was worthless to him. What did it contain but probably some clothing. Stuff that he could replace easily with the money he carried. It would be foolish, at best, to get caught trying to claim replaceable possessions. Baxter's still staying one ploy ahead of us, he thought.

Sam carefully looked over the area once more. If Baxter was here by chance after all this time, Sam would notice. There was no one. Not one individual that looked remotely out of place. And no one that resembled Baxter. He cursed the possibility that Baxter might have shown up while he had his head buried in an article in Time and missed him. Naw, he was aware, he thought.

Sam approached the suitcase. With it in hand he returned to where he had waited. Laying it on the bench he carefully opened it. He was nervous. If it was not Baxter's but someone else's, and he got caught prying about it, he would be embarrassed, worse, trouble. He was right about the contents. There was nothing in the bag except clothing. He rummaged hurriedly. It appeared to be American style apparel. But no identification as to its owner. Frustrated, he took the bag to "lost and found." Inquiring if anyone had asked about it, he received a negative reply in halted English. Sam made a request that the luggage be held for the authorities. Again he got a negative. He reflected on what Menendez and Captain Dickson had said about cooperation in Columbia. Another dead end he moaned. But he had Baxter in Columbia. At least that was something. He would start over again. He left the suitcase with the attendant and headed for the concourse. On his way out his searching eyes focused on everyone that remotely looked like his man. Not a sign of anyone resembling Baxter.

Briefly he worked the cab line. No one had seen the gringo. His thoughts turned to Baxter's moves to this point. They were anything but consistent. He knew they wouldn't be. He did not have a clue as to what Mark might be up to. Standing alone, in this sublime and strange atmosphere, desperate, Sam wondered if he wanted to be a cop anymore. Hell, he said to himself, what else would I do.

He approached the Aero Mexico Airlines counter, hoping that Baxter just might have.

"Yes sir, may I help you?" the attendant said. Impeccable English.

First came the badge, then the photo.

"Yes sir, that man booked passage to Mexico City a little more than three hours ago. The plane is taking off, er, just about now."

"That SOB," Sam said.

"Is he a friend of yours?" the young man said. His eyebrows raised.

"Not exactly," Sam answered. "Get me on the next plane out of here," Sam requested.

"To where?" he asked.

"Mexico City, dammit."

"Yes sir." His fingers, moving robotically, tapping out the request on the computer.

Sam held onto the packet containing the ticket as he searched his pockets for the change to call Mexico City.

"Let me speak to the chief," he said, to the watch commander.

Menendez said, "Yes I know, he's headed back this way, am I right?"

"Goddammit, Menendez, how's come you guys know every move our man makes, but you can't nab him?"

"We will when he arrives back here," Menendez said. Sarcastically. "He's on a flight right now. Am I right?" he repeated.

"Yes, he's on his way back, the sly bastard," Sam said.

"As a matter of fact, Sam, we've got a man on board the plane keeping an eye on Baxter. When he steps off, he'll be greeted with a welcoming committee. If you wish, we'll even have a Mariachi band there."

"Don't be funny Alfonso. Just slap the cuffs on and lock him up until I get there." Sam was tired, exasperated.

CHAPTER 13

Mark did not board the flight back to Mexico City making the flight one passenger short of a full compliment. He remained behind, in order to deceive the police into thinking he was on his way back to Mexico City. Knowing that the authorities were now on his trail and knowing that they were capable of finding out his habits from his time in Columbia, Mark checked into a hotel that they could not trace from his past, The Capitola.

Mark hadn't contacted Alexis since his departure from Mexico City. Only one brief conversation that had ended in frustration. He knew she would be in a state of worry, or worse. She could be difficult when she was angry. The heavy breathing and silence. He hated that. He was slow in making the call. But, it had to be done. If they were ever to be together, he had to keep her informed. Deliberating on what he would say, he reached for the telephone on the night stand. The last thing he wanted from her was her inability to understand why he was running. But then, she was female. He knew that they think more rationally than men. He read that somewhere.

He was counting on her being home. He struggled with the operators accent in order to get her to dial the number for him. Just getting that far considering South America's telephone system was an accomplishment. He was of the opinion that when you leave the United States, you leave the planet, in so far as common sense was concerned. You'd know that if you ever tried to buy a bottle of aspirin in a Safeway supermarket in Canada.

His thoughts, in a state if confusion, were rambling out of control.

After ten minutes and three attempts to reach her, he heard that familiar purr.

"Hello," she said.

"Hi, it's me."

Silence.

"Listen Alexis, I know you're upset. I haven't got time to discuss the situation. I just wanted to let you know I'm all right. That is, if you care."

"Mark, you know I care, but ..."

"Don't go into it Alexis. I love you. I'm doing this for us. That's it. Listen, I'll get in touch with you later. Just how, I'm not sure, but I will."

"Mark, please come back. Give it up. Won't you?"

"Not a chance honey. That's definite. It's for us."

"We don't have a future Mark. You'll be running for the rest of your life."

"I'll figure a way. Leave it at that. I'm going to hang up now. I think of you everyday, a lot everyday. I'll see you. Bye"

He pressed the disconnect button. The phone went back to a dial tone. He sat on the edge of the bed staring at the telephone wishing he could somehow climb through the lines and get to her.

For the next two days he sat in his room. The hotel had no kitchen or means to serve him food. He left only for grub which he brought back to his room. The chow was awful. Worse than he'd remembered. He had difficulty communicating what "food to go" meant. He paid extra for the ceramic plate they let him take to his hotel with a solemn promise to return it.

His clothing began to resemble that of one pushing a grocery cart through the streets. Soiled and rank he decided on the morning of the third day to claim his suitcase. The one with the gold "MB." It would be better to have his own clothing than to be spotted shopping.

Approaching the "Lost Baggage" area from a distance, he cautiously scanned the area for any unusual activity or characters hanging around the small office. He did not know what this guy Weston looked like, but he had to chance it. He waited for more time than he would have liked. Feeling confident he approached the office. There was no one about the area.

He thought about what Alexis had said. He mulled over the possibility of being captured and the consequences. He envisioned himself spending countless days and nights in confined, gray surroundings. Enclosed, guarded. And for what. Some lousy money. He cursed to himself. He cursed the fact that he was running. This was, after all, a rotten, cruel and dangerous world. His thoughts carried him away. Thinking better of the idea, he left. Walking away, he changed his mind. His clothing was important. A comfort zone for him.

An irritable itch on the back of his neck began to bother him. It began to burn as an insect bite would. Instinctively, he slapped at the back of his neck with his open hand hoping to quell the vermin. It intensified. Again, he swatted. He rubbed the hair that curled in a little ball on that part of his neck with his index finger. He felt nothing unusual, but the irritant persisted. A stranger at the far end of the baggage claim appeared and stared at him. Mark acknowledged the individuals presence. He didn't recognize him. The spot on his neck became an obsession. It wouldn't let up. It burned with a fury. He was positive he had been attacked by some tropical menace. Or was it? Wincing in discomfort and reluctant to move from his location, but out of necessity, he was compelled to inspect the intrusion. In the restroom, in front of the mirror, he turned one way then another in order to locate the burning area. Nothing. It was as if he was not supposed to discover the injury. The stranger he watched a minute earlier entered the room. Mark cringed at his presence. The man glared at Mark, then went for the urinal. Mark dampened his neck with cold water. Some relief quitted his anxiety. The burning ceased. It was the first time anything like this had affected and engulfed him. The incident, was it an omen, he wondered?

Again he returned to the baggage area. He quickly retrieved his suitcase and returned to the hotel. His clothing reeked with a putrid odor reminiscent of the lingering smell of sweat on unwashed clothing, unbathed bodies. At least, that's what he thought. A warm shower and clean clothes would rejuvenate him.

Showered and freshly clothed he lay on the bed, an overhead fan slowly spinning clockwise, cooling the room, his mind churned with the tempo of the blades. He felt alone, dejected, rejected. A move had to be made. He still had enough money in his possession to go anywhere. But where? Anywhere he pleased. He wondered if he was tiring of the perpetual subterfuge. It seemed a mistake. Alexis' words rang in his ears.

Deep in thought, he heard a slight tapping on the door. He froze. A paralyzing chill enveloped his body.

"Yes, who is it?

Another tap.

Again he asked. "What do you want?"

"The FBI, open up."

There was no escape. No exit. From his room he would have to fall two stories in order to flee.

Mark cracked the door slightly. "What's up?"

"FBI, are you Mark Baxter?"

"Yes, why?"

"We want to talk to you."

Two young neat types, impeccably dressed individuals, sporting sunglasses, stood just back in the hall away from the door. Both held up their ID's.

Mark stood aside and allowed them to enter.

"Mr. Baxter, we have a warrant for your arrest." Without saying another word, they spieled off his Miranda rights.

"For what?" Mark asked.

"Suspicion of illegally possessing government money. Leaving the scene of a crime, and other criminal violations"

"Explain it to me."

"We have sir, Come with us,"

One of the agents reached for his handcuffs.

Mark threw a punch to the gut at the one nearest him catching him by surprise, He immediately bent over groaning. Mark let go with an uppercut to the jaw. The officer fell backwards hitting his head on the night stand knocking him out cold, The second agent lunged at Mark grabbing him from behind around the neck. Mark threw him over his shoulder. Then pounced on him as he lay on his back. They struggled rolling back and forth. Mark managed to top his opponent. Punching wildly to the agents face, blood spurted from his nose and mouth, Without let up he pummeled the man's face until he succumbed to the fury. Kneeling on top of his victim, Mark lunged his knee to the officers groin. He moaned in agony.

Mark reached into the agents coat and retrieved his pistol. Holding the business end of the pistol, Mark lobbed the butt to the officers head, knocking him out. He then turned his attention to the agent lying unconscious by the bed stand. He removed his weapon. He repeated his action against the agent with the butt end to his head. Both agents lay unconscious bleeding but breathing.

Mark stood over the two agonizing at the carnage. Pulling the bed cover back he stripped the sheets and tore them into strands. Dragging the agents together, back to back, he secured both their hands and arms tightly. Then bound the unconscious men together by their feet and legs then gagged both, stuffing balls of the cotton sheet into their mouths. For extra incapacity, he handcuffed the pair to the bed railing.

Peering through a tiny crack in the door opening he could not make out any unusual activity in the hallway. Mark retreated going straight for the closet, grabbing the small valise containing the money, the suitcase with his clothing, that he had never emptied, and departed.

The elevator opened into the lobby which he casually strolled through, exiting the hotel, not bothering to check out. He hurriedly climbed into the taxi, that was available for hotel guests.

"To the bus depot," he requested.

"Si."

There was no conversation on the way. Mark was totally consumed by the events of the past half hour. He began to tremble. He knew he had just added to his problems.

Departing the cab he made an elusive move toward the entrance of the depot. Looking over his shoulder, he watched the taxi pull away and disappear out of sight. He turned and commissioned another taxi, ordering the driver to take him to the train depot. Again, no conversation. His concerns were easing a bit over what he had perpetrated on the agents. It was either he or them, he rationalized. An hour had passed since the events in the hotel room. He surmised that the two men were coming around to consciousness, struggling to free themselves. An urgency compelled him to decide quickly what to do. His mind still muddled. His neck ached where the agent had grabbed him. How the agents had located him so quickly since arriving in Columbia gave him pause.

In the train depot he approached the ticket window. He bought passage to Pereia. A city he knew well, a ride of five hours through the rugged Andes. Crowded, odorously noxious, he sat hemmed in among peasants on hard, seasoned planks. He felt a camaraderie with them. Travelers in all, to where, who knows?

Jack Bates had been diligently tailing Sam, keeping him within sight at almost every turn. However, Bates was unaware that Sam had departed for Bogota because Jimmy took advantage of Jack's nodding off to slip out for a quick one at the bar next to Sam's motel. With their guard down, Sam had returned to the police station to confer with Menendez. In turn he left for Bogota Columbia.

Jack arose from his short nap alarmed to discover Jimmy's absence. Knowing where Jim would have gone he entered the saloon to find his comrade casually sipping on a Modelo Negra.

"Dammit, Jim, what the hell are you doing here. Is Sam still in the motel?"

"Damned if I know. I thought you were keeping track."

"For Christ's sake Jimmy, I was sleeping. What the hell were you thinking? Let's get out of here." Jack was livid. He grabbed Jimmy by the shoulder and pulled him off his stool.

"Hey, get your hands off me. I was taking a break. What the hell were you doing sleeping?"

Angrily, both men walked side by side to the Trans Am.

"Go check to see if he's still in his room."

"How the hell you suppose I do that." Jimmy asked.

"Knock on the goddammed door. It ain't rocket science."

"What the hell am I supposed to say if he answers?"

"Excuse yourself, you made a mistake. He'll think you're an employee or something. You think he's going to shoot you?"

"OK, OK, I'll be right back."

Jimmy returned. "No answer."

"All right, let's get down to the station and see what you can dig up. That's probably where he's headed. I don't know where else he'd go."

Jimmy was inside the station house, again, for what Jack thought was an eternity.

Returning and climbing into the drivers seat, Jimmy said, "He's left for Columbia. My man tells me that Baxter fled sometime ago. About the time that we were witnessing the accident. Are you going?"

"Goddammit, I guess I'll have to. You really screwed up man. How long ago? Did they say?"

"Earlier today. Maybe a couple of hours."

"OK Jim, If don't see you for a while, hang in there. After you letting Sam get out of our sights I shouldn't make this offer, but if I'm successful in catching up and score with the money, I'll contact you and square up. All right?"

"Yeah, sure Jack. Good luck." Jimmy knew that scenario would never happen.

Jack departed company with Jimmy and took a flight to Columbia two days after Mark. He had to acquire more money and that took time contacting his people for more funds to be wired to him in Mexico.

Upon arrival in Bogota, Jack hadn't the slightest clue where he was going to go or what he was going to do. He was just there. Hoping for some miracle in running into Sam or Mark Baxter.

Sometimes miracles never seem to cease. Disembarking the flight Jack entered the seating area for departures. Sitting off to one side sat Sam Weston waiting for his transport back to Mexico City.

Since Sam had no contact man in Bogata up to that point he wondered why in the hell he ever decided to go to Bogata in the first place. Except that he was told that Mark was there. After two days Sam recognized that his best chances to catch Baxter would be to be as close to Menendez in Mexico City as possible.

Because of the incident with the FBI, InterPol was now involved It had become an international crime. Mark's picture was now plastered on every police bulletin board around the world.

Jack glanced at the stat board. Sam's flight was to leave in forty five minutes.

Immediately Jack secured a ticket back to Mexico City. Why, he wasn't sure. But his best guess was that Baxter had returned there in order to elude Sam's pursuit. Anyway, staying in Bogota wasn't going to do him any good. There was only one man in the fiefdom that knew what was really going on and that was Mark Baxter.

Mark arrived in Periea exhausted. His clothing saturated with smoke from the train's engine, bleary eyed, looking haggard. He hired one of the town's three taxis requesting the nearest accommodations. The dilapidated rusted hulk of metal squealed to a halt amid a cloud of dust in front of a bleak tan adobe structure connected to a string of buildings on what appeared to be the towns main street. A dirt road. The sun baked buildings suffering from age and the elements continued to peel and crack, pieces of which, lay about at the base of the buildings littering the sidewalks, if you could call them that. To Mark it looked like a blessed haven. Even through the dust that swirled skyward from every footstep found its way into every crack and interior, including ones nostrils. Colorfully dressed shawl draped Andean people sauntered aimlessly in all directions. Some sat quietly with their backs against the buildings, their knees tucked up under their chins, peacefully napping. Their wide brimmed hats keeping the sun at bay.

His accommodations were sparse. Lying quietly, resting, wide awake his mind churning, Mark could think of nothing else but where he would go from here. The visions he conjured up covered the entire globe. He knew it would have to be off this continent. A place where no one cared about your existence. A place teeming with humankind. A bustling city of many nationalities. Where one could get lost in the crowd. A place where freedom of movement was uninhibited. He thought of his short stay in Hong Kong at the time he was recovering from his wounds inflicted in Vietnam. That's where he would go. It felt good. It was a positive decision. He had some knowledge of Asian ways. He liked it there. He liked the people. They were energetic. Warm, hospitable. His mind blurred. A peaceful comfort enveloped his being. He fell asleep.

Sam, waiting for his flight back to Mexico City was unaware of Jack Bates presence. Jack lingered out of sight behind Sam leaning against a tiled wall. All the while not taking his eyes off of Sam for a second.

Tired from his two days in Bogota, searching, then finding out that Baxter had returned to Mexico City, Sam sat with his chin resting on his chest half asleep, occasionally raising his head to see what was going on around him. Between one of his nodding off periods he heard his name called out on the P A system. He jerked upward looking around in confusion. It repeated, "Mr. Sam Weston, please report to the main ticket counter."

Sam aroused, stood and proceeded to the check in counter with Jack on his heels. "I thought I heard my name called." He told the attendant.

"Are you Mr. Weston?"

"Yes."

"They are asking for you at the main ticket counter. Downstairs."

"Thanks." He headed post haste to the destination. Jack Bates followed close behind, keeping enough distance to remain incognito. It wouldn't have made any difference to Sam since his attention was riveted on finding out what he was wanted for.

"I'm Sam Weston," he informed the attendant.

"Yes sir, there's a phone number you are to call."

Menendez answered. "Sam, he said, am I glad you got the message before you returned. He continued, Baxter was not on the flight that just arrived. He has duped us again. Apparently he remains in Bogota. There's no sense in returning."

"What?"

"Yes Sam, our man was not on the plane. He's still in Bogota. Do you understand?"

'Well, then, that saves me a trip. I'll take it from here. Thanks Alfonso."

"You are welcome senor. Good luck. By the way, we have made a contact in Bogota for you. He is not with the police. Remember, they won't help. Our man is an ex-narcotics agent whom we have used in the past, but have not been in contact with lately. His name is Hector Torres. We have a phone number and an address for you. He is expecting you to call."

"You are a genius Alfonso. That will help a lot. Thanks."

"You are welcome. Please keep us informed."

"1 will."

After disconnecting with Menendez, Sam dialed Torres' number.

"Yes."

"Mr. Torres, this is Sam Weston. You are expecting my call."

"Good. Mr. Weston I would like to meet with you as soon as possible. When will you be available?"

"I need some rest. Can we get together this evening? I'm going to look for another room somewhere here in Bogota."

"Of course. May I make a suggestion for accommodations? They are near my residence. A hotel. The Capitola."

"Fine, fine." Give me the address. "Let's see, it's two o'clock now. What if I call you around seven this evening?"

"That will be OK. But you stay at the hotel. I will come at seven. We can talk there."

"Good. I'm looking forward to meeting you."

Precisely at seven o'clock Sam heard a knock on his door.

Standing in the entry was a short, rather disheveled individual. The scars on his face evidenced a bad case of juvenile acne. He tried to cover most of his disfigurement with a heavy beard. Otherwise his warm smile and mild manner disarmed any negativity from first sight.

"Mr. Torres, please come in."

"Ah, Mr. Weston, I have heard good things about you, A fine investigator they tell me."

"Right now sir, I'm a very frustrated sleuth." This guy we're after, Mark Baxter, is a better phantom than I am a pursuer, May I call you Hector?"

"Of course, Sam, if you don't mind."

"Ditto." Sam said. "Can I offer you a cup of coffee?"

"No, that's OK, thanks. Where are we with the chase? Tell me. Perhaps I can shed some light onto the situation. Not that I have any specific information right now. But I am familiar with this city and all the venues of hang outs and the means of departure, if he has left town. I understand that he is an ex-DEA agent and that he is also familiar with Bogota. As a matter of fact many of the agents still use this hotel for their stay in Bogota. That is why I chose it for you. Perhaps he was here also. If so, maybe we can find someone that saw him. Just a guess."

"1 haven't made any inquiries yet," Sam said, "I was just too damned pooped to get any information when I arrived. I crashed as soon as I hit the room. But I appreciate your directing me here. It may perhaps be of value. I can tell you what has transpired so far. I tracked him to Mexico City. Just missed collaring him, when a traffic accident interfered. Then we got word that he flew here, then back to Mexico City, which he didn't. We think he may still be in Bogota, but not positive."

"Menendez faxed me a photo of Baxter," Torres said, "and I took it upon myself to make some inquiries while you rested. I checked all of the outgoing flights since this morning. Nothing. Then I visited the bus terminal. Nothing. I struck pay dirt at the train station."

"If my man there is right, Baxter got on a train for Periea. A small town across the mountains. It is an isolated town of about fifty thousand. There's an airport there. He'll probably use it when he decides to leave. Mind you, I'm not positive that is where he went, but I'd bet a lot of money on it because the photograph was positively identified by our people. He would have arrived there sometime this afternoon. We can fly there if you wish and check it out."

"Well, that is interesting. How soon?"

"This evening, if you wish. It is an hours flight. There are two every evening. We could be there by midnight."

"OK, let's go. It sounds like something he'd do."

"I'm not sure, but would you like to run around this huge city chasing your phantom when perhaps he's not here."

"Like I said, let's get going."

"Good."

Jack Bates hadn't slept for more than twenty eight hours. His perseverance was beginning to show signs of deterioration. Somewhat relaxing in a corner of the lobby in the Capitola he cat napped. Or rather closed his eyes for mere seconds. He was not going to lose Sam in an unguarded moment. Jack, you might say, had the endurance of a pack of African Wild Dogs. He wouldn't give up. He would eventually get his quarry no matter what the odds.

He saw Hector Torres, a man he would later come to know, enter the hotel lobby and approach the front desk. He also heard Torres ask the clerk for Sam Weston's room. He waited for Torres to enter the elevator. A minute later Jack ascended to the fifth floor and put his ear to room number 26. The voices were mumbled. He could not make out what was being said. He was satisfied that he recognized Sam's voice.

At the end of the hallway the hotel management had positioned a couch against a wall surrounded by two large potted ferns. From that position Jack could observe any movement in or out of Sam's room. Jack waited, a newspaper he had read earlier conveniently lay on his lap.

When the two men exited Sam's room and turned toward the elevators, Jack took the stairway, two steps at a time, entered the lobby and waited for the elevator to discharge its passengers.

As Sam's cab pulled away, Jack jumped into a second taxi and ordered the driver to follow handing him a ten dollar bill. "Don't lose them."

"Si, senor."

Jack tried to stay alert, but exhaustion took precedence. He nodded off on occasion, which helped. At the airport the driver came to a stop behind Sam's taxi. The driver leaned back over the front seat and gave Jack a nudge.

"We are here, Senor. The people you are following are just now getting out of the taxi in front of us."

"Thanks." Jack handed the driver another ten dollar bill. "Keep it."

"Gracias, Senor." To a cab driver in Columbia a ten had the value of a fifty in the US. He was pleased to say the least.

Jack followed Sam and Hector at a distance, keeping a low profile. He waited until both men had secured passage to their destination.

After the pair disappeared out of sight. Jack inquired as to where, "the two gentlemen had purchased tickets to."

"Peria, sir."

Boarding the small craft, Jack tried as best he could to look inconspicuous. However that may be, it would be difficult at best not to stand out like a beacon in a lighthouse among the local dark skinned people. In fact, Sam did notice Jack but paid no heed.

Within the hour the flight prepared for the landing, announced by the Captain.

Upon disembarking Jack lagged behind the two men keeping them in sight.

"Let's see if Baxter has booked passage out of here before we seek accommodation," Hector said.

Sam exposed Baxter's photograph to the only person at the one ticket counter inside the airport.

"Thanks," Sam said after getting a negative response.

"Appears he's still in town," Hector said.

"Looks that way, but if he isn't it wouldn't surprise me." Sam said.

Jack followed Sam and Hector.

The two men proceeded into town experiencing the same stifling reception that Mark had encountered with the dust that permeated the towns environs. Jack followed close behind keeping the two at arms length.

Mark lay uncomfortable in the hot muggy room. His skin felt as if a thin film of sticky glue covered his body. Even the bedding had an air of musty dampness. He jumped to his feet and headed for the shower. If you could call cold water a way to bathe. He lathered, jumping into then out of the chilling water thinking of nothing but the Orient. It consumed his thoughts easing some of the discomfort. He made up his mind as he vigorously see sawed the towel back and forth over his body. He was excited. Nothing else seemed to matter at that moment.

Climbing back into his soiled reeking shirt and pants. Mark departed for the airport with the satchel in hand that contained the thousands of dollars he would use for the voyage. Later he would replace his clothing.

Mark was totally unaware that he had just missed being spotted by Sam, Hector and Jack. Their paths had crossed by inches as the taxis passed each other going in opposite directions. Call it fate. Call it luck. But it happened. Sam and Hector were engrossed in conversation. Jack was cursing the dust descending upon him from the taxi ahead.

Mark found out through the ticket agent that in order to get to Hong Kong he would have to fly first to Lima, Peru. Change planes there, then one more stop in Oahu, Hawaii.

Eighteen hours seemed an awful long time from Peria to the city of his choice. Mark produced his passport and received the usual scrutiny.

The brief flight to Lima went off without a hitch. His departing flight to Hawaii was some three hours distant. He could purchase some decent cloths in one of the clothing stores in the airport complex. Choosing some fine threads escalated his spirits. It seemed wonderfully ironic to him to be able to walk into a fine haberdashery looking like a street person and exiting looking like the king of Monaco. It suited his style.

Mark was always aware that his brief interlude from being pursued was temporary. His good sense told him that the authorities would always be at his heels.

Mark had never before been to Hawaii. Stepping off the plane into the gentle warmth of the westerly trade winds overwhelmed him. Never before had he experienced anything as breath taking and exotic as that first wave of warm gentle air flowing in from the tropical Pacific Ocean. The intoxicating sweet scent on the air from the flowering Plumeria trees, the vibrant colors, the palms gently swaying in the winds, all captivated him. And again, it was moist here too. However, most welcome.

Time passed quickly. Feeling fresh after showering in the mens room and donning his new clothes it was almost as if he had a new start, a new beginning. Invigorated, he returned the smiles from the stewardess', who greeted him with a complimentary comment upon entering the aircraft.

He settled into his window seat and prepared for the long flight to Hong Kong. He purchased a novel entitled "The long Journey" at the news stand before departing hoping to glean some insight from its contents. Perhaps.

Mark started to open the book to begin reading, but before he trained his eye to the text, he glanced out of the window at the scene beneath the rising aircraft. His eyes and imagination were captivated by the portrait below. The ocean beneath the airplane near the shore provided a scene of a yellow, light blue green pool. The island appeared to be edged with an arc of yellow, a reflection from the sand beneath the water, which in turn blended subtly to a light green further outward. From there, ending abruptly, a demarcated line showed dark blue that extended beyond the horizon. He wanted to go back to bathe in the surreal colors.

He read for a while. Occasionally glancing down at the endless expanse of water that seemed to stretch forever in all directions. The vastness overwhelmed him as it had when flying to Vietnam years ago. He spotted the tiny image of an ocean liner off in the distance. He had never taken a cruise and wondered what life must be like on that ship far out to sea. Boring perhaps. He returned to the story. Soon his eyes began to tire and water. The text blurred. He laid the book down in his lap and nodded off. He slept fitfully sitting upright. He listened to the drone of the engines. The pulsating seemed erratic. First revving, then subsiding. He guessed that the computer was making adjustments to keep the craft on a steady course and speed. Time seemed to stand still.

Finally he fell asleep. He was totally exhausted from the past few days. His dreams were bizarre. Strange people and scenes. The running. The mayhem at the hotel in Bogota with the FBI agents. The hurried escape to Peria. Living in soiled clothing. Being subjected to finding his way around strange surroundings. His sense of routine, of regularity and sanity totally upset. He awoke suddenly to the sound of the engines pulsating, first whining very high, then slacking off seemingly not running at all, barely heard. He looked out the window into heavy fog. The "Fasten Seat Belts" sign was on. The stewardesses were busy hustling up and down the aisles checking the passengers seat belts. He heard the Captain announce "Prepare for Landing." The passengers stirred anticipating getting off to meet loved ones, weary from what seemed a terribly long confinement.

The ship broke through the clouds. The giant city below stretched beyond the horizon. Crawling up and over and around the hills that surrounded the metropolis. It seemed as if the earth's entire population was set down in one place. Directly below in the dark green bay lie a myriad of small islands all separated by large expanses of water. Ships by the hundreds, large and small, of all shapes and configurations. Freighters, Junks, Pleasure craft, all working their way in different directions and destinations.

Finally the aircraft touched down, the thump, followed by the reversal of the engines struggling to bring the mammoth machine to a slower pace. Still racing, the craft made a turn to the left. Mark thought the plane would tip over from the force of the angle. Now it slowly taxied to its berth among the hundreds of stalls. It seemed to take an extraordinary amount of time to reach its berth. The terminal and its environs were cavernous. He thought he would never find his way about the airport and surely not in the city.

Stepping into the passenger waiting area it was the largest airport he had ever encountered. The brightly lit plastic signs directing travelers to their baggage was at best confusing in French, German, Italian, Chinese, Arabic, Spanish and a few he had never seen before. Shoulder to shoulder people of many faces competed for the exits. Voices over the intercom ordered the masses to different destinations in strange unrecognizable tongues. He walked for fifteen minutes or more through bland but brightly lit tiled tunnels to what he hoped would deliver him to his baggage. Turning right, then left, as if in a maze, never seeing the light of day, he seemed to be getting nowhere. In the distance he could make out what appeared to be baggage carousels and exits to the outside, There were yellow and green vehicles, taxis waiting for fares. After latching onto his one suitcase he walked to the exit. Taxis by the hundreds, shuttle vans of all makes and colors advertising their owners, were double and triple parked, blocking traffic, apparently oblivious to the chaos around them, blatantly ignoring the confusion while they waited their cargo.

Oriental women and men everywhere holding up signs, some with names of hotels and inns, enticing the sojourners to stay with them, some with the names of targeted arrivals, assisting them to their destination. In all the confusion, order seemed to prevail. As soon as the taxis and vans were loaded to capacity they pulled out into a steady stream of traffic, some allowed to merge smoothly into traffic, others having to force their way into the stream of vehicles.

Mark wasn't in any particular hurry or concern where he was going. He had no reservations and was not sure just where to stay. Any cab or van would do at this point. He headed for a young woman with a charming smile driving a clean white short version of a limo who touted the advantages of a hotel he had never heard of before. "The Excelsior." Mark thought, not bad, sounds classy.

Like all the others, the driver knew what she was doing when entering traffic. She plunged right in missing the rear of the cab ahead by inches and forcing the van following to slam on its brakes with a corresponding blast from its horn. It did not seem to matter about the intrusion she caused, horns were blaring from every direction.

At first she advanced the limo ahead by inches then leaped forward in lurches with Mark holding on to his valise with the money. Slowly and systematically they left the hysteria and the gray air pollution behind to memory. Their carriage picked up speed as it traversed the wide streets and tree line boulevards of this sparkling skyscraper city. Everywhere people. A sea of heads. A profusion of signs advertising anything and everything one could imagine. It was an open society with no apparent restrictions. It was exhilarating. Mark was excited.

Along the boulevards row upon row of tall buildings reaching for the sky. Standing elegantly, their glass and marble facades reflected the sunlight like dazzling diamonds. The endless variety of tropical trees bent gently in the warm wind, much like Hawaii. Leaving the super structures behind Mark found himself motoring down narrow lanes lined with weather worn dilapidated wooden buildings. Their age forgave the hardly discernible ragtag signs that hung precariously from above their sagging doors. The appearance of the inhabitants changed with the neighborhoods. Along the gracious boulevards the people were well dressed. Men in three piece suits, ladies in smart well tailored dresses and pant suits. In the run down areas it looked as if they were on the last rung of existence. Oh well, he thought, it's the same everywhere. Just another reason to hang onto the money and make the best of it.

Relaxed and enjoying the ride he spied the Excelsior Hotel in the distance. It had the appearance of an elegant old world edifice. The taxi pulled up to the front that was shrouded with heavily foliated trees forming a tunnel to the entrance. The marble exterior and bizarre cupid figures complete with wings clung to the face of the building at different angles giving the impression that they were about to flyaway at any moment.

Inside soft pastels of coral, pink and delicate green foam greeted new arrivals. Large padded mahogany furniture including the registration counter lent a sense of richness. Off to the right of the reception area a three tiered carpeted stairway with broad rounded polished wood railings led to a balcony that surrounded and overlooked the main floor. Live colorful flower arrangements placed strategically grabbed the eye with their beauty. Plant leaves were as large as elephant ears. Above all was a sky light made of stained glass that directed the suns brilliant rays throughout the lobby and accounted somewhat for the abundance of outrageous color in the flowers and magnified the size of the plants leaves. It was a microcosm of a paradise. It was tropical.

Mark requested a suite using another alias, Jeff Chimes. He was pleased when the bellboy opened the door for him to enter. It was every bit a compliment of the lobby. The same decor greeted his eyes. Soft colors, fresh cut flowers adorned the tables and the mantel over the fireplace. He wondered why a fire place here in this tropical paradise. "It's ambiance," the bellboy said. "It's never used." The bed was gargantuan with a puffy floral throw. A view of the bay left him breathless. This is how he wanted to live from this day forward. Hong Kong would become his new base.

The phone rang twice at Alexis's condo before she picked it up.

"Hello."

"Its me, Mark. Before you say anything Alexis, I want you to know that you've been on my mind almost constantly."

"Mark, where are you?"

"I want you to join me," Mark said.

"Mark, I want to see you so badly, I need you. I'm scared."

"I understand. I need you too. I want you with me, I'm in a situation for the two of us to be together without worry or concern. I can work it out. I believe my location precludes anyone finding me. I'm positive of it. Will you consider it?" "Of course," she repeated, "Where are you?"

"I can't say right now. You've got to know that the authorities are listening to this conversation. I'm going to hang up shortly. I'll contact you soon. Be on the lookout for any communication from me. 1 love you, 1 love you." he repeated.

He didn't give her a chance to respond. He placed the receiver in its cradle. He knew she would be furious, or curious, perhaps totally frustrated.

Mark laid back on the bed trying to relax. His neck ceased to ache. It was the first time in more than two weeks that he felt all together. But he wanted Alexis. It would not be complete until then.

CHAPTER 14

The FBI had a new charge against Mark Baxter. Resisting arrest and assault to commit bodily harm on two of their agents.

Listening intently for any communication with Alexis, the agents waited patiently by their surveillance equipment.

"We've got something, we've got him." One agent said to another who was chomping on a Hero sandwich.

"Got what?" he said, his words muffled with a mouthful of salami.

"Got Baxter talking to Alexis. what the hell you think I'm listening for reports on the weather. Can't pinpoint the exact location, the conversation was too short, but it's from Asia."

"Are you sure it's Asia. How in the hell."

"He's got money, he can go anywhere he damn pleases. He said he wanted to hook up with her. She responded positively. Let our people know right away. He said something about contacting her through the mail. Let's assume for now that it'll be through the postal service. Notify them to snatch any correspondence from the Far East to her."

"All right, I'm on it."

"Keep it to ourselves. Don't let the locals get wind of this."

The police at the lake kept a keen eye on Alexis's movements. An officer was assigned to do just that. He complained about having to almost live in his vehicle. Her shopping excursions were followed. Her supervisor at work was informed to be on the alert for any contact with Mark. They too picked up on the conversation from their tap, but could not determine where the call originated. They, like the feds were most anxious to get their man. InterPol had also intercepted Mark's call to Alexix.

Mark Baxter, ex Navy Seal, ex DEA agent, good guy was diligently being pursued by every authority on the planet.

Despite that, Mark tried to take his mind off of his predicament by spending the next couple of days much like a tourist rather than a man being pursued. However, constantly looking over his shoulder, he visited some of Hong Kong's famous sights, indulging himself to the fullest. He was especially fascinated by the diversity of religions. Buddhists, Muslims, Christians and Taoists. To that extent the number of different nationalities. More Chinese than any other, but on any street at any time one could cross paths with ethnic peoples, nationalities, tongues of every country. A varied skin color from white to brown to yellow and all the shades in between. English was the dominant language due to the British influence for the past one hundred and fifty six years. Hong Kong was one of the largest cities in the world. The sprawl covered many square miles. Even though the English language is the major method of communication, Oriental architecture was the predominant theme.

Mark couldn't help notice the attention he was getting from indigenous women. He could sense their penetrating eyes as they passed. It embarrassed him when he caught them turning their heads to get a last look. He thought of Alexis. He wanted to be with her, here. To share this beautiful and wondrous place with her.

He found himself leaning over the wood railing on the gigantic Star Ferry that plied the enormous bay. As it quietly slipped through the sparkling blue green waters, he enjoyed the warm breeze that swept delicately across his face and soothed him. His thoughts turned. How to get Alexis to Hong

Kong. How to retrieve the money in the vault in Mexico City and how to carry such a large amount of cash with him.

Concentrating on all of the aspects of those concerns caused him to totally blank out on the subjects. He changed his course and enjoyed the ride.

Walking about the ship he discovered a large relief map outlining the environs of Hong Kong, Kowloon and the islands that occupied the bay. The map also indicated the ferry's routes, One island caught his attention. Tung Lung. It was not a scheduled stop. Matter of fact it looked as though the island was uninhabited. It was located Northeast of the City and some distance away. Perhaps twenty miles distant. There were no other islands in the proximity of Tung Lung. It was isolated. He wanted to know more. He wanted to investigate Tung Lung.

Before the ferry returned and docked at its assigned berth in the harbor, Mark approached one of the ships crewmen. A young Chinese, handsome in his neatly pressed blue and white gold braided uniform. In the ensuing conversation with his new acquaintance, the young man voluntarily answered every one of Mark's questions with enthusiasm. He disclosed that Tung Lung Island was occupied. But was seldom visited. A fishing village off the beaten track. A row of houses, you might describe them as shacks, that lined one side of a poorly paved street. It was not governed by any particular authority. Just there for the convenience of a few fishermen. A small store for basic necessities and fishing gear for the fishermen. "And yes, it is sometimes used as a tourist hideaway by those that want to disappear from the world for a few days, weeks or months. It is not advertised in the Travel business, An enclave of grass huts with thatched roofs and scarce amenities, like electricity.

It had been a long, somewhat bitter sweet day. He enjoyed for the most part his adventuring and his conversation with the young crewman, but remorseful, alone.

Back at the hotel, reading several of the local newspapers that littered the foot of his bed, Mark familiarized himself with every bit of news and events that were or would be taking place in the city for the upcoming month. He noted several religious ceremonies and parades complete with dragons and fireworks that honored deities past and present. All of which would draw large crowds to celebrate the coming events. His plan was beginning to formalize and congeal. He befriended one of the desk clerks, bribing him with a few dollars for information. During his stay these past three days he dined regularly at a particular restaurant and became friends with a Hostess. From these contacts and events to come, Mark finalized the blueprint for getting Alexis to Hong Kong. The isolated island, Tung Lung, would be involved in the conspiracy.

Mark composed a letter to Alexis outlining the plan she was to follow in order to meet him in Hong Kong. He enclosed enough money for her passage and informed her of a date and time to leave the lake. He planned it down to the minute when she would arrive in Hong Kong. Mark's plan included enough time for her to acquire a passport, secure passage and arrive as he instructed. Mark longed for the two weeks to pass.

Inquiring at the UPS office he was promised that his vital package would reach the addressee in three days. The clerk even guaranteed the time of day it would arrive. She would be home at the time to receive it. Saturday morning next.

Mark returned to the hotel and immediately called Alexis.

"It's me."

"Hi darling"

"Sixth day, AM." Mark said. "1 love you." He disconnected.

Alexis, confused, stared at the receiver, listening to the dial tone. "Sixth day, AM," she repeated aloud. What does he mean, she thought as she placed the receiver in its cradle. She repeated in her mind, Sixth day, AM. Sixth day, AM. Saturday morning. It came to her. Saturday morning. It was three days away. She wouldn't have long to wait to find out if that's what he meant.

Next morning Mark set out to visit Tung Lung Island. Venturing down to the port he happened onto a remote dock in the harbor. A faded sign hanging askew on a rickety shed advertised, "Boats for rent, by the hour, day, week." Inside the small cluttered shack that served as an office festooned with fishing nets, many of which had apparently spent many days in salt water, hung haphazardly on the walls. Several well preserved large unrecognizable sea creatures dangled in and about the netting as if caught or were about to be snagged by the webbing. An old seaman who looked as weathered as his nets and sporting a scraggly goatee greeted Mark with a smile. Mark's impression was that this was the place to do his business. The old gent recognized Mark as a Westerner. He spoke in English.

"What can I do for you, Mister." The grimy, faded and wrinkled Captain's hat that perched cockeyed on his head bobbed up and down as he spoke.

"I'm here to do what you advertise out front."

"How long you need it and what kind."

"Something that'll get me over to Tung Lung safely and back."

"That'd be a power boat. In and out drive. Full of fuel and ready to go. A twenty one footer. That do?" He said succinctly. He had dealt with westerners before. Mark could tell. No dealing. Just the details.

"How much?" Mark asked.

"Twenty American dollars by the hour. Seventy five by the day. How many days you need. If more than three I can make a better deal."

"Let me ask you. How long you think it'll take to get over there, spend a couple of hours and return?"

"You can do it in a day. If the bay is calm. Thing is, the water can turn nasty without notice. But the craft is sturdy and reliable. If you know what you're doing. Got boating experience?" Without taking a breath, he continued. "Just so you know, the bay is patrolled regularly. If you get into trouble keep your life vest on. Somebody will come along sooner or later."

"To answer your question, I've got enough experience. And thanks for the safety tip."

"Good then, she's sitting right there." He pointed to a good looking craft Mark recognized as a Tahiti. He owned one once. "Looks like a jet drive to me with a 454 Olds engine." Mark said.

"Tis that. Better than an In and Out. No prop to bung up. Drafts inches instead of feet."

"I know." Mark was pleased. He was familiar with the boat.

Mark handed him two twenty dollar bills, American. The old man smiled. He liked US currency. "I'll settle up with you when I return if you need more."

The engine rumbled, then purred to an idle. With the gear shift in neutral, he goosed the accelerator with a light tap. Mark wanted to hear the 454's growl. Eager, responsive. A sense of power. Letting up on the pedal he allowed the engine to pop-pop-pop, through the exhaust pipes, as it warmed. The gurgling of air and water mixing at the stern along with the light rocking motion reminded him of his days on the lake sitting behind the wheel of his own Tahiti. Mark glanced out over the large expanse of water where the boat would cruise. Unfolding the map the old man provided, Mark took note of the direction from where he sat. Satisfied, he tucked the map under his leg to keep it from deserting the boat on the trip to Tung Lung. In reverse the craft eased out from its berth. Out in the open he shifted the lever forward and again gunned the engine with a tap of his foot. It was ready. He pressed hard. The craft surged forward as the bow rose. The jet drive struggled for just an instant as the stern dug in. He could feel it's eagerness to level out. The roar from the engine and open exhaust was deafening, exhilarating. The bow plained out and came level with the stern. It was as if a giant arrow had been released from its restraints. The boat sped forward, on course, as it slipped through the heavy sea water with ease. The noise level decreased as he let up on the accelerator. The cool wind rushing past his face was refreshing.

The rooster tail from the jets propulsion could be seen from a distance. Mark raced by several slower craft in the bay, not hot dogging. Just making time. People waved, recognizing that they would rather be with him than where they were plodding slowly to their destinations. Mark responded by raising his arm and hand above the windshield to acknowledge their awareness. He was having fun. A long time in coming.

It took almost thirty minutes to reach the island. He located an empty space along side an oily pier post and eased the boat to a stop. A young dark skinned man on the dock motioned for Mark to throw a line.

"Thanks."

His assistant did not say a word. Just smiled and nodded.

"You gonna be around?" Mark asked.

He nodded again without a word. He obviously understood English, Mark thought.

Mark handed the youngster a five dollar bill. "Keep an eye on it for me, can you?"

The man scowled. "1 don't need your money. But I'll look after it anyway. I'll be fishing."

"I didn't mean to insult you. 1 appreciate your help. Where's the main part of town?" Mark asked.

He pointed over his shoulder to the stand of palms swaying in the breeze. "Not much of a town. What are you looking for?"

"Nothing in particular. Just wanted to see what was over here. I've passed it many times and was always curious." Mark said with sincerity in his voice.

"Well, there's some small stores over the rise there, behind the palm trees. Then beyond that there's a," He hesitated, "I call it a recluses place on the beach about a quarter mile from the stores."

"OK, Thanks. I'll be back in about an hour, maybe sooner. Again thanks for keeping an eye on the boat. You need anything? I'd be glad to pick it up for you."

The young man's eyes lit up. He smiled again. "Well, yes, I could use some number four trebles. Here, I'll give you the money."

"No, no," Mark said. "I'll get them. Where?"

"Second little shack you come to on the right side of the street"

"OK, see you in a bit"

Mark recognized the tackle store immediately. It had taken him three, four minutes to reach the "business" section of the village from the dock. It was small, neat and well stocked with fishing gear. Matter of fact it reminded him of a typical fishing tackle store back home. The walls were carefully arranged by category and there seemed to be plenty of everything a fisherman would need or want. Mark made his purchase and exited.

The elderly man that rented Mark the boat was exact as to the contents of the town and it's general condition. Ten or so old weather worn wooden buildings, side by side, no space in between, a common wall for each, a rutted gravel street running the length of the frontage with a dirt alley in the rear. The village was completely surrounded with palms and a heavy layer of ferns that intruded on anything and everything in their path. A few grassy areas scattered about refused to give in to the ferns encroachment. It was a peaceful and pleasing stage.

Mark made note of the area, especially the route from the town down to the dock. It suggested that there was only one best way to get there. The very same path he used to get from the dock to the village center. Every other route was hindered by vegetation disallowing passage.

He tucked the small sack containing the hooks into his pocket and proceeded toward what he wasn't sure he would find. After walking for a time through an open area, beyond the village, he again was greeted by a heavy growth of palms, ferns and high grass with razor sharp edges. Another ten minutes passed before he saw the blue green waters of the sea in the distance through the palms. Brushing back the grass as he waded through the undergrowth, the lacerations began to bleed slightly and stung with a vengence. He shucked it off with a grunt. The discomfort disappeared by the sight of the tops of what appeared to be thatch roofed huts in the distance silhouetted against the sea.

From his perspective they appeared to be square configured structures crowned with pyramid styled roofs. The sea beyond completed this paradisical scene. Awestruck, he knew immediately that this had to be what he was looking for. He paused in his tracks. He approached slowly. Cautiously. Standing just outside of the enclave, it was eerily quiet, deserted. There wasn't any sign of activity. Only the soft resonant sound of the sea rolling onto the beach. The wave's crests were low and gentle. The only other visible disturbance came from the palm's fronds bending with the wind.

Mark entered the compound, searching every niche with the curiosity of a cat. There were ten bungalows in all. Each one stood like ghostly spirits, all constructed the same and featureless. The huts outer walls were covered with grass attached to wooden studs. The same grass he had passed through. Up on stilts a three step stairway rose from the sandy ground up to the front entrance. A tropical style roof was covered with a heavier weave of thatch, spilling over the eaves giving the appearance of a vegitated waterfall. Each one appeared to be well maintained and welcoming.

After determining that none were occupied he approached one nearest to a stand of palm trees, close to the beach. The surf resounded in his ears. He rapped on the wooden door. No one responded. He turned the door knob carefully.

It was unlocked. He peered in, his head just inside the opening. He was surprised with what he saw. A neatly furnished room, with cane furniture, floral cushions. A smoked glass topped cane coffee table in front of the couch. An easy chair. A bed completely made up with a night stand. Wooden vertical venetian blinds on three open windows. One on each of three walls. A small kitchen, complete with a camp type stove with four burners, a refrigerator with a generator along side. A small sink. He walked in. It was right out of Robinson Caruso. Behind a door in one corner was a clean well stocked bath, toilet and shower. He returned to the center of the room, twenty by twenty, he estimated, turning in a circle, he smiled. "This is it," he said aloud. He stood there for a few seconds more, taking it all in. He bathed in the room's charm and comfort. He saw Alexis in his mind. Damn how he wished she were here, now.

He exited and began examining each of the other huts. No one here nor anyone that would appear to be in charge. He wondered if this place were real. Was it some kind of ruse. But it was real. It was here. On the beach. A deserted beach surrounded by coconut palms, some leaning out over the water. It couldn't have been better. Even had he known about it beforehand he couldn't have planned it any better. His excitement heightened, exploded.

He rushed back to the little village. Entering the fishing tackle store again, he approached the clerk that had helped him earlier.

"Hi," he said. "Can I ask you a question?"

"Of course," she said.

"What's with the ah, grass shacks over on the beach? Are they for rent?"

"Oh yes, What you do is occupy anyone of your choice, that is, anyone that is unoccupied, then once a week Mr. Yamamoto will drop by and register you and collect. Simple eh."

"You mean, you just pop in and take one? That's kind of casual, isn't it?"

"They are seldom used, so it doesn't pay for Mr. Yamamoto to sit on the property to wait for someone to show up. There are no reservations. He comes over once a week, religiously, to see if there's anyone there. No phone service you know."

"He's Japanese? What a mix here." Mark commented.

"I'm Filipino, does that make any difference?"

"Oh god no, I was just commenting. I think it's great. Thank you very much. I'll probably see you again."

"You're welcome." She said with a warm smile.

Mark returned to the dock. The young man was sitting alone concentrating on his fishing line that hadn't moved in a while. The boat still tied securely to the pier.

"Any luck?" Mark asked.

The young man turned, startled. He didn't hear Mark approaching. He had that same disconcerting look as before when Mark tried to give him money.

"Sorry," Mark apologized for surprising him. "Got your hooks."

"Thanks."

"Thank you for looking after the boat."

"No problem. No, I haven't caught a thing, yet." He said, responding to Mark's question. "Some days are slow. They're probably further out today. I'm about to quit."

"Well, then, the hooks will come in handy for another time." Mark said.

"Yep."

Mark stepped down into the cockpit, released the line and started the engine. The motor responded with a burst of energy that assisted in easing the craft out and away from the rickety pier. The roar from the engine within the sturdy boat promised a quick and safe passage back to the mainland. The young man waved as Mark sped into the distance.

Sam and Hector had exhausted every angle in their attempt to discover Mark's whereabouts in Peria. Their attempts to locate his whereabouts or departure was met with one negative after another. At the airport, the bus depot, the train station, car rental agencies, anywhere that he might have used to escape Peria. Two days had passed without a lead. Mark had disappeared without a trace from the remote Andean town. It looked as if they had reached a dead end. Sam was perplexed, frustrated, feeling a sense of failure. at the end of his rope.

Jack patiently waited. And waited. He followed them discreetly wherever they. Sam and Hector, ventured. He knew from their relentless scurrying from place to place that they were having little success in locating their man.

It took Sam twenty minutes to reach home base by phone. Telephone communication from Peria was listless to say the least. No one or entity was in a hurry to reach the outside world. It was their way. Purposely.

"Let me speak to Dickson." Sam said curtly. He didn't recognize the voice.

"Who's calling?" The voice of the unknown asked.

"Weston, let me speak to the Captain."

"Oh, yes Sir. Hang on."

"Sam, where in the hell are you? We've been trying to reach you for two days."

"Captain, I'm in Peru, Peria. Ever heard of it? I've followed Baxter to this point, but he's disappeared."

"Sam, I can tell you he's not in Peru anymore. We've got information that he's in Asia."

"Asia, well that makes sense," Sam said sarcastically.

Dickson chuckled. 'Thou seem a little out of sorts, Sam."

"A little my ass, I'm about to squeeze this receiver into powder."

"OK, OK, I can understand your feelings. Calm down."

Sam responded. "How do you know he's in Asia. Where in Asia?"

"We're not sure. Could be in Singapore, Tokyo, Hanoi, anywhere. Hell, for all we know he could be in Ulan Bator. From a wire tap, we determined it was in the Orient, but just exactly where is a mystery. He's quick on the phone. Ten words or less then he hangs up. We're narrowing it down. Rationale tells us it would probably be somewhere where he could disappear with little language barrier. Big city. Lots of diversity in the population. Make sense?"

"Hong Kong." Sam interjected.

"Yes, we're looking at that very carefully. Loose there. Easy entry. This guy could give us fits if that's where he went. In any event Sam, we're under some pressure from the people upstairs to call off the chase and let the feds and Interpol handle it."

Sam's emotions exploded. "No way, Goddammit Captain. I'm into it this far, I'm going all the way. Even if I have to do it on my own. Christ, I've sweated this thing out until all I've got left is the holes in my shoes. Get those guys heads screwed on right. By the way, I need some traveling money." Sam didn't give a thought to how that might come across considering what the Captain had just relayed about calling him back.

"That's one of the problems Sam. They're complaining about the cost of this pursuit."

"Money is secondary here Captain. It's principle that counts. Our reputation is at stake. We'll look like a bunch of chumps, wimps, small town bunglers if we give up now and let somebody else take over and succeed. C'mon, make them see it as our right that is foremost. The crime happened in our jurisdiction. Besides, I've been so close to collaring him that it's incredible to think I won't pretty soon. I'm learning his pattern. He's almost like a known quantity at this point. Well, except maybe for this latest escapade."

"I understand Sam. It's not that they've chiseled it in stone that they won't support you. It's mostly on the table for discussion. I'm sure I can persuade them to go a bit farther." OK?"

"OK, but don't scare me like that, please."

"Just letting you know. Mind you, the pressure is on."

"So, you think it's Hong Kong?" Sam said.

"It seems to make sense. The language is predominantly English. It's the business capitol of the Far East. A diverse population. He could blend in easily. With the recent take over by China things are politically in a state of confusion. We think the authorities are concentrating on more important things than looking for a fugitive from the US. Getting into Hong Kong is easier than say, Singapore, Tokyo or other destinations. We're placing our bets on Hong Kong. So if you were to depart for any other place, it would be our first choice. Do you agree?"

"I'll agree on anywhere, if it means that you'll keep me on the case."

"We're going to notify the authorities of your pending arrival. We do have a contact there. His name is Twange Hong. He's located at the central police station. That's where you will start. Perhaps they'll have something for you by the time you arrive." He is a Lieutenant, I believe. Give me an address to wire the money. I'll have it there by tomorrow for you."

"Thank you, sir. Here it is." Sam read off the address of the local police precinct.

Jack Bates, whose patience had rewarded him in the past, was about to be compensated again.

Alexis eagerly awaited Saturday Morning's event. The one that Mark had advised her to anticipate.

At nine thirty A.M., on a cold, overcast Tahoe Saturday morning, December 15th, a UPS delivery truck pulled into the complex's parking lot. Most of the occupants were either just rising from their beds or sitting quietly having breakfast. The usual fare for a weekend morning. Quiet, serene, peaceful.

As is their way, the driver gingerly hopped from the open doorway of the van holding a large envelope. Locating the correct address, he hurried to the door and knocked. Express delivery people always give the impression that their current mission is the most important one on their route. Maybe it's the good salary they make.

The door opened slightly. "Package maam."

Alexis signed the etch a sketch metal binder held by the driver, that he turned in her favor. "Thanks." He said and disappeared into the van which departed in such a rush that it begged for an answer to the sense of urgency.

Anxious, with enthusiasm, fingers trembling, she unsealed the envelope. Carefully, she pulled the inner envelope out. Recognizing Mark's handwriting, she thrilled as to what might be inside. She was touching something of Mark. She was aroused, spuriously.

Inside, the contents revealed a letter, a packet of money. She laid the money aside and began reading Marks words.

"Let me express how much I have missed you. How much I love you. How much I want to see you and be with you. I know this has been difficult for you. And myself. We will celebrate when I hold you in my arms. Feel your tenderness. Soon. For now please follow the instructions below. Memorize them, then destroy this letter.

FIRST, he instructed, use the money to secure a passport. Apply for it in San Francisco. Apply for an "Emergency" passport. It usually takes three days to acquire an "Emergency" passport. Otherwise it takes about three weeks. While in the City acquire an airline ticket to Hong Kong via Honolulu, Hawaii using a travel agency in San Francisco. Fly Singapore Airlines. Departing Dec. 24th. Arr. Dec. 25th. Schedule I've seen says arrival at 10:30 AM, on the 25th, SECONDLY, upon arrival in HK, taxi to the Excelsior Hotel. At the front desk there will be a message for you. In it you will be given a phone number to call. You will be instructed to a certain address. There you will be greeted by a lady, (Can't use her name here). She will recognize you. She will give you another address. Take a taxi to that destination. I will meet you there on the 25th.

REMEMBER, THIS IS IMPORTANT. When in San Francisco change cabs several times in your travels from place to place. Be alert to being followed. Change cabs as many times as necessary if you are suspicious of a tail. Changing cabs is not fail safe, but it can make it difficult for anyone following and could throw them off. The same goes for traveling in HK. December 25th will be a very busy day in HK. Parades, festivities. It should be easy to lose a tail in the confusion. I will be aware of your arrival and presence here. So take your time. I love you. Good luck. If for any reason I am suspicious of a tail on you when you arrive, and consequently do not meet you on the 25th", as instructed above, return to the Excelsior, secure a room, and I will work out a way of getting together at a later time.

Alexis put the letter aside. She stared at the packet of money lying on the table. The wrapping partially obscured the denomination. It was clear though that they were not one dollar bills. They were one hundred dollar bills. A lot of one hundred dollar bills. More than she had ever seen before. She hesitated to touch it. She sensed that by accepting the currency she was committed to the crime and conspiracy. By handling the money she was now as guilty as Mark. It was dirty money. I'll gotten. It remained untouched. She reread Mark's message.

Excited, she paced back and forth reading and rereading, at the same time formulating plans for leaving her job, traveling to San Francisco, making arrangements to be with Mark. She returned to the coffee table, picked up the bundle of money and began counting. It was more than enough to see her way to her destination. Much more than enough. In her hands the money took on an aura of power, freedom, a lifestyle she had always dreamt of. She felt as Mark must have when he first discovered the wreckage and its contents.

Alexis couldn't contain her anxiety. By noon, she managed to bathe, dress, make-up, pack a few belongings and begin her journey to The City. She eased out of the parking lot in her red convertible, heading north. The long way. Around the North Shore of the lake, one that she knew well and one that might, just might, throw off anyone that would be following. She kept an eye on the rear view mirror. At no time was she suspicious of any pursuing vehicle. For the first time in more than an hour she relaxed as she entered Interstate 80 in Truckee.

The officer that was in charge of keeping track of Alexis had left his post for a quick ten minute trip to the deli down the highway, south of Alexis' condo. It had been quiet all morning. Ever since the package was delivered. During that brief spell Alexis innocently slipped away. When he returned he agonized that Alexis' Camaro was gone. He knew that a severe reprimand was forthcoming, especially since he had observed the UPS driver deliver a package to her address hours before and should have been aware that something was up. Murphy's Law he thought. He immediately informed the watch commander to put out an All Points Bulletin for her vehicle. It would be to no avail. She had gone in the opposite direction from the South Shore. The direction he was sure she had ventured. The feds, long ago, had left the responsibility of physically tracking Alexis up to the local police. The FBI's interest lay mainly in wire tapping. A mistake. They too, were unaware of her departure.

"Get someone else out there and bring Smith in." Dickson relayed to the watch commander. "Let's hope she's just on a joy ride. God Bless Smith if she's not."

"Yes sir."

The admonishment that ensued with Smith standing at attention in front of Dickson, went, "What the hell were you thinking man?" Dickson asked. "Didn't you report that she received some kind of package by UPS this morning?"

"Yes." Smith replied.

"Didn't that alert you to be aware that something was up?" Dickson asked angrily.

"It was like a morgue out there after UPS left. I was only gone for ten minutes. I'm entitled to eat, aren't I?"

"For Christ's sake yes, but this was a critical time. You know better. Goddammit, Smith, you're one of our best officers. How in the hell could you have let this slip by?"

"I know it doesn't do any good to apologize sir, but what can I say."

"You can say you agree to a three day suspension without pay. That's what. Get out of here."

CHAPTER 15

Alexis was nearing San Francisco at four thirty in the afternoon. Traveling west, some twenty miles from the city she observed a dense line of fog, a progressing armada of low lying clouds rolling in, seeming to swallow the metropolis. A common sight in the Bay Area. The sun, subdued by the invasion, struggled to provide the ambiance that is so much a part of San Francisco's charm. A city of beautiful, magnificent and uniquely designed skyscrapers and bridges. Row houses, painted in warm pastels, scroll over the hills and basins. The fog enshrouding the bay and Alcatraz Island with its stark structures was barely visible. It wasn't the prettiest day for her arrival. Nevertheless, she was in awe of San Francisco's skyline as she approached on the Bay Bridge from Oakland. It raised her spirits.

During the entire trip she never once had an anxious moment for fear of being followed. She was alert to that.

She soon discovered how frustrating and confusing it can be maneuvering the streets of this great city with its one-way demands, avenues that angle off obliquely, dead ends, culde-sacs, steep hills, varied ethnic sections, fast moving traffic, the ever present construction hazards and distracting scenery. Because Mark had always driven on their visits to the city, she as a passenger, was new to this adventure. It was a miracle, she thought, that she ended up at Fisherman's Wharf where she spotted a Holiday Inn. She gave a sigh, pulled into the underground parking facility, turned off the ignition, sat there, and quietly thanked her good fortune. It was enough for one day.

Sunday she rested. Her good sense told her to keep a low profile. So far, so good, she said to herself. Alexis laid back in her room, resisting the temptation to be out and about. There would be no business conducted at the passport office on Sunday and to walk in the Wharf area would be folly. No need to take any chances. There would be enough danger at the passport office, Monday.

Sunday dragged. She read the Examiner, front to back. Every section. She detested sports but learned the names of some of the Forty Niners. Mark would be proud. She watched TV. She peered out from her forth floor window at the activity below. It was busy. She was safe, for now.

She also prepared for the next day's activities. At the front desk, she secured a map of the city. Back in her room, with the telephone book spread open on the bed, Alexis looked up the name of several travel agencies. Using the map, she picked one that was around the corner from the hotel. She could have used the services of the agency within the hotel, but thought it better to separate her activities in order to create subterfuge in case of any follow up investigations. Again, Alexis made good use of her intelligence.

At six AM Alexis arose from her slumber. Dressing in her usual manner, a smart business suit, she called ahead for a Taxi. With her credentials she entered the Passport Office. As expected, she encountered no difficulties. The application process went smoothly, without a hitch. She was assured the passport would be ready within three to four days. Professional appearance does make a difference, she thought. Asked where to mail it, she indicated that she would pick it up personally. The clerk agreed. That done they bid each other good bye with, "Have a good day." Alexis felt her confidence building.

Within an hour she was back at the hotel. At the front desk she paid for four more nights lodging, anticipating the amount of time before the passport would be ready. From there she walked the short distance of two blocks to the travel agency she had chosen from the yellow pages. At first, things went as planned. The greeting, the information she provided the agent. It seemed to Alexis that the agent was having difficulty in making arrangements on the particular day that she wanted to depart. She spent what Alexis thought an extraordinary amount of time clicking on various screens in order to consummate the purchase.

"Is there a problem?" Alexis asked.

"I'm having difficulty arranging passage on SAL on that day. You might have to fly another airline and arrive at a different time."

"No, that's impossible. I have to arrive as I specified. Someone is to meet me and I will not be able to contact them in time. They are away on business and incommunicado."

"Well, I'm doing the best I can. SAL is completely booked on that day, on that flight."

"I don't care if I have to ride in the baggage compartment, get me on that flight."

"The only way I can do that is if there is a cancellation."

"I'm willing to pay double the fare. Can't we ask for a volunteer to take another flight? Isn't there a passenger list? I'll call myself."

"Well, yes, that's possible. But first I have to secure it then get the airlines OK. Maybe they'll attempt to persuade a passenger to cancel. How can I get in touch with you to let you know?"

"How long will it take?" Alexis asked.

"1 don't know. Can I call you?"

"No, I'll call you. This afternoon."

Alexis was perturbed. Tense. Nervous. Everything was going fine until this. She returned to the hotel. Paced the floor. At every turn she wanted to pick up the phone to call and find out the results of her request. She fantasized about having to take a different flight, missing Mark, being alone in Hong Kong, both running around trying to locate each other.

Then it occurred to her that she knew where to go in Hong Kong. The Excelsior. Even if she had to take a later flight or another airline, surely he would eventually realize that something had gone awry. Surely he would follow the plan that he laid out for her. If she could arrive as close to the time as specified the plan would only have a slight glitch in it. She still would follow his directions and meet as planned. If it came to that, Mark would just have to bear with it until their meeting.

That afternoon Alexis contacted the travel agency.

"No, I have not been able to get you on that flight." The agent said.

"I'm going to be around for the next three or four days. Please keep trying, will you." Alexis asked.

"Of course."

"I'll call about this time each day. Like I said, I'll pay anyone for canceling and taking another flight. You will communicate that to the airline, won't you?"

"There is a very good chance that they'll be able to do that. But I would like to have your telephone number in order to let you know right away." The agent requested.

"That's OK. I'll call." Alexis hung up.

On Tuesday, waiting for the passport, and for the airline to confirm her passage on the flight she needed, both uncertainties became too much for her. Sitting in the room, she decided to venture out. She needed a break. Leaving her red convertible in the underground parking garage she enlisted a taxi to Marin County and the seaside community of Sausalito. There she spent the day amusing herself by shopping and strolling through the shops and boutiques. It was a hiatus that relieved the stress of the past two days. She almost felt renewed until the urgencies to be met within the next few days came to mind.

Back at the lake, the police and the FBI were ragging on each other for the misstep. The FBI came down hard on the locals. The locals in so many words told the feds to shove it. Smith, the officer that blew his assignment went into seclusion to avoid the wrath from both sides. The All Points Bulletin failed to turn up any evidence of the red convertible. Alexis was not aware that that event was in the process. Sam was waiting in Peria Peru for Dickson to wire him the money so that he could head for Hong Kong. Even though Sam wasn't sure that that was where Mark had fled to.

Jack Bates was biding his time while keeping tabs on Sam. He was again at the mercy of Sam's movements. Jack's people had no idea where Mark Baxter was nor did anyone else know for sure for that matter. Asia was a large and mysterious place.

CHAPTER 16

Wednesday was a crucial day for Alexis. She arose early. At eight o'clock she was on her way to the passport office. Taking a cab she arrived there just after it opened. At the counter she was greeted by the same person that had taken her application on Monday. Alexis appreciated the warm familiar smile once more.

"Miss Cottier your passport is ready."

The clerk couldn't help but notice Alexis' deep sigh.

"Are you surprised?" The clerk asked.

"No, just relieved. I've had a very frustrating two days. This is the first thing that has gone right."

"I'm sorry to hear that," she said.

"Thank you for your help." Alexis offered.

"1 hope your adventure goes as planned." The clerk said.

Alexis looked at her with an expression of query. "What makes you say that?"

"Oh, no reason. 1 just thought that. Well, when a person applies for a passport they're going somewhere. 1 am always a bit envious of those because I wonder where they're going. Traveling is so exciting. I meant no intrusion."

"I didn't mean to be offensive," Alexis said.

"No offense taken. Good luck. Have fun." The clerk said.

Alexis departed with another "Thank you." Smiling. "I hope so." She said.

With her passport secured she had only one other detail to deal with before her departure to Hong Kong. The airline ticket.

It had been her intention to return to the lake to gather her belongings before departing for the Orient. However, during her stay at the hotel it occurred to her that returning would quite probably be the end of the adventure. Mark had been so adamant about secrecy that it sunk in that she should just stay in San Francisco until her departure. She wondered to herself why he hadn't told her to do so. Maybe, she thought, he knew she would do that without his having to instruct her. The thought made her feel good about herself. She had enough money to purchase anything she would need for her trip. She had already decided to terminate her employment. The condo would be safe, when and if she returned. She could see to that by calling Leslie, her close friend, and co-worker. There was no reason to go back.

It was Wednesday, the 19th of December. Alexis dialed her office and asked for Leslie.

"Leslie, Hi."

"Alexis?"

"Yes, it's me."

"Where have you been? Roy is furious. He's called your home several times trying to find out what's going on."

"Oh Leslie, I'm so sorry. I meant to call earlier, but I really haven't had a chance. Tell Roy that I'm leaving my job. And I really apologize to you. Please forgive me. Something has come up and I've got to take care of it."

"It's about Mark isn't it?"

"I can't say right now. It's very important. I'm probably going to be sorry, but I've just got to be with him."

"Where?" Leslie asked.

"I can't say right now." Please forgive me. I love you and don't want to lose your friendship."

"Alexis, what on earth are you doing? It's not worth it. Jeopardizing yourself like this."

"Yes it is. He means so much to me. I've got to get to him and bring him back, If I can."

"Alexis, you're crazy."

"Maybe. Listen I'm going to send you enough money to pay for three months mortgage payments on the condo. Will you see to it?"

"Yes, of course. But when will I hear from you?"

"I don't know. It will be a while. Just look after the house for me. I'll make it up to you when I see you next. And please, please don't mention this conversation to anyone. You hear, no one. Just tell Roy that I'm sorry about being so, ah, remiss in not letting him know in advance about my leaving. I will explain to him someday."

"I'm going to hang up now. Look for my letter in the mail. And, oh yes, destroy the letter after you receive it. Especially the envelope. OK."

"All right. Good luck Alexis, I love you. Please be careful."

"I will."

Alexis called the travel agency once more. Again they had nothing to tell her. They were working on it. She was assured that they were.

Sam received the money from Captain Dickson. He and Hector departed for Lima where Sam purchased a plane ticket to Hong Kong, thanked Hector for his services and bade farewell. Jack Bates followed. Still keeping a low profile and out of Sam's awareness. Jack was good at keeping his distance. Never once did Sam have any suspicion that anyone was on his tail. Why? For one thing Sam was not looking for anyone pursuing him. There would have been no reason to. Secondly, Jack Bates' training and experience at the DEA stuck with him. He was good.

Thursday, December 20th. Sam Weston was snuggled in his seat in business class, somewhat relaxed, but with his ever present distrust of an airplanes ability to stay aloft. His mind wandered through the past couple of weeks events. He squirmed in his seat at each slight bump the aircraft experienced with air turbulence. He squirmed even more when the thought of having to be called off the case crossed his mind. He was aware that he would have to succeed within a very short time. There would be no more excuses. Dickson would have to pull the plug and recall him if he wasn't successful soon. Those in control of the purse strings would demand it. Thoughts of "them" were bitter ones.

Jack Bates sat confidently three rows behind Sam, casually reading the droll airline magazine. The airlines route maps were more interesting than any of the features. A novel that he purchased in the terminal, titled, "The Ultimate Pursuit" lay without attention on the unoccupied seat beside him. He would get into it later, he thought.

The tower at Hong Kong's Airport put Sam and Jack's plane in a holding pattern. It made one pass over the bay which gave both a view of the city below. As with Mark, both men were astonished at the sprawl. Sam's thoughts were mixed. He wasn't sure if Mark was down there and if he was, where would he start. He was counting on Twange Hong for a lead. Any lead.

Not complying with the orders from the stewardess to remain seated until the craft came to a halt, some passengers disobeyed and started the usual chaos. Many of them popped up to retrieve their small bags as the craft taxied to its assigned space. It had been a long flight and many were anxious to get off. Two hundred or so people jostling impatiently all with one idea in mind. To be first to leave the experience. Sam sat, watching, knowing that time was on the side of confusion. Jack bumped his head on the overhead compartment attempting to get to his carry on.

Jack Bates was first at the baggage carousel. He was pleased when he spotted his gray leather suitcase approaching while Sam had a look on his face as if his was on its way to Tokyo. Jack never took his eyes off of Sam and waited out of sight until Sam retrieved his luggage from the conveyor.

Sam headed out of the building lugging his one very heavy bag, occasionally heeding to one side in response to the bags weight. Should have rented a cart, he thought to himself Jack followed, stepping on Sam's still warm footsteps.

"Thanks for automatic doors," Sam said aloud.

A fellow passenger responded, "Yes," recognizing Sam's plight and carrying a lightweight suit bag thrown over his shoulder.

"Thank god for automatic doors and waiting taxis," Sam shot back.

His new acquaintance smiled.

"You want to carry this thing for me?" Sam said kidding.

"No thanks, I've learned to travel light. I used to do that. Carry everything in my closet. No need. You only use so much. A suit, some underwear, socks and a toothbrush."

"Looks like I've got a ways to go before that sinks in." Sam said.

Outside there was an odor neither could identify. It was, in fact, a mixture of a hundred cultures mixed with salt air and a thousand meals being prepared at the same time within a few square miles of each other.

Sam dropped his bag on the sidewalk and hailed for a taxi.

"Where to," the cabbie asked, pulling along side the two men.

"The Hong Kong Hilton."

"Yes sir, throw your things in the trunk." The driver made no attempt to leave his seat as the trunk lid popped open.

The cab was an extended vehicle with two rear facing seats.

Sam's new acquaintance hoisted his bag into the trunk. "Don't mind if I share the ride with you, do you? I'm headed for the Hilton too."

"No, not at all, jump in." Sam said.

Jack, looking as if he were about to be a stranded rat on a sinking barge, jumped into the rear facing seat along with his baggage. "Looks like there's room for a third, you guys mind."

"No, the more the merrier," the stranger said.

"Where you headed?" Sam inquired of Jack.

"Hong Kong for starters," Jack answered.

Actually Jack had no idea where he was headed. "Hong Kong for Starters" was a stall.

"I'm afraid we haven't introduced each other. I'm Sam Weston." Sam extended his hand to the stranger he met exiting the terminal.

"Jon Dexter, nice to meet you."

Both Sam and Jon looked at Jack. Jack hesitated. "Jack Barton, nice to meet the both of you."

"You here on business Jack?" Sam asked.

"No, just pleasure. I travel somewhat. Never been to Hong Kong before. Never been to the Orient. Inherited some money a while back and I'm going to spend it. Worked all my life. Never took time out to enjoy. Just want to have some fun. Kind of postponed it you might say."

"1 see. And what did you do for a living?" Sam asked.

"Drove a tow truck. Big rig you know. Only picked up the big stuff. Eighteen wheelers and the like. Worked the Interstate in Spencer County, Arkansas. Big rigs pay good when they're down. Big outfits can't afford to have them off the road too long. Got to get em hauling again. Call me, I'm the best around. A hundred bucks or more a haul. Do about four or five a day, sometimes. All cash, under the table. I don't pay those assholes in Washington any more than I have to. Yes sir, those pork barrel projects don't get much of my money. No sir. Don't believe in it. Never have. You got any idea how much of your taxes go to things that you don't get any benefit from? You know what the Navy pays for an ashtray? The Air Force pays six hundred and fifty bucks for a hammer that you can buy at the hardware store for six bucks. It's a crime I tell you. And we let them get away with it. What the hell's going on? He continued. That's why I decided to start spending my inheritance, before those eggheads in DC find out about it and figure a way to take it away from me.

"And you Jon, what's your visit about?"

"Business. Just some business. Men's clothing. I have a small chain of clothing stores back in the Midwest. I'm here arranging for some merchandise. They've got the best and least expensive to buy. He was reluctant to say 'cheapest'. I buy about eighty five percent of my merchandise here and have it shipped back ..."

Jack interrupted, "Say Jon, I paid seventy five bucks for this rag I'm wearing, what do you think?"

"I don't judge a person by the clothes he wears." Jon said.

Sam turned to Jack in an attempt to change the subject hoping to diffuse Jack's 'dumb as a stump' question. "Where are you staying, Jack?"

"Where's this thing headed?" Jack responded.

"The Hilton."

"Well, I'll be damned. So am 1. What a coincidence. Had Merv Schuster, at the travel agency back home fix it all up for me in advance. I'll be damn. Maybe we got something in common. What do you think, Sam? Halfway around the world and I meet a stranger that's staying at the same place. Must be a hundred possibilities and here we are. Boy, wait til I get back and tell em about this one." Jack kept Sam at bay with his deception.

Sam had just about enough of this guy. What he didn't know was that he was going to get a lot more. A whole lot more.

Tired, Jon ignored both men, turned away, staring out of the window.

The taxi now picked up speed. Rushing through heavy traffic like a bullet. It reminded Sam and Jack for that matter, of their experiences in Mexico City. Sam was on the edgy side. He still had a slight scab on his forehead from the accident.

Sam, tired of Jack's long winded outbursts, turned his attention to the rolling screen of faces on the broad sidewalks. As they passed he couldn't help but notice that the faces and the signs advertising individual businesses were so close together that they all became a blur.

Without warning. the taxi's nose dipped suddenly, the driver pushed firmly on the brake pedal to avoid a child that had lurched into the street, having escaped his mother's grasp. Missing the boy, the driver thrust his foot to the accelerator throwing Jack from his rear facing seat toward Sam. Sam wasn't having much luck riding in foreign taxis.

The abrupt motion caused Jack's pistol to launch itself from his shoulder holster landing in Sam's lap. Sam reacted quickly hunching back into his seat, startled. "This yours?" Sam asked, pointedly, offering the revolver to Jack, handle first. "Is it loaded?"

"Damn, I'm sorry about that. Naw, 1 just carry it for protection. Never can tell what you might run into when you're traveling."

"Looks pretty mean to me." Sam said. "What is it?"

"1 don't really know," Jack answered. "Mr. Perkins, at the gun shop said it was a .38. I don't know one from the other, Like 1 said 1 just carry it for protection."

Sam wasn't convinced. He didn't like this guy, now he finds out that he's carrying a piece. "If I were you, I'd strap that thing in."

"Yeah, probably a good idea." Jack said sheepishly.

Jon's eyes were as round and wide as the dome light in the cab.

As a result of the incident, no one bothered to continue the round of asking each other what they did for a living. To that end Sam did not disclose his reason for being in Hong Kong nor what his occupation was. Jack knew.

The taxi pulled up in front of the Hilton. Sam motioned for Jack to exit first. Somehow, Sam felt uncomfortable with the thought of Jack at his back. The new arrivals were met by the customary aide in the customary simulated military uniform although much more adorned with gold braid.

Sam was thinking of the .38 revolver. A snub nose one at that. To Sam, it meant, one thing. This guy was no sojourning country bumpkin. He was concealing a vicious weapon cherished by dirt bags. 38's are a death sentence for anyone unfortunate enough to be on the business end. The slug makes a neat little hole when it goes in, comes out carrying enough meat to make a large stew. You don't want to be the victim. of a .38 bullet. You might just as well stick your head between your legs and kiss your, you know what, sayanora.

The big guy in the red uniform carried all five bags into the hotel under his arms clutched in his Yeti sized paws. A skip loader couldn't have done more. Sam was convinced he must be a Mongolian, a descendent of Attila The Hun. "We got guests," he barked to the clerk behind the reception desk made of wood and marble, festooned with computer monitors at ten or more stations.

The three newcomers stood in a square configured atrium. Thirty stories rose above them. The sky an azure blue, was visible through a domed skylight. One balcony stacked upon another, each with a hanging garden of lush, flowering vegetation. It was warm, moist, pleasantly comfortable. Definitely equatorial. Beautifully tropical. Red, Green, Blue and Yellow Parrots perched on the bottom arc of metal rings suspended out from various balconies on selected levels provided more outrageous color to the scenery. The bird's sharp calls echoed throughout, almost intrusive. From the domed skylight rays of sunlight penetrated a sheer curtain of mist above the skylight that bounced off of the tiled floor and danced along the surrounding balconies.

Scurrying about, in their neatly pressed white uniforms, were stewards, bellhops, caterers, and servants. Sam knew that the expense of staying here wasn't going to set well with the boys back home.

Jack wasn't saying much, trying to recover from the incident of the revolver landing in Sam's crotch. But he wasn't asleep either. He noted the room number given Sam by the clerk. Bade farewell to Jon and apologized to Sam for the incident in the cab.

"It's all right Jack. Just keep track of that thing. My advice is to leave it in your room." Sam was relieved to be rid of him, at least for the time being.

"Good idea." Jack said knowing full well the piece would be with him at all times.

As soon as Sam departed for his room, Jack requested the room next door. It was available. Besides his packing a weapon, Jack also had in his bag of tricks all the paraphernalia necessary for eves dropping. Devices he had confiscated before leaving the DEA. Entering his room Jack took note of its environment. He listened for any movement next door but was not sure if Sam was there or just resting. It had been a long day, he was exhausted but, he needed to get into Sam's room to set up a bug. At all costs he had to keep tabs on Sam. Jack called down to the desk and requested that the clerk give Sam a message from his headquarters. In so doing, he, established a pretense to be someone at the Lake trying to get in touch with Sam.

The phone rang in Sam's room.

"Front desk sir." The voice said.

"Yes, what is it?" Sam answered.

"A message from your office sir."

"Read it to me," Sam requested.

"Can't sir. It is to be handed to you personally," the clerk answered.

"Personally? What the hell."

"Yes sir, the individual said it had to be handed to you personally. Not to use the telephone to communicate it."

"OK, OK, I'll be right down."

Sam had been resting. Lying on the bed in his shorts, He threw on his trousers, a shirt and headed for the elevator.

Jack, with his door slightly ajar, watched as Sam entered the conveyance.

Jack observed the numbers over the elevator entrance descend in order. Working the lock on Sam's door, using two metal probes, he successfully opened it and entered. Just as fast as he had gained access he attached a wireless listening device under the night stand that harbored the telephone. Checking the hallway for any activity, finding it empty, he left, locked Sam's door and returned to his room. In all the time that he had been tailing Sam, this was his first opportunity to relax and wait for Sam's next move. Sitting in his car was a thing of the past. At least for now.

The message was innocuous. It said in essence, 'Let us know when you arrive.' Signed Dickson.

"I thought they had something." He said aloud. He ripped the note in half and asked the clerk to discard it.

The APB on Alexis's red convertible failed to produce any results. However, local law enforcement, the FBI and the DEA were looking for her up and down the West Coast. Trains, planes, buses and her Camaro were targeted. Everyone was aware that because she was absent from the lake, she must be either on her way to meet Mark or else she was holed up waiting for the right time to depart. Even though they had temporarily lost contact with her, the authorities knew she would eventually show herself somewhere, someplace.

CHAPTER 17

December 22nd Alexis checked with the travel agency to see if they had succeeded in getting her a seat on the Singapore Air Lines flight to Hong Kong. It was just two days before departure. Each time she inquired, she detected a bit of loathing in the agents voice. Most probably because Alexis had become somewhat demanding and irritable in their conversations. On each occasion she was told that her chances of flying on that day on SAL was futile. No one was willing to give up their seat, especially on Christmas Eve. That flight had been booked months in advance.

"I have another flight out on Christmas Eve if you are willing to take it." The agent said.

Alexis was silent for a moment. "When? Who? What time does it arrive?"

"United. It will get you there just three hours later than the SAL flight. Do you want it?"

"1 don't have any choice, do 1." She said, resignation in her voice.

"I'm sorry, we tried everything, but sometimes ..."

"That's all right, I understand." Alexis interrupted the agents last words. "Yes. Tie it down. I'll be right there to pick it up."

Upon returning, she had to abandon the idea of meeting Mark as planned. The next day, the day before departure would be an anxious one. Alexis wasn't one to tolerate intensity. The past five days had been filled with just about as much strain as she could bear. Her only escape was the concept of seeing Mark. It kept her in balance. One more day, she thought. One more day.

The police were on heightened alert. They were sure she was going to make her move within a day or two. The place of departure would probably be an airport. The San Francisco Airport was the logical choice. One agent commented that there were more eyes looking for Alexis at that location than passengers. They had Mark Baxter somewhere in Asia. They didn't have Alexis anywhere, yet. But, she was their best bet to locate Baxter. Any airline that had flights going to the Orient was staked out by at least one observer.

December 24th. Alexis exited to the underground parking garage to take one last look at her red convertible before departing for the airport. She loved that car. She then walked up to street level and around to the front of the hotel where a taxi would pick her up. The cab driver secured her luggage in the trunk while Alexis sidled into the rear seat of the vehicle. The trip to the airport in South San Francisco was routine. She nor the driver spoke to one another. Although she did see him looking into the rear view mirror, with smiling eyes. Wishing.

The Skycap at the entrance tagged her bags, checked her ticket and directed her to the appropriate gate.

"Gate B," he said. "Your flight leaves in an hour."

Slinging her purse over her shoulder, clutching her small carry on, she headed for the assigned gate.

Upon arriving at the portal, she couldn't help but notice the crowd of passengers. The flight must be full, she thought. There wasn't a seat available in the waiting area. Many Orientals heading home for the holidays she guessed.

From off in a corner, an FBI agent spotted her immediately.

On his two-way, the agent could hardly contain himself. Just above a whisper, excited, he communicated, "I've got her. I've got her."

"This Riley?" The voice on the other end asked.

"Yes, it's me. I've got her. United Airlines. Gate B. Flight 601, leaves in, ah, about forty five minutes."

"OK, OK, we'll get Shipley down there right away. Hang in there. You all set to follow?" As if he didn't know. "You two stay with her to her destination. Understand. Don't let her out of your sight for a second."

"Got it. We'll be all right."

Alexis stood with her back to Riley. Leaning against a tiled wall, she clutched her small valise while waiting for an available seat prior to boarding. Riley's intense stare bore into Alexis causing his eyes to water, burn. He was afraid to glance anywhere but in her direction. Shipley finally showed up. Riley discreetly pointed to her. Shipley smiled.

Agent Shipley then went to the pre-boarding counter, flashed his identification, and informed the attendant that she was going to have to bump two passengers. She nodded. Five minutes passed before the airline clerk announced the names of two individuals to approach the counter. There were words. Harsh and clamorous words. The two would be passengers grabbed their bags in a flurry. With a continuous crescendo of boisterous and abusive curses they hustled away.

The feds did not inform the local authorities at the lake of their discovery.

But Interpol was not sleeping. Their man at the gate noticed the activity taking place in and around the FBI agents. Then he caught a glimpse of the beautiful brunette they were concentrating on. He knew instinctively that she was Alexis Cottier. The photo in his pocket verified it.

Interpol was alerted. Interpol notified Twange Hong who in turn notified Sam Weston who called headquarters in the States and informed Dickson of Alexis' pending arrival in Hong Kong. The elation among the different agencies on the case was tantamount to an energy field bursting with exuberance. All were expecting to be the capturing entity. But, as yet they still were not aware of who they were dealing with. Mark Baxter.

CHAPTER 18

After a brief stop over in Honolulu, all the passengers were tucked in for the last leg of a long flight. Some watched movies, read, slept, chatted with neighbors, concentrated on the ceiling or gazed down into the empty expanse of water below. Alexis who hadn't dropped off in any fashion of slumber sat quietly, reading, working her crossword puzzle, occasionally stared off into space. Wondering.

Riley was positioned across the aisle from Alexis. Shipley sat six rows behind her. It would have been impossible for her to leave her seat without their awareness. When she did use the restroom, both squirmed in their seats for fear of her disappearing.

December 25th. Mark prepared himself with his usual flair for the subterfuge. His beard now more than two weeks in the blooming. An indistinct baseball cap and dark glasses would have kept anyone at bay in so far as recognizing him. At least not without close inspection. However, no one would be looking for him. They were concentrating on Alexis.

At ten thirty AM on the 25th of December at the Singapore Air Lines arrival gate, Mark positioned himself some distance away, but within easy viewing of the exit where Alexis would appear.

Excited, Mark waited patiently. He watched the Lockeed L-IOll that she was supposed to be on taxi toward the accordion like structure that would attach itself to the side of the craft like a giant vacuum cleaner which then would assimilate a sucking maneuver to transport the passengers out of the airplane and into the terminal. One by one, appearing tired, somewhat disheveled, they came out from the tunnel into the seating area. Two hundred and fifty of them. On occasion he thought he spotted her. A close likeness but not quite. He worried for the moment that he'd forgotten what she looked like. How could he forget. Still he did not see his beloved Alexis. The steady flow of traffic stopped. A pause of minutes. Then two stewardess, the pilot, the Engineer appeared. Alexis had missed the flight. He was sure of it. He cursed. He waited still more until the area was empty. Realizing that something went awry, Mark slipped out of the terminal and into a waiting cab.

Sam Weston and Twange Hong also prepared themselves for their quarry's arrival. Prior to the 747's arrival at the United gate there were more police in plain clothes than passengers waiting to board a plane that had not yet arrived. Every agency that had an interest in the case had a man or men waiting for Alexis. Had she known of such a reception committee, she probably would have fainted, perhaps would have had to be forced off of the craft.

The huge 747 loaded with holiday relatives and revelers set down on the runway just three hours after the L-1011 at the SAL Gate. The Boeing then taxied to its berth and unloaded its cargo of passengers. Alexis was spotted instantly by every agent, cop and gumshoe assigned to the case. Like a battalion of warriors engaged in a siege they followed her to the baggage claim and customs. Some of the authorities involved were not aware of the others presence. In some respects it would have made an excellent Key Stone Cops comedy.

Alexis who had memorized Mark's instructions was concentrating on accomplishing that deed to the letter. Even though she was three hours behind Mark's schedule. She secured her suitcase and passed Customs inspections easily. Customs was not informed of her identity nor were they aware of the attention she was receiving by the lawmen.

On the concourse, Alexis hailed a taxi. Six blocks from the airport, she asked the driver to pull over near a telephone booth. Deceptively she said, "I need to make a phone call." Standing in the red booth, she feigned dialing a number. She watched as a parade of vehicles passed. She pretended to be in a conversation while watching for any semblance of the same vehicles passing the booth more than once. Five minutes passed. Alexis was aware of one dual occupied automobile that slowed conspicuously as it passed. Also one that was parked across the boulevard near the booth.

Alexis approached the taxi and paid the driver, requesting that he depart immediately. "What about your luggage?" the driver asked.

"Keep it. I'll pick it up later at your office. I can't handle it right now." She noted the cab's number and put it to memory for later retrieval.

"OK Lady, Women." The driver commented.

Alexis began walking slowly at first. Then she picked up the pace. She thanked herself for wearing flats instead of heels. Every so often she would pause to gaze into a window as if shopping. Capitalizing on the window's reflection to see behind her, she judged that there was, maybe three vehicles in all. She trembled with fear. She froze, terrified. She fought a tendency to panic. Then she remembered Mark's words. "Change taxis. And keep changing as many times as you feel necessary." She gathered herself. Still extremely frightened, she continued to walk. She sensed her pursuers following slowly just behind and out of her view. She knew, eluding them was going to be difficult. She kept reminding herself to follow Mark's advice.

Looking over her shoulder she spotted a taxi approaching. She waved it down. Jumping in, holding her purse and valise close, she ordered the driver to tour the city. No particular destination in mind. After several minutes she informed the driver that she thought she was being followed.

"Can you lose them?"

"Yes maam, I'll give it a go." His Australian accent made it obvious where he was from.

With that, she sat back unaware that he was going to give her the ride of her life.

The driver used back streets and alleys to avoid the myriad of parades and festivities occurring simultaneously on the avenues and boulevards. He sped, weaved in and out of his lane, darted into and around oncoming traffic where it inherently could not be justified.

She gasped and held her breath repeatedly. In a state of astonishment she clasped her hand over her mouth, amazed at the driver's skill avoiding pedestrians she thought had no chance of escaping a collision with the cab. After ten minutes of the driver demonstrating his skill, she came to the conclusion that he knew what he was doing.

Glancing behind her, she could detect no trace of the police's pursuit which eased her concern. She and the taxi had lost the hounds.

"You see them?" He asked.

"No."

She handed the driver a hundred dollar bill with a "thank you, keep it," and departed the vehicle. The driver, startled, said, "Thank you, maam." The emphasis on, Thank you.

Alexis waited patiently in a doorway before hailing another taxi. It didn't take long in this bustling city.

"Where to?" he asked. Smiling.

"The Excelsior Hotel."

Only Detective Hong could have predicted that Alexis would lose them in Hong Kong's massive congestion. Not Sam. Not the FBI. No one could have followed the Aussie with his skills. Certainly not Jack Bates who was one of the interested parties. All were left in the dust of Alexis's cab. All were cursing their luck. Mark was right. Hong Kong was all dressed up for the Christmas Holidays. Parades, festivals, open air markets. It was a good day for getting lost in traffic.

Hong kept apologizing to Sam. Sam kept his temper. The pair drove in circles for some time avoiding closed avenues and streets.

Riley and Shipley, the FBI agents succumbed to their knowledge of having blown it. They prepared for being called upon the carpet.

Alexis kept an eye on the taxis rear window. Still, not a sign of anyone following. She relaxed in the well worn back seat. It seemed to her that the driver was having difficulty containing his desire for her, noticing his eyes fixed on the rear view mirror much of the remaining time to their destination.

The taxi pulled into the circular drive in front of the hotel. She dismissed the cab driver after paying twice the fare for his services. "Thanks for the ride."

The doorman looked perplexed at Alexis' not having any luggage.

"I'm not staying. Just inquiring." She said to him.

"Yes Maam." He said, bowing and opening the large gold framed door for her to enter.

Alexis went straight for the reception desk. She introduced herself asking for any message for her. Without the slightest hesitation, the clerk reached into a bank of boxes on the wall behind him and retrieved an envelope, handing it to her.

Backing away and turning toward a sign indicating "Telephones" she read the contents. It was a terse note. "Welcome to Hong Kong. (622) 888-1212."

"Hello." The voice answered.

"I'm Alexis. I was asked to call you when I arrived."

"Yes, yes." The voice responded. "I'm to give you an address. Are you ready?"

"1032 University Avenue. Do you understand?"

"1032 University Avenue." She repeated.

"Yes, that is right." The phone immediately disconnected.

Mark sat forelorn in his room wondering if she had arrived. He hadn't heard anything from Sherrill. He worried that Alexis had missed her flight and was still on the other side of the world. His mind racing, trying to come up with a solution regarding contacting her with new instructions.

Alexis hired one of the taxis' that occupied the hotels designated stand.

"Where would you like to go?" The driver asked.

Alexis remembering what Mark had said about changing cabs often, replied.

"Downtown."

"We are downtown, Miss." Where downtown?"

"The financial district." Thinking offhand. "And be quick."

"All right." Came his reply.

They traveled for some distance before Alexis ordered the cab to let her off at the next corner.

"We're not there yet." He informed her.

"That's OK. I'll get out here. Thanks."

The taxi pulled in behind another cab parked waiting for a fare.

Alexis paid the driver before exiting, thanking him again.

In one continuous movement, she departed one taxi and entered the taxi that had been waiting and ordered him to the address she had received on the telephone.

"1032 University Avenue." That's all she said. The cabbie didn't respond except to put the vehicle in gear and drive off.

From her perspective it seemed to be another long excursion from nowhere to nowhere.

She felt that she had seen every part of Hong Kong at this point. Because of Hong Kong's many narrow alleys and avenues it seemed endless. In reality, she had unknowingly been traveling in the same general vicinity since her arrival.

Arriving at 1032 University Avenue, Alexis was surprised that it was an Oriental restaurant. She was apprehensive. Entering through the glossy red double doors, she stepped into a seating area of bright green vinyl benches. Glancing into the dining area the tables were covered with pristine white linen cloths. A single yellow or alternating purple flower adorned ceramic bud vases, along with sterling utensils. Paper lanterns in a variety of colors hung throughout. Chinese stencil art on the walls above each table added to the atmosphere. She could smell the sweet aroma of Chinese cuisine. Alexis was greeted by a woman of about forty.

"How many?" She asked Alexis.

"I was told to come here for a message. I'm Alexis Cottier."

"Oh my goodness. I'm sorry. I was expecting you but had no way of recognizing you. My name is Sherrill. Come this way." Sherrill pointed to a multi-colored beaded curtain behind her, "Paul, take over for a while." Sherrill requested of a young man standing close by.

"Come Alexis, it's not busy right now. I do have a message for you from Mr. Baxter."

Alexis, exhausted by this time, was pleased and at the same time wary of the hospitality. Sherrill seemed just a bit too friendly. Her suspicions would prove to be frivolous.

Alexis began to warm up to her host after being offered a refreshment of tea and pastries. The British influence, Alexis surmised.

"You've no doubt have had a very busy day, or may I say, perhaps a very busy two or three days." Sherrill said.

Alexis wasn't much for idle conversation at this point. "Yes, I have. If you don't mind I would like to get on with my stay here. I really appreciate your kindness, but you can imagine how anxious I am to see Mark, er, Mr. Baxter."

"I can't imagine." Sherrill said jesting. "Of course, let us get on with it. Mr. Baxter left this envelope for you. I've kept it in the safe until just a while ago knowing you were about to appear. I'm sure his instructions are as complete as his character." Alexis looked puzzled. Shrugging off Sherrill's comment, she opened the envelope.

"Hi babe. Welcome to Hong Kong. I hope all went well for you. I have been sending out positive thoughts for your safety and for us to be together at last. Now that you have met Sherrill, trust her. She will help you. She also will take care of you for today. Get some rest and tomorrow we will be together. Tomorrow morning, Sherrill will escort you to the dock area. Don't worry, sherrill knows where. There, an older Japanese fellow, Mr. Yamamoto, will take you by boat, to an island. I will meet you there. Love, Mark."

It was a bitter-sweet communication. She thought for sure that she was going to see Mark today. At the same time, she was suspicious of "Sherrill." What kind of relationship did Mark have with her. Stop, she scolded herself in silence. Mark had been here for less than a few days. How much of a relationship could they have developed in that amount of time? Sherrill was a ten, or nine at least. Euro-Asian, blue-green eyes, high cheekbones, tanned, beautiful body. Hmmm. Alexis again shrugged it off. She assumed that it was because she was lonely and in the care of a stranger.

Mark stayed put in his hotel room. He still had no idea what was going on. Surely she had missed her flight. He had no way of knowing that she did make the trip and had received his note at the reception desk.

In order to keep their association from the hotel personnel he made no attempt to ask if she had arrived. He kept brainstorming a myriad of ideas as to how to secretly get in touch with her back in California.

Sam Weston, Twange Hong and Jack Bates, working alone, were at an impasse. Sam figured that because he had lost Alexis in the pursuit, he would have to communicate that to his boss, Dickson. Sam was sure that Dickson would be disgruntled and call Sam off the case. Sam decided to delay any contact with Dickson, stalling for time. Twange Hong went about his business, with assured confidence, and the wisdom that something would develop. Knowing that with all the eyes out there, someone would pick up on Alexis and off they would go, again. Hong tried to soothe Sam's ego by reiterating Sam's reputation, over and over. To the point that Sam was getting tired of hearing how good he was. Jack Bates tried to relax in his room, listening for any evidence of Sam's movements. That is, when Sam was in his room, which wasn't very often. Sam spent most of his time at police headquarters. Jack was spending a lot of his time in his car, again.

December 26th. The sun, brilliant this morning, rose over the bay. A warm breeze accompanied a humid air. Alexis slept uneasily. But rested. She knew though, that the change in time zones, would catch up with her. But, that was not what was on her mind. She could have lost three days sleep. It wouldn't matter because today she was going to see Mark. Her clothes mussed, with no changes at hand, made her feel terrible. She cursed leaving her suitcase in the first taxi. That too, seemed to fade into oblivion. She was going to see Mark today.

At eight thirty Alexis heard a tapping on her bedroom door. The apartment over the restaurant was comfortable, cozy. Alexis was surprised by how quiet it seemed inside even though the restaurant was located on one of the busiest streets in the city.

"Alexis." Sherrill called out courteously.

"Yes, I'm awake, come in."

"How did you sleep?" She asked as she entered. "I've got some clean undies for you. I washed them out last night as you slept."

"Oh my, I was thinking about that. Thank you so much. But the rest of me is a disaster."

"I've also got some things you might want to wear. I noticed that we are about the same size. If you don't mind Oriental fashion. And I've got scads of makeup. I think we can get you together just fine."

"You are a lifesaver, Sherrill. How can I ever thank you?"

Sherrill's demeanor and disarming charm, her anxious to help attitude, completely diffused Alexis' suspicions about her relationship with Mark. The two women began bonding immediately. They chatted about things. Mark came up in the conversation on several occasions. Sherrill openly talked about Mark's sweetness. How much he loved Alexis.

"Even though Mark just happened into the restaurant a couple of days ago, I feel like I've known him for years." Sherrill said.

"That's Mark." Alexis answered. "You can understand how anxious I am to see him. It's been too long for us to be apart."

Alexis wasn't sure whether Sherrill knew why Mark was in Hong Kong or even if she knew of the trouble he was in. She decided not to investigate the subject.

"I'll give you an hour. Then we must be off. Our Mr. Yamoto will be waiting. You do know about Mr. Yamamoto, don't you?" Sherrill asked.

"Mark mentioned him in his note." Alexis answered.

"OK then, an hour. Can you make it?"

"Yes."

At nine thirty a sharp knock on Alexis' door alerted her to Sherrill's earlier statement, Alexis was more than ready. She would wade through a river of crocodiles to get to him.

The two women left the restaurant through the back door. They stepped into an alley, where Sherrill's black Jaguar was parked. Both were unusually silent. Sherrill drove steadily for twenty minutes before the atmosphere changed from that of a cosmopolitan metropolis to the shabby environs of a wharf area. The familiar scent of sea air permeated the atmosphere, with a hint of fish odor and the pungent redolence of oil oozing from the dock's creosote soaked pier-posts and planking. The tropical sun bore down as the morning progressed.

The old Chinese with the cocked captain's hat greeted the two ladies. Sherrill spoke first.

"Where's Mr. Yamamoto?"

"He's not here yet." He answered, as a matter of fact.

Alexis was suspicious of a conspiracy between Old Captain's Hat, Mr. Yamamoto and Sherrill. She had no way of knowing that Mark had coordinated the plan that would get the two of them together on Tung Lung. She kept telling herself to trust these new acquaintances, that they were there to take care of her, and to go along with the plot.

Disgruntled, Sherrill gave the old man a cringing look. "Have you heard from him?"

"You know he's not about to jump for anybody. He takes his time."

"We'll wait in the car." Sherrill said.

"Whatever. His boat is ready." The old man pointed to a cabin cruiser tied down at the end of the dock.

Mark tried to reach Sherrill at the restaurant to tell her that Alexis hadn't arrived as planned. He was taken aback when informed that Sherrill and a lady that arrived yesterday left earlier. He didn't know who the lady was or where they were going. Mark knew. His disappointment in missing her evaporated with the thoughts of seeing her. It had to be Alexis with Sherrill. He was sure of it.

Mark was beside himself. For a second or two he turned in circles trying to think. There was only one place Sherrill would have taken Alexis. Why didn't he think of this before, he said to himself. He then realized it was because he thought for sure she was still in California. He waved the first taxi in line and jumped in and barked out his destination. "And be quick."

Yamamoto, a pleasant elderly gentleman, dressed formally in a black suit, white shirt and a garish yellow tie, and bowler hat, apologized for his tardiness. Actually, he arrived only five minutes after the women.

Bowing courteously, "Please forgive me." He said. "If you will please follow me, we will be on our way."

Sherrill, gave Alexis a warm hug and wished her luck. 'Look me up later, if everything goes all right."

Alexis turned and waved to Sherill as she walked down the dock to Yamamoto's cruiser.

Mark had missed Alexis's departure by an hour. Old Captain's Hat informed him.

"You wanna go over there again, my friend?"

"Of course, let me have that Tahiti, if it's available."

"It is." He said.

Mark released the lines throwing them into the craft and jumped in. Without so much as giving the engine time to uncoil, he thrust his foot down on the accelerator. The engine roared, the stern buckled under the strain, digging into the water. Within seconds the bow obeyed the law of physics, met the plain of the sea as it sped off, to Tung Lung.

Mr. Yamamoto escorted Alexis onto and off the cruiser as if she were royalty. Arriving at the island, they slipped into his rickety golf cart, and rode without saying a word to one another, to the secluded group of huts. She was electrified, in awe as she gazed upon the scene. It was paradise. The calm blue-green sea lay outstretched beyond the deserted white sand beach. The palm's supple fronds danced in the warm, temperate breeze that crossed the island. The grounds were smothered with elephant ear size ferns. Vines entwined themselves around the tree trunks. Each strand rising on its own course struggling to reach the light in the canopy. Serenity, seclusion and warmth. It was too much for one to absorb in a single exposure. If Mark had been there, she would have fainted, she said to herself.

Yamamoto escorted her to one of the more secluded huts amongst a group of palms. Upon entering, Alexis gasped. It was Shangri-la. It certainly would be when Mark arrived. A scenario she had no idea was taking place at that very moment.

Yamamoto asked her if there was anything else he could do for her.

"I can't think of a thing, except if you could make Mr. Baxter appear magically."

"I think Mr. Baxter will be along shortly. I will wait at the dock until he shows up. If he does not arrive I will not abandon you here by yourself."

Alexis beamed. "I hope so. Thank you so much."

Yamamoto excused himself and disappeared over the rise, his cart silently wending its way back to his boat.

Mark's Tahiti slowed to a crawl, the engine barely more than idling, propelled the craft smoothly along side the dock. Yamamoto was descending toward the dock when both men spotted each other. Yamamoto broke into a wide grin. Mark knew instantly what Yamamoto was communicating.

"Is she here?" he shouted as if to confirm Yamamoto's silent message.

"Yes. The far cabin, in the palm grove." He said.

"Thank you, thank you, thank you." Mark repeated in exultation.

"Here, use the cart. It will get you there faster." Yamamoto offered the key to the cart as the two met on the dock.

"I'll be forever indebted to you sir."

"That's all right young man. Enjoy."

Mark transcended the quarter mile as fast as the little vehicle could muster. Alexis did not hear the electric conveyance approach their love nest to be. She was too busy getting used to her new surroundings. Exploring and delighting in every nook and cranny inside the cottage.

Mark burst through the door. Alexis turned startled.

Mark opened his arms to receive her. "Come here you beautiful thing."

"Oh my god." She ran to him. They enfolded each other tightly, their arms entwined. They pressed together. He searched for her lips with his. Both moaned softly, feeling the euphoria, the ecstasy, experiencing the thrill of near sexual gratification. He pulled away from her momentarily, looking, just looking. His eyes not missing a detail. Then he began anew, kissing her face, her neck. Their lips met again in a long passionate renewal of their love.

"Oh, am I glad to see you sweetheart. Man I thought this day would never come. I've wanted to see you, hold you so much for so long." Mark said.

Alexis' eyes, misty with tears, pulled him to her again. She begged for his lips. He responded. He could feel her body surrender to desire. "I want you so much." She said.

Their sex was longing, burning, gentle, touching, fulfilling. They spoke not a word during the encounter. She reminisced, thinking of his gentleness, vivid memories of his caring. The most important thing was how much she loved him. She needed the sexual intimacy to assure her that he had not forgotten. To be loved like a woman. Mark tended to her every need. And his.

It was complete. They were together once more.

"1 will never let us be apart again." He vowed.

"1 couldn't take it any longer." She said.

They lounged in the warmth of the bed for nearly three hours, talking, playing, making love.

In time the conversation became more serious. Directed to the matter at hand. The passion of the last three hours faded into the reality of Mark's situation, and now hers. It came down to pointed questions from Alexis.

'What are we going to do? Where will we go Mark?"

"We are not going anywhere for the time being. We're going to lay low for a while. Now that you're with me, we'll take another approach to avoid detection until the matter cools off."

"And how long do you think that will take."

"I really don't know. Six months, a year, maybe more. We will just have to be careful, stay incognito, you might say. There are any number of places on this planet to seclude ourselves. Any number of people willing to help you, provided the price is right. I have contacts around. Especially in the southern hemisphere. Somewhere where extradition would be a problem for the authorities. Now that you're here I can think more clearly. Just give me a little time. Let's enjoy the moment. This place is perfect for now."

She interjected. "It will be perfect until complacency sets in or until you get antsy and restless and want to get going. And that won't be long from now. I know you Mark, I know how you think. I have a feeling that we will be running forever. Not just six months, a year or more, but forever. That doesn't appeal to me,"

"Let's talk about it later. I just want to look at you for now. To know that we're together. Spend time together. Although, he chuckled, I don't know of much to do around here. I guess unless you like to fish or swim. One thing for sure, it'll give us time to plan. The fridge is stocked. How about something to eat."

"Right now food doesn't appeal to me. I wish we already had a plan and were following it."

"Too soon. Too soon."

CHAPTER 19

The authorities were stalled. Each one, in their individual enclaves, all brainstorming ideas as to her whereabouts. Actually there wasn't much thought crunching to do. It was obvious. So Sam decided to retrace his steps.

"We've got to get to the cabbie that picked her up. If we can get some info out of him, maybe we can take the second step, then the third and forth, if necessary, to find her. She had to leave a trail. We have the cabs ID number. At least that's where I'm going to start. If you come up with something better, let me know."

"I would be surprised if there was only one taxi involved." Hong inserted.

"Who knows, miracles do happen. That's where I'm headed." Sam said.

Sam checked in with the taxi company and gave them the license number and the identification number on the taxi's trunk lid.

"I don't have any idea." Was the answer Sam got when he asked the driver who first picked her up at the airport. "She just walked off down the street that's the last I saw of her."

"What street? Where?"

"Eleventh and Commerce."

"Is that a place where other cabs hang out regularly for fares?"

"Yeah, a couple of guys like that spot. It's busy all the time."

"Can you give me any names?" Sam said.

"1 only know two, but there are several others."

"Let's start with the two."

"Ah, Lo Chang and Mia Kweng."

"Thanks."

"You're welcome."

Sam checked his map that Hong had furnished and located Eleventh and Commerce.

It was a busy intersection. The streets were littered with yesterdays festival debris. Teams of men in white overall uniforms were busy cleaning up the mess.

Three cabs were parked in an area marked "For taxicabs Only." The drivers all were engaged in their favorite pastime activity when idle. Reading the newspaper.

Sam went directly to the first cab in line, stuck his head through the passenger window.

"Where to?"

"Nowhere. I'm looking for Lo Chang and Mia Kweng."

"What for?"

"Police. I want to ask them some questions."

"What police, you don't look Chinese to me."

"You gotta be a chinaman to be a cop here? I'm Sam Weston." Sam flipped out his ID.

"Lo's in the third cab back of me."

"Oh, by the way. Did you pick up an attractive brunette here yesterday."

"No, but I'd like to."

"You know if any of your compatriots did."

"We don't get together everyday and discuss who picked up who." The cab driver said.

"Look wise guy, this is serious business. I'm going to be around. So if you hear of anyone that picked up a very attractive Caucasian lady yesterday, I want to know about it. OK?"

"All right, I'll check into it for you."

"What' s your name?"

"Lee Hui. The last name is pronounced, wee. Get it? Lee wee. My parents were strange."

"Not funny to me." Sam said.

Sam poked his head into Lo's cab. Dispensing with any confusion up front, he displayed his ID, introducing himself.

"You Lo?"

"Yes, what can I do for you."

"You know of anyone of your fellow cabbies that picked up a beautiful brunette lady yesterday."

"I think it was Charley. He couldn't stop talking about the beauty he had yesterday. Maybe him."

Sam got excited. "Where's Charley?"

"He's out on a fare right now."

"What's Charleys cab number?"

"Ninety six."

"Does he always come back here after dispensing with his passenger?"

"Yeah, unless he picks up another fare on the way in."

"Whats he look like?"

The cabbie shrugged his shoulders, turned up the corner of his mouth. "He's from Australia. Ordinary guy."

"That it? How long has he been gone?"

"Fifteen minutes, maybe twenty."

"Thanks, I'll wait around."

"Your choice."

Sam felt uncomfortable just standing around. He paced back and forth. Checked out the merchandise in the window of a feminine boutique. Noticed that he needed a haircut. Got excited with every cab that passed.

An hour passed. No number ninety six.

An hour and a half expired. Finally number ninety six pulled in behind the other taxis. Sam rushed over opened the front passenger seat and jumped in. Performed his usual police ID routine and again introduced himself. Charley scooted closer to the drivers door.

"You Charley?" Sam asked.

"Yes sir. What's up mate?"

"You picked up a lady yesterday. A brunette. A knockout. Where did you take her?"

"Oh man. She was something. You know, the kind that gives you the shivers. What a face, body. An animal. Man, I wanted her so bad."

"Not as bad as the police want her. Where did you take her? Just answer that."

"I figured so. She asked me to shake a tail. 1 drove like a son-of-a-bitch through traffic."

"Goddammit Charley, Where did you take her?"

"The Excelsior Hotel."

"Did you see her go into the hotel?"

"You bet your butt. 1 watched hers until she disappeared inside."

"Thanks Charles, my man. You have no idea how much I love you."

"What."

"Don't take that seriously, just a grateful thank you."

"Oh, ok."

"By the way, where's the Excelsior?"

Charley gave him the address and complicated directions. Sam screwed up his lip.

"Thanks, I'll check my map."

Sam crossed the busy intersection to get to his vehicle, violating the 'Walk, No Walk' icon.

He rushed through traffic, stopping every now and then to look at the map. He sped through traffic rushing to the hotel as if he expected to catch her standing at the reception desk, checking in.

"Do you have an Alexis Cottier registered?"

The clerk ran through the register.

"She checked in yesterday." Sam said.

"No Alexis Cottier."

"A brunette. A very attractive brunette." Sam said.

'We don't register our guests by the way they look."

"Who was on yesterday?"

"I was, for one. Why?"

Sam pulled out his ID. I'm looking for a brunette lady, Caucasian. "Now, tell me who was on besides you yesterday."

"There were three of us. Shawn, Cherry and me."

Sam hurumphed. "Where's Shawn and Cherry now?"

"In the office. I'll get them."

Sam waited. And of course, Jack Bates was waiting outside. A lot of time in his car. The floorboards were getting messy with candy wrappers, empty cola cups, a few coins and the ashtray brimming over.

Shawn and Cherry appeared from out of nowhere. Both wide eyed. The police were outside they were told. They thought they were going to have to explain the hemp purchase they'd just made.

"Hi, I'm Sam Weston. I need some information. Maybe you can help me."

Both individuals appeared relieved.

"Either of you see or talk to a very attractive brunette lady yesterday. Say around noon, maybe a little later."

"1 did." Shawn said.

"Did she check in?"

"No. 1 just gave her a note that was left for her."

"Do you know who left the note?"

"Mr. Chimes."

Sam described Chimes. He pulled out a photo of Mark. He knew it was Baxter.

"Yes, that's him."

"Is he here. I mean staying."

"He was. He checked out yesterday."

Sam rolled his eyes. At the same time his adrenaline surged. "You didn't by chance peek at what the note said, did you?"

"No sir. No way."

"Do you know what kind of car Mr. Chimes drives?"

"He doesn't, he always takes cabs as far as I know." He looked at the other two. They shook their heads in agreement.

Sam continued. "How long was Chimes here?"

"Ahhhh, a couple of days, maybe a week."

"Any of you ever talk to him?"

Cherry interrupted. "Didn't talk much. He came and went. I know he likes Chinese food. He brought it in regularly in a take out container."

"Chinese food. There must be a million Chinese restaurants in Hong Kong." Sam blurted.

"Emerald Palace." Cherry said.

"That's the name of the place?" Sam asked excitedly.

"Yes, that's the name I always saw on the bag. I go there often."

Sam got the address and was off. Jack Bates followed.

'Welcome to the Emerald Palace. How many?" Sherrill asked.

Sam brought out his identification. At the same time exposed a photo of Mark.

"Ever see this man?"

Sherrill hesitated, looking at Mark's image. "I'm not sure, I see so many Americans that I could be mistaken."

"What makes you think he's an American?" Sam was suspicious of her statement. "He could be European."

"Well, yes he could be. I just assumed that he is because you're an American."

"I could be Canadian. Look again. Have you ever seen this man?" Sam repeated.

"No."

Sam knew that she was acquainted with Baxter. She looked away when she responded negatively. Sam recognized that trait in almost everyone when they're lying. They can't look you straight in the eyes.

"Listen to me Miss, ah, what is your name, by the way?"

"Sherrill, I own this business."

Sam continued. "This is a very serious matter. If you are not telling the truth, it could mean trouble for you down the road. You understand. This man is a fugitive from justice. He's wanted by just about every police organization on the planet. I have reason to believe that you know him. He frequented your business several times these past few weeks. I have witnesses." Sam was bluffing. "Think about it. Here's a name and telephone number to call if you change your mind." Sam gave her Twange Hongs phone number.

"Who's he?"

"One of your own. Police. He also would like for you to cooperate."

Sam parted, circled the block, traversed the alley behind the restaurant then headed straight for the nearest phone.

"Twange Hong please." He asked.

Twange eventually answered. "This is Twange."

"Twange. This is Sam. Remember me."

"Don't be funny. Of course."

"I've got something. A chinese restaurant, the Emerald Palace, the owner, Sherrill, knows our man Baxter. She responded negatively when I showed her Baxter's photo, but she's lying. I ran this lead down from some employees at the Excelsior Hotel. He took food back to his room from the restaurant. He goes by the name of Jeff Chimes. Any way, I want a tail on Sherrill. I think she'll try to reach Baxter to let him know we're hot on his trail. There's an alley behind the restaurant. A Jaguar is parked near the restaurant's back door. It could be hers. I want a lookout at that location, front and back real quick. Can you accommodate that?"

"You have been busy. Yes, I'll get some people on it right away."

"Twange, I'm going back there now. Sit it out near the alley. I figure she'll use the Jag, if it is hers to reach Baxter. Have you come up with anything on his girlfriend?"

"Not a thing. She's disappeared, just like him."

"Well, I do. She picked up a message at the Excelsior, yesterday. She's not staying at the hotel, but Baxter was. I figure they've connected, because he checked out yesterday also. They're on the move. Maybe out of town. We have to keep some surveillance on the departure arenas, just in case."

"We're doing that."

"Good. Right now, I'm counting on this Sherrill to lead us to them, if they're still around. Damn, I hope so."

"I'll get a couple of people over there right away. In the meantime, stay in touch. You took too long before this call to reach me. I would like for you to call in at least twice a day. The reason for that is, I'm getting the message that I am personally responsible for his capture. That's the way we work over here. Once you're assigned to a case, my people want to know what's happening by the second. No offense intended."

"OK, but get me a cell phone. Then I can call you six times a day. Running around looking for a phone ain't gettin it."

Sam returned to the restaurant. Nearing the alley behind the restaurant, he saw a black Jaguar pull out. It turned right, into his direction. He recognized Sherrill as she passed. Sam made a quick U-turn, missing two oncoming cars, and sped off in pursuit. He followed two, sometimes three cars behind. Trailing her some distance away, he spotted a traffic light turn yellow which she successfully drove through. He was tempted to run the light, but thought better, He waited, cursing the time it took to change back to green. For a minute or two she was completely out of sight. He stuck his head out of the drivers window in the hopes of seeing her. No Jaguar was to be seen. Then, as luck would have it, he caught up with her four blocks away. She was sitting, waiting for a red to change. It was then that he decided he would have to chance exposing himself, by sticking as close as possible to avoid another miscue.

As he pursued, Sam's thoughts wandered back to Mexico City. Things like, how long had he been on this case, six weeks, seven weeks. He had lost track of the actual time. It seemed like a year. How close he was to concluding it in Mexico City. How close he was to Baxter in Peru. The way Mark had eluded him in Columbia by faking a flight back to Mexico City. He felt a failing in his ability. Here I am in the Orient and I'm not closer now, than I was back there. Am I losing my touch?

Sherrill led him out of the city to near the bay and the port area. He lagged further behind. There were no traffic signals in the district. Just an occasional stop sign. He could afford to hang back a little.

Sherrill parked near Old Captain Hat's shack She disappeared inside. Sam waited. It was ten minutes before she reappeared. Sherrill backed out of her parking spot and headed Sam's way. He ducked down, lying flat on the seat. He heard her pass. For a time Sam sat contemplating whether or not he should follow her or visit the interior of the shack.

He knew where he could find her. Something took place in the shack He had to find out what transpired there.

"Can I help you?" The old man asked.

"Maybe. I'm new here. I'm a travel agent. I have several outlets back in the states. I was wondering if you could tell me a little bit about some of the islands in the area. I'm always looking for something new to offer my clients. You know. interesting places. Something different than the usual fare. I would imagine that you have intimate knowledge of that."

"It could mean more business for you. I've obtained a lot of useful information by asking the local people about their surroundings."

The old man was more than accommodating. A sense of helping. Lending his expertise. His ego had been inflated.

"Yes, I know of a few. Here on Hong Kong Island at North Point there are many nice resorts. A few are secluded. Then there's Tap Island around the peninsula. A very nice place. It is not well known. On Basalt Island there is a quiet resort. But it caters mostly to the elite Chinese. Very expensive. And Tung Lung Island. It is the closest except for North Point. Tung Lung is kind of deserted. Probably not even the locals know about it. I mean the small resort there. An old gentleman, Mr. Yamamoto owns the property. He's retired and not very active anymore. Once in a while someone runs across the resort and they spend some time. Grass huts, real secluded. A fishing village mostly."

"Tell me more about this Tung Lung Island."

"Like I said already. There's not much there. Just some huts. A small village. For fishing. Mostly native peoples live there."

"How do I get there?"

"It's about a forty five minute boat ride. Big Green doesn't go over there. No business."

"Big Green, what's that?"

"The ferry. You are new here." The old man stated explicitly.

"I see you rent boats. Can you help me? 1 want to see this Tung Lung. How do I get there?"

Old Captains Hat directed Sams attention to a large map on the wall.

"Follow me. I'll show you."

Sam walked around the counter to the map.

"See here, this is where we are. There's Tung Lung," pointing it out.

"There's a lot of space between here and there. Is there any landmarks out there that I could use. A person could get confused." Sam said.

"It is very simple. Once you are out of the harbor, look directly Southeast. It will be on the horizon. Follow the coast. C'mon I'll show you from the dock." The old man escorted Sam to the edge of the pier. He directed Sams attention to the peninsula where the land seemed to end. "That peninsula is Hong Kong Island. When you reach that point look Southeast. The land you see on the horizon is Tung Lung. Head straight for it."

"What's the fastest way to get there?"

"I got another ski boat. Big engine. Jet drive. It'll get you there in about forty five minutes. My other Tahiti is over there now. A guy rented it yesterday. Second time he's been over there."

"A man, you say, rented your other boat yesterday." Sam exposed Mark's photo. "Is this the man?"

"Yes. American. Young. Why do want to know what he looks like."

"Competition. Always someone trying to horn in on your business." Sam said.

The old man continued. "Yamamoto took a lady over there before he rented the boat. I figure they are a couple spending some time alone."

"Oh." Sam took note of some dark clouds off to the East. "Looks like we're getting some weather."

"Could be. It's a long way off." He said unconcerned. "You ever pilot a boat before?"

"Yes, I'm familiar."

Sam debated whether he should notify Hong before taking off. Thought better and did so. However, he wanted this collar alone. If there was an arrest to make. Using the public phone on the outside wall of the rental shack, Sam asked Hong if he had anything further. Hong responded negatively.

"Where are you Sam?"

"Down by the bay. I'm checking something out. You know about Tung Lung Island?"

"Tung Lung. My God Sam, that's way out there. What's up."

"Just a hunch. I'll let you know if it has any substance."

"We've got patrol boats. If you need help let me know right now. I'll send one over. Maybe I ought to have one pick you up and take you there."

"No thanks. I don't want to waste your time and money on a false lead. Just so you know where I'll be this afternoon."

"OK."

Sam headed out following the old mans directions. He didn't like deep water. Wading across a stream, OK. Dark water, no. Sam rounded the peninsula, aimed his sight to the Southeast. There it was. On the horizon, like the old man said it would be.

Pressing the throttle to the floor, the boat planed more so. With less resistance it leaped across the smooth surface. The island grew larger by the minute.

He wasn't sure what to expect.

Sam eased the boat to the side of the pier. A little forward, then backwards bringing the craft along side and even with the walkway. On the opposite side of the dock, tied down, was the other Tahiti.

He checked his weapon before stepping off onto the dock, making sure that one shell was in the chamber, the safety off. A light drizzle began to fall from the dull gray clouds. A mist swept over the island aided by a stiff wind out of the East.

Sam trotted up the hill towards the village. Inquiring at the tackle store he was given directions to the tiny resort.

Nearing the area he took note of the terrain. Soon he was within sight of the huts. He paused, using a palm trunk for secrecy. Looking for some activity, he was pleased to find none. Not a soul in sight nor any sign of anyone inhabiting the area. That in a way was good and bad. If they were here, where were they? He said to himself. Sam took the time to look carefully at all the structures. One by one. All appeared to be vacant. And then he spotted it. It was tucked away in the palms. The only one that had towels drying on the porch railing.

The surf broke easily in this part of the bay. A peninsula that jutted out on the Eastern side protected a long inwardly sweeping beach. It was here that Mark and Alexis had been enjoying themselves. Yesterday was filled with lounging and sharing the joys of lovemaking. Visiting the beach last evening, they took a long and leisurely walk in the soft sand. The eighty two degree water affectionately bathed their feet as they splashed along the shoreline. They were becoming relaxed and off their guard.

On occasion, Alexis attempted to talk Mark into returning to the lake to turn himself in. She persisted in rationalizing that, "Mark you haven't robbed a bank. You didn't steal it from an innocent person. It's drug money. Dirty. You'll probably get off with a slap on the wrist."

Mark's response. "That sounds all well and good to you, but how do I repay all the money that I've spent, answer that." He continued, "How do I explain some of the mayhem I've done with the feds. Those things will not be excused." Alexis mused, seemingly perplexed.

Carefully, with slow deliberate steps, Sam descended on the hut, his pistol in hand. He used a tree trunk within ten feet of the cabin for cover. From there he rushed the last few feet to the rear of the cabin. With his back against the structure, holding the pistol with both hands, he worked his way around to one side of the cottage. With his ear to the wall he listened for any sign of life inside. As yet he hadn't heard any movement, nor any conversation. He decided to take the pair, if they were in there, through the front entrance. Hunched over, he ducked under a side window. As fast as his feet would carry him he slipped around to the front of the hut. He turned quickly, He climbed the three steps to the front door. Turning sideways he slammed his shoulder full force against the door. The door sprung open crashing against the inner wall. He thrust his weapon from side to side. The cabin was empty. Sam examined every corner of the interior. There was no outward sign that it was occupied by Baxter or Alexis.

His eyes looking for detail spotted a wallet lying on a table near the bed along with some coins. Sam opened it. There in all her striking beauty was a photograph of Alexis. The waiting would begin. Sam positioned himself in a cushioned rattan chair facing the front entrance.

It was nearing two o'clock before Mark and Alexis started back to their hideaway from their mid day walk and lounge on the beach. Both were in a cheerful happy mood. Holding each other as they walked, their arms around each others waist. It was their second full day together. The sun disappeared, hidden above a thick layer of clouds. The gloomy gray sky now degraded to heavy ominous looking black clouds. The air was still, warm, humid.

Neither of them were aware of a weather report that indicated that an unusually late season typhoon was generating itself into an angry rage out in the western Pacific.

Sam thought he heard voices approaching. He went to the partially open window and espied the pair coming toward the cabin. Sam became rigid, tense. Sitting back in the chair, he waited with his revolver drawn, cuffs ready to be applied.

Mark left Alexis's side to open the door to let her in. Always the gentleman, she thought. Both were partially inside when Sam greeted them.

"Welcome home Mr. Baxter, Miss Cottier. You are under arrest. Get face down on the floor." The nose of Sam's nine millimeter pistol positioned just two feet from their noses.

Neither Mark nor Alexis said a word. Alexis let out a shriek, swooned and fell limp, to the floor.

Mark hesitated. "Get down on the floor, I said." Mark reluctantly responded.

"Who the hell are you?" Mark snapped from his lying position.

"The name is Weston. South Tahoe police." Sam ordered, "Put your hands behind your back, I said. Stay still." Sam read the two their Miranda Rights, from memory, while putting the cuffs on Mark. "You have the right to ..." Mark muttered something under his breath. Sam could not make it out.

Mark wanted to know what he was being held for. As if he didn't know.

"You know damn well what for. Just keep quiet until I finish here."

Just then Jack Bates burst through the door. His pistol pointed at Sam. "Thanks Weston, I'll take over from here. Drop your weapon. Drop it, I said. You two stay put", directing his order to Mark and Alexis.

"What the hell," Sam said, as he lowered his arm, dropping his piece on the floor.

"Kick it over here." Jack ordered. Sam complied. Jack picked it up and placed it in his back pocket.

Sam muttered. "Who the hell are you anyway?"

"Doesn't make any difference who I am. I'm here for the money. You can have both of them."

What Jack Bates didn't know was that the 'money' was in a vault in Mexico City. His assumption that Baxter carried it with him was without basis. Just as the last few years of his life had been.

Mark tried to get a look, twisting his head, over his shoulder to see who this other party was. "Bates, you bastard." Mark recognized him. "How'd you get involved in this?"

"Lie still Baxter or I'll put you out. Don't move a muscle or I'll waste you."

Sam, confused said, "You two know each other?"

"In a way." Mark said.

Alexis fainted again. Lying quietly face down on the floor.

"Get her some water." Mark barked.

"May I?" Sam asked Jack.

"Yeah, easy does it."

Sam walked to the sink. He dampened a dish towel that was hanging on a rack and returned to apply it to her forehead. Jack was standing off to the side, near Alexis, waiving his pistol back and forth keeping his eyes on Sam.

"You OK babe?" Mark asked with his arms crossed behind his back cuffed.

Alexis was totally in a state of unreality.

Jack stepped back as Sam neared. Instead of leaning down to tend to her, Sam held onto one end of the two foot long towel and smacked Jack in the face. The towel made a cracking sound as it struck his eyes and blinded him temporarily. Jack, startled, raised his pistol to fire, Sam grabbed the gun barrel and wrested it from Jack's hand.

The two men swinging wildly, struck each other with solid blows. Furniture was knocked around as each kept busy throwing punches, wrestling on the floor, defending themselves. Mark seeing the fray struggled to his feet and joined in. With his hands useless cuffed behind his back, he kicked Jack hard in the stomach putting him to the floor, groaning. He turned to Sam who was standing, wobbling and dazed from the pounding Jack had given him. He then thrust his knee to Sam's groin. Sam buckled over and fell to the floor, unable to respond. Mark turned his attention back to Jack who was on his knees shaking his head. Mark let loose with a powerful kick to Jack's head. Blood squirted from his nose and mouth. Jack went out. Sam, unresponsive, lay motionless in a fetal position, holding his crotch. Mark ordered Alexis to relieve Sam of the keys to the handcuffs.

Alexis trembling had risen to her knees, screaming for Mark to stop.

"Get the keys. Open the cuffs."

Alexis grappled with the keys, her hands trembling. It took a minute for her to find the key hole. She freed Mark.

Mark took possession of their weapons. Gave one to Alexis and ordered her to keep both men constrained. To make sure, Mark pummeled each one to the jaw, knocking them into unconsciousness. He used Sam's handcuffs to hamstring Sam's arms behind his back. Mark used the second set of cuffs to disable Jack. Furiously, Mark tore bed sheets into strips to bind Jacks' arms behind his back. He rolled both men on their stomachs and bound each mans legs tightly, spoiling their ability to walk. They were not going to move for a while.

Mark and Alexis grabbed their essentials. Wallet, purse and money. She reached into the open closet grabbing onto a couple of light nylon wind breakers and fled.

It had started to rain during the fracas and now it was raining hard. A monsoon specialty. The wind blowing erratically and stiff. The palm trees were bending to its will. Nature was on the loose.

Outside, the pair hastily made their way to the dock and the Tahiti. Mark observed the other Tahitis' docked on the opposite side of the pier, realizing it had to be both Jack's or Sam's. He released the lines that secured the boats allowing them to drift away.

Alexis lowered herself into the boat. She was silent. He recognized that she was in a state of shock. Almost helpless. Soaked from the downpour and wind's chill, she trembled, shaking uncontrollably. Mark realized her fragility. He tried to soothe her with encouraging words.

"It'll be all right. Please Alexis, try to relax. It will be all right. I'm so sorry for what happened back there. I had no choice but to free us."

Alexis tried to get the words out. She stammered. Her lips quivering, tears in her eyes. She had never experienced anything so violent as Mark's actions. She had never seen Mark in that light before. Had no idea Mark was capable of such brutality. "Mark, Mark I'm scared. You scare me."

"What else was I to do?" Mark tried to explain as the boat skipped across the water, knifing through high waves, the bow, slamming hard, down on the water's surface. The raging wind sweeping across the open water, with nothing to hinder it, picked the craft up, almost out of the water, at times pushing it off in skewed obtuse angles. Mark struggled to control it's forward motion. The sea was angry, churning, keeping up with the wind. The boat began taking on water. The waves coming across the bow spilled into the craft.

"Get the life preservers." Mark yelled out over the roar of the struggling engine and howling wind.

Alexis was frozen to her seat, afraid to move for fear of being thrown overboard by the erratic behavior of the boat, she remained motionless.

"Alexis, we need the preservers. Get them. They're under one of the seats." It was the first time he could remember being angry with her.

Still she hesitated. "Look under your seat. Please Alexis, it means our lives." That phrase struck home.

Slowly she turned from her position and removed the bench seat in the rear. Clutching onto an orange jacket, she slipped her arms through the straps and buckled the snap. She handed one to Mark. He almost went overboard trying to enter his. She recognized his predicament and snapped the buckle while he man handled the wheel.

The boat's progress slowed with the extra weight of water inside. Mark decided it was too far to the mainland to fight nature's offering. The wind's fury and the sea's swells were too much for the small craft.

'We're going back Alexis. We have to or we'll drown out here." He shouted. Mark spun the steering wheel around. Nearly capsizing the vessel in the process, Tung Lung was within sight, yet far enough that he would have to put all of his energies to bear to return safely. But now he had the wind at his back. The boat, although encumbered with the weight of the water inside handled and maneuvered more easily. Instead of bucking the waves he now was moving with their favor. Still the sea pounded and thrust them erratically.

Reaching shore, Mark piloted the boat onto the sand beach at half speed, aided by the wind and high surf, it ground to a shushing halt. Disembarking, they ran to shelter under a grove of palms. They huddled together, cold, soaked, exhausted, unable to think rationally or consider their next move.

The storm raked the island furiously without concern for anything in its path. Palm fronds broke off, sailing into oblivion. Bits and pieces of debris swirled in the air, unleashed to fend on their own. The din of the gale overwhelmed any utterance from either. How long it would go on was unpredictable, incomprehensible. They clutched each other in the hope of easing their fright.

CHAPTER 20

Just prior to the storm gaining strength, Lieutenant Hong joined the crew of a patrol boat and headed to the island in the belief that Sam might need help. Sam had been too secretive for Hong to believe that something of importance was "just a hunch."

It was a large craft, with an expierienced crew, capable of handling the storm. It arrived at the pier right after Mark and Alexis departed. The crew tied off the frigate, disembarked all but a standby crew and headed to the compound of cabins. Three crewmen in all, descended upon the hut where Sam and Jack were coming around to consciousness.

Both were released from their bonds. Sam immediately ordered Jack arrested. The charge, he said, "Was interfering with a peace officer, assault with a deadly weapon, mayhem on a police officer and whatever else I can think of." It would stick. Jack Bates was in custody. This time with stainless steel handcuffs instead of cloth bed sheets.

Sam informed Hong and the crew of the occurrence that took place earlier.

"I have no idea if they made an escape or if they are still on the island. All I know right now is that my head and crotch need a rest." Sam was beginning to believe that this trip really wasn't worth it. The emphasis on "really."

The storm continued to rake the island with a vengeance. Mark and Alexis toughing it out, continued to huddle together under the threatening trees.

He knew they couldn't remain out in the open much longer. Alexis was wearing down, shaking, uncontrollably. The village couldn't be far off the reasoned, even though they landed in an area of the island that Mark had not visited during his short stay. He had to get her under cover. Dry and warm. Reconnoitering the situation, Mark estimated they were north of the village. Maybe a mile or less.

"Alexis, we've got to get to shelter."

"Yes," she said meekly.

"Let's get out of here. The village can't be far. You've got to try to make it."

"I'll try."

With the wind at their backs, the pair worked their way through the undergrowth of ferns, staying within the groves of trees for protection. It was pouring rain. Both were weak from the experience. They had gone about a quarter of a mile unexposed. As yet hadn't detected any sign of life. In the distance through the hard driving rain and mist, Mark saw what he thought to be a shed standing alone under some trees. An out building of some sort. Alexis was faltering, barely able to walk. Mark picked her up in his arms and carried her the last few yards to the structure.

The tiny building contained some tools for harvesting coconuts, a ladder, a ragged set of overalls hanging from a nail driven into the wall, some garden implements. It was dry, out of the wind and downpour.

Hours passed. The wind subsided and the rain had stopped beating on the roof. There was a light drizzle as dusk engulfed the island. The storm ebbed leaving the island drenched and wind blown. Mark opened the door of the shed. Palm fronds covered the ground. Those that managed to fight off the storm, still attached to their host, were dripping sparkling beads of water left by the storm. Dark and threatening clouds continued to blanket the sky. Looking around, Mark discovered that their shelter was isolated. Not a sign of habitation within sight.

Mark turned to Alexis. "If we can get back to the boat, if it's still there, we can get off the island."

Alexis didn't respond as if unaware of Mark's presence.

"Did you hear me?"

"Yes. Mark, I'm exhausted. I don't think I can make it."

"We can't stick it out here. We've got to try."

"Give me a little time." She begged.

"Alexis, we don't have the luxury of time."

She raised from her sitting position. Struggling to compose herself, she assented to make it back to the boat.

Under the cover of darkness, the pair hugged the forested landscape in their attempt to reach the place where Mark beached the craft.

Remembering that he drove the boat hard onto the shore, the bow cutting deep into the sand, he hoped the storm hadn't dislodged the vessel and scurried it out to sea. Reaching the sight, Mark saw that his luck was holding. The boat had been freed, but the surge of waves kept it broadside against the beach, the surf lapping the starboard side.

Mark assisted Alexis into the boat, then pushed it out and away from the shore, climbed in as the craft slipped into deeper water.

With Jack Bates in tow, the storm subsiding, Sam, Lt. Hong and his crew set out to search the island for Mark and Alexis.

Sam said, "If we had a goddammed army over here we might catch the bastard." Sam was miserable, hurting, physically and mentally.

"Thou are letting negativity enter your aura Mr. Weston." Hong said.

"Something better enter my aura, Hong, and dammed quick." Sam said.

"You must remain confident and in control my friend. Remember time is on our side and Mr. Baxter is scared and on the run. No matter what you think, the odds are with us. We have the initiative, the benefit of surprise, and the freedom to pursue at our pleasure. He must always be burdened with guilt and fear, running and looking over his shoulder. That gives us the advantage. Our minds are at peace. Mr. Baxter is fighting right from wrong. It is a difficult position to be in. It keeps him preoccupied and confused even though he may not realize it. Also he is now burdened with additional baggage. His women. She will be the mill stone around his neck. A choke hold."

"You are a philosopher aren't you, Hong."

"All of us Chinese are philosophers, Mr. Weston. That is why we, in our slow and methodical ways are ahead of you westerners in many respects. You are materialists, we are spiritualists. There is a difference, you know. You want everything now. We are patient, for we know it will come eventually as long as we have concern for our being. The future cannot be rushed. The only thing that we have not been able to control is our birthrate. Could it be that we are hornier, as you say, than you westerners."

Sam looked at Hong with a raised eyebrow, responding, "You're also comedians, eh Hong."

Hong smiled. "Perhaps."

Mark and Alexis, making their way back to the mainland, rounded the island in an attempt to execute a shortcut, when they were spotted by the crew that stayed aboard the cutter.

The crew chief radioed Hong that they had a suspicious craft in sight. There was a man and woman aboard. "We are in pursuit."

As the Tahiti sped away, the cutter, a much faster craft, overtook the pair. Running along side Mark and Alexis, the Captain ordered them to stop.

He had no choice but to obey. Looking down the barrel of a fifty caliber canon and several rifles, he succumbed to capture.

A sprinkling of rain drops began to pelt the ship's deck. Ominous dark clouds once again formed off to the East.

The crew secured a line to the small boat and walked it to the stern of the mother ship where it could be safely towed back to Tung Lung.

Mark and Alexis were escorted below deck in to what appeared to be a map room. A large conference table dominated the center. Ocean charts, some rolled up, some laid out covered the glass top table.

Alexis hadn't said a word during the ordeal. In shock, exhausted, frightened. Mark continued in his attempts to soothe her fears by using words of confidence. "Let me do the talking."

"Yes." She murmured. "But isn't this a good opportunity to turn yourself in? I can't take anymore of this."

"Strength babe. We're getting a free ride. When the time is right, we'll be on our way. Have faith. For now just do as you've been doing. Act as though you don't understand why we're being detained. Let me do the talking. If you're asked a question, try to answer with a question. I know you are good at that. If you falter, I'll break in and help you. OK."

"Yes, but ..."

A ship's officer entered the room. The hash marks on his sleeve made it appear that he was the authority on board. "I'm Lieutenant Yangsing. I've come down to chat with you for a minute. We're going to try to make port before this regenerated storm hits." He was very articulate. He continued, "1 overheard some of the conversation between you and your lady friend. Your attempt to escape is futile."

"We weren't trying to escape. We were trying to beat the weather. We were making good time before you interfered."

"If we hadn't, you wouldn't be safely aboard sir. Quite possibly you would be swimming with the fishes. Maybe worse."

"That's conjecture on your part lieutenant. I'm an old hand at sea. Let me inform you that I am an agent of the United States Government. A member of the Drug Enforcement Agency. That's what I'm doing in this part of the world. Working with your government, your people, looking into some nasty business. Sources of drug production, trade, pipelines. You understand lieutenant? 1 can't go into detail, but that's it in a nutshell."

"1 see." The lieutenant didn't appear to be impressed. "Excuse me sir, I have a couple of questions to ask you."

The wind, now stronger than during the first storm surge caused the ship to heel hard to port, throwing Mark, Alexis and the lieutenant against the wall. Charts slid from the table and crashed to the deck. An overhead lamp swung violently from left to right. It felt as though the craft were about to capsize. The second storm was upon them. The gusts of wind hit the cutter broadside. The ship shuddered from the propellers rising above the water line. A mountainous wave poured over the port side engulfing the main deck. Water poured to the innards through open hatches.

The winds blew powerfully sending wave after wave over the bow and sides engulfing the deck and down below. It was a swirling chaos sometimes coming over the bow, then the stern, and abeam causing even this big craft to struggle to make headway to shore.

From the impact of crashing into the wall, Alexis could not raise her right arm above her shoulder and complained to Mark that she was in pain. She supported the arm by cradling it with her left hand holding the arm close to her body.

Lieutenant Yangsing recovering after being thrown to the deck saw that she needed attention. "Miss, you are hurt. Let me try to get you to the first aid station." Sloshing through ankle deep water the lieutenant assisted her to what consisted of two closets with a chair and a cot. A medicine cabinet with basic supplies. Alexis was taken by the man's compassion. Something she hadn't seen in Mark for a while. It occurred to her that Mark was at times preoccupied with himself. In her state of confusion, she mused, had all the pressure on him begin to show a lack of concern for her? The man she so desperately loved. Her gentle and kind man. She wondered in delirium.

The ship continued to heave in all directions as it churned through the angry sea. Up and down, side to side. All hands on board were holding onto something, having a difficult time maintaining their balance.

The waves smashing against the pilot house window made it impossible for the crew to make out any signs of approaching land. They were struggling with the instruments, Sonar, radar and compass.

The storm grew more intense as the minutes passed. No matter what the crew did to control the craft the sea interdicted with its power and manipulated the cutter. Huge swells, some fifteen feet high, battered the boat, coming in astern, thrusting the boat forward in great leaps. It seemed that the storm's fury had unleashed itself on this one area, perpetrating its fury on the boat and its occupants. At the helm, the master was barely able to hold onto the wheel.

Suddenly the ship foundered on a sand bar a hundred yards off shore. It lie heeled nearly sixty degrees, completely disabled. Water poured into the hull from the starboard side. The ship was breaking apart from the pounding on the sea bottom. Some of the crew were thrown overboard. Below deck, Mark and Alexis struggled with the abrupt halt of the craft. Their surroundings were confusing. A twisted convoluted arrangement. Water was rising hip deep. Debris floated throughout. Paper, plastic, tables. The Lieutenant was out cold after hitting his head on the edge of the chart table. Mark grabbed onto the back of his shirt, pulling him from under the water.

The pain in Alexis's shoulder disappeared as a result of the terror. All that mattered was survival. She exited the room entering the cluttered and water filled hallway. From which a stairway led up to the main deck. Mark wading in the deep water just ahead of her, beckoned for her to follow. Alexis had swallowed a good amount of water. Panic stricken, she choked and gasped for air. Mark grabbed her around the waist, pulling her up the stairs. Here too, debris crowded the surroundings. Crew members could be heard shouting orders in Chinese. Others screaming for help. Mark held onto Alexis while trying to sustain his footing on the slanted deck.

A large chunk of decking had broken loose. Mark reached out, snagging the flotsam and held on. Another wave engulfed the piece of wood sending it below the water. Mark took advantage of its position and lifted himself onto the plank. Letting loose of her temporarily, she went under. Mark seeing that, quickly snatched Alexis by the hair and pulled her on board with him. The 'raft' bobbed around the ship for a time, then slowly retreated.

It seemed like hours but in reality it took only thirty minutes for the current to deposit them onto the shore. They lie quietly, the rain pelting them in the downpour. Somehow that didn't matter. They were safe from drowning. The rain was just an inconvenience. Not a word was spoken between the two. They were alone.

For a time they lie quietly regaining their senses. Alexis spoke. "Mark this is enough. I want to live. No matter what it costs I'm turning myself in. It's not worth it. I know how you feel about this whole matter, but to me it's not worth it. As soon as I can I'm going to the authorities and be relieved of the burden I've placed upon myself. Do you understand?"

"Yes, seeing you hurting is tearing me apart. I'm so sorry it has turned out like this. I guess I'm resigned to the fact that it's not working. Maybe because we were saved twice today means that I'm supposed to give in to my determination to get away with it. Believe me honey, it has been hell these past few weeks. There were moments when I thought it was a grand adventure. But it is a nightmare. I'm sorry I dragged you into it. I'll do whatever it takes to secure your innocence. If I have to do time, well, then I'll face it. Let's get up to the village and into some shelter. I'll try to make contact with that guy Weston. He's probably still at the cottage. Is that OK?"

"Yes, please Mark. It's for the best."

Sam, Hong and the men remained in the cabin to wait out of this second surge of the storm. Sam was prepared to continue the chase, although he was a bit puzzled as to where he would start. He was sure the pair had made it off the island and back to the mainland.

After securing cover and safety for Alexis, Mark made his way back to the cottage. His thoughts ran the gamut of whether he was doing the right thing. Then, he thought of Alexis and the turmoil he had created for her and himself from the beginning. He was convinced that it was the only way to keep her. Even considering what may lie ahead for them.

The weather continued its ugly persona as he approached his fate. The little hut seemed empty and quiet as he neared. Wet, disheveled, cut and bruised he climbed the few stairs to the front door. He was exhausted both in spirit and energy.

At the door he spoke loud enough to be heard over the wind and rain. "Anybody in there?"

Sam was the first to answer by opening the door. "Baxter, what the hell."

"I'm here to turn myself in." Mark was meek in his utterance. Defeated, his voice was without dominion.

"Come on in. Sam had a look of shock and disbelief in his welcoming. Where's the lady?"

"In the village. She's waiting for us to return," Mark said.

Sam immediately announced that Mark was under arrest and began reading him his rights. Mark listened attentively. He held out his hands for Sam to snap on the handcuffs. "You're familiar with these." Sam said as a matter offact.

"Yeah, I guess so." Resigned.

Hong tapped Sam on the shoulder. "What did I tell you about being patient. It only happens in the Orient, I suppose."

Sam glanced over his shoulder at Hong. "Eh."

Mark described what had happened during the last few hours. Their attempt to escape the island, Being picked up by the patrol boat and it's fate. Their near death experience and miraculous return to the island on a piece of planking. He expressed his regret as to the demise of some of the crew, to which Hong immediately dispatched another cutter to the area to search for survivors. And yet another to pick them up as soon as the storm subsided.

CHAPTER 21

Sam was beside himself with excitement.

The storm was now all but over. Only the outer fringes of lingering clouds swirled with calm winds and light rain. The recovery boats arrived to retrieve their quarry, surviving crew members, Sam, Jack and Hong.

Back on the mainland Sam communicated with Captain Dickson at the Lake, calmly relating the events that took place and Baxter's surrender.

"Captain, sir, Mark Baxter is in custody. He turned himself in. Miss Cottier is also in custody. I'm going to finish my business here in a day or two and we will be on our way back. Do you have any instructions other that to just get back?"

"Excellent Sam. Excellent. We're anxious to see you and your people. Good work my man. I knew you would do it. Never doubted you for a minute. I'll get the word out. Been tough, I'll bet."

"Just a bit." Sam answered. "I'm looking forward to getting back to some normalcy. If that's possible."

"Well Sam, you deserve a vacation. We'll see to that. We're very anxious to see you." Dickson repeated himself.

Sam finished his business in Hong Kong with the authorities while Mark and Alexis were held in custody. Alexis was not dealing with being incarcerated very well. Twange Hong took care of arranging transportation back to the states, including two escorts, just in case. The one positive on the return was First Class accommodations. Mark and Alexis barely spoke during the long flight. Hardly glancing at each other. It was not a happy time for either. Sam busied himself with the report that would be required. It consumed all of his attention on the return trip.

The group, were received by an entourage of official types, including the FBI, at the airport in Reno. Ironically, where the adventure originated. The feds insisted on taking over, but Sam kept them at bay. "This is my baby fellows. You'll get your time after I release them to detention. I'm taking him in."

Reluctantly, they backed off. They followed in their government issued black Chevrolet Suburbans up to Lake Tahoe.

Mark and Alexis were separated and incarcerated again. It tore at her. Being isolated from one another for the first time, officially, since their relationship began. It was devastating for both.

Alexis's friend, Leslie, posted bond for alexis, which allowed for her release.

Remorse and shame was tearing at the fabric of Alexis' self-esteem. Her sense of being honest and playing the game of life by the rules. She was overwhelmed with what appeared to be the loss of everything she held important, dear and sacred.

The following day, Mark was taken to a stark, dimly lit interrogation room furnished with one bare stainless steel table and two hard and uncomfortable contoured black plastic chairs. Under intense pressure, for five hours, he was quizzed with the same questions, repeatedly. To which he gave the same answers repeatedly. He revealed only that, yes, he was at the scene after the accident, nothing more. Mark knew how to handle the strength of their questioning. He had been in the 'questioning' chair many times during his days with the DEA when he interviewed some of the worst dregs of society.

Later that day he stood before a judge to be arranged. He was indicted on one count of stealing government money. The other alleged charge that was proposed was, leaving the scene of an accident and not reporting it. It was dropped for lack of evidence. He heard the magistrate announce that his bail would be set at one hundred thousand dollars. Of which he did not have nor did he know of anyone capable of furnishing it.

Mark requested that a public defender be assigned to the case, pleading the inability to pay for an attorney. A bailiff standing near, who Mark knew, whispered that Alexis had been released on her own recognizance after bail had been made. Mark smiled. "Thanks."

The time passed agonizingly slow in his cell. A week, two weeks, three weeks. The weeks turned into a month and a half. Alexis visited almost every day. Assuring him that all was well with them. That everything would be "OK" in the end. Even though, they discussed the possibility that he would be put away for some time. How much, he refused to speculate.

"It's something I would rather not think about." She would tell him.

Mark was fortunate in one respect. His case was on the docket very early, considering the load of cases waiting. His court appointed attorney visited nearly as much as Alexis, gathering mounds of information from Mark. Mark liked his attitude. Especially his assurances that he would do the best he could to get the situation resolved.

"Mark, I think you ought to consider a plea bargain. It will go much easier if you do."

Mark refused. "All they have is circumstantial evidence. I did admit to being there, but nothing else. All they've got are my prints and a lot of other prints. Anybody could have come along before or shortly after me and absconded with the money. That's what they're after." Up there in the mountains, where I thought no other human was within miles, I have been surprised when another hiker came out of nowhere."

"I know, but it's unlikely that anyone else was on the scene but you. You are the only one that appears to have been there and able to take the dough. There is no evidence to indicate that another human being was any where near the location. They're going to pound away on that scenario."

"They can hammer away all they want. They've got to prove it. I don't think they can." Mark said.

"OK then, we'll base our case on that. That you were there and were returning with the intent to report it. The reason you didn't was that on your return you heard about the accident on your car radio and there was no reason to get involved, that's all. But if push comes to shove, please consider a plea bargain. Maybe we can get off with a year, possibly two at the most. By the way, where is the money?"

Mark didn't bite on the suggestion. "What money?"

"All right then, the schedule on the docket is next week. I'm nearly prepared. I'll finish up this week. Wish us good luck."

"It's not a matter of luck. If you are prepared, then I'm not worried. They've got to prove it. That's the bottom line."

The jury was selected and seated. The opening statements were routine, as proclamations go. The prosecution swore that they could prove that "Mark Baxter, the defendant in this case was the only person at the scene after the crash of the subject aircraft. That he and he alone discovered the cargo. Furthermore, that he and he alone discovered the money aboard and through his wonted and inexcusable greed took what was legally the governments currency and fled. That he left the scene of a tragedy and failed to report it. That possibly lives could have been saved had he reported it in due process. Instead, he allowed the authorities to discover the site sometme later."

The judge interrupted and admonished the prosecutor. "We're not here to discuss any alleged charge other than that of absconding with government money. I don't want to hear anything regarding leaving the scene of an accident or any thing else. Just prove your case on the possession of money belonging to others. Is that understood?" The judge turned his attention to the panel of jurists. "The jury is to ignore the prosecutors statements about leaving the scene of an accident and not reporting it."

Mark sat, with concern, listening. Thinking from what he had just heard the judge say, the governments's case was substantially weakened.

He occasionally whispered some of his thoughts to his attorney. Alexis, sitting behind Mark, fidgeted nervously, apparently irritated and worried. For a time, it looked as though the prosecution was making very valid and intrinsic accusations that could be proven. Occasionally she would catch Mark's attention and show concern for the negative proceedings. Mark would smile assuring her that things were going to be all right. Even though he hadn't the slightest idea what the outcome would be.

The prosecution really didn't have much to go on. They didn't have the total amount of currency they knew was on the aircraft. They didn't have any witnesses. They did have one briefcase with some of the money, but no prints on the case. What they did have was a tire identification and a fingerprint from the aircraft. That's about it. The basis for their case was purely circumstantial. But, they did have an ace up their sleeve. At least they thought so. They reasoned that a wiretap on Alexis' phone would be their trump card. During the proceedings, the prosecution pointed out that they had enough evidence to convict from their wiretap of Alexis's telephone. That the conversation between she and Mark conclusively proved that Mark had taken the money and was on the lam. Alexis, according to their conversation, begged for Mark to return and turn himself in, and relinquish the money.

Mark's attorney picked up on their statement regarding the wiretap and requested to approach the bench for a conference. In the ensuing discussion with the judge, Mark's attorney requested to know whether the authorities obtained a judge's order for a wiretap. If so, to see it and introduce it as evidence. The prosecutors stated that they were in the process of acquiring the court order. The judge, disgruntled by the delay, ordered a recess until such written evidence could be entered into evidence.

The attorney accompanied Mark back to his cell to inform him of his knowledge of wiretaps and their consequences. "We might have something here. As you know Mark, wiretaps are a sensitive subject with judges. They dislike them because they're hard to prove. Most of the time a judge will throw them out as inconclusive evidence because of, who's voices can you identify as factual. If he doesn't, it is not good for our case. In addition to that, wiretapping an innocent person is illegal unless there is substantial evidence that the individual being wiretapped is guilty in a narcotics case. And narcotics were certainly a part of this case. At least from the government's standpoint."

However, Alexis was not a suspect in this case. Only an accessory. I just want you to know that if he accepts the wiretap it's going to be very difficult for us to win. In that case then, I suggest, as I said before, that we plea bargain. It will be the only way to reduce your sentence. That is if you tell them where the money is."

"Fine." Mark didn't elaborate. "I'll consider it. What money?"

The following day in the courtroom, the judge asked the prosecution for the judge's order for the wiretap. The prosecution begged for time. They hadn't been able to secure the order.

"You've had enough time." The judge responded. "Either you have it or you don't."

The prosecution requested to approach the bench. Doing so, it was revealed that they had searched the records thoroughly for the order but could not, as yet, find it. "Your honor, we need more time to secure it."

"Granted. You have until noon today. If not, 1 will declare a mistrial. As a matter of fact, I'll throw out the case and release the defendant. Is that understood? Illegal wiretaps are not of much use in my court. They've caused too many innocent individuals to be put away and forgotten as a result of false evidence. For another, I disapprove of them because they're misused and misunderstood. Period. In addition to that, all that you've got is some wishy washy evidence. Don't waste the courts time unless you can show more concrete evidence. You're toying with ipso facto."

Noon arrived. The prosecution team had a definite dejected aura about them. When asked for the order, the lead prosecutor announced that it was not available.

The hammer slammed hard on the bench. "Case dismissed. The defendant is free to go."

Alexis let out a scream. Mark sighed and slumped in his seat. His attorney glanced over at him, smiled. "How about that"!.

Alexis ran to Mark and leaped in his arms. "Oh my God. How could this be?"

Holding her close, Mark extended his arm and shook his lawyers hand. "Yes, How could this be? After all that I've, we've been through."

"You are one lucky man is all I can say."

Sam heard the news immediately. "Oh man." The ball point pen he was using slipped through his fingers hitting the desk with a thud. Placing his elbows on the desk, he cradled his chin atop his clasped hands, and stared at the facing wall.

Just then Ron Blamebridge knocked on Sam's door.

"Come in."

"I just heard Sam, I'm sorry."

"Sit down young fellow. I need some company."

"Well at least you got Bates. He'll pay."

"The least, after all." Sam said.

"What about Miss Cottier?" Ron asked.

"Oh, her. She was vindicated after the fact. They couldn't see any reason to prosecute. She had nothing to do with the situation. We know that she was determined to get him to return. In our interview with her she said over and over that she begged him to come back. Never once did she mention anything about money. She intentionally went to Hong Kong to get him to come back. How about that?"

"The feds. Are they going to press charges against him for the fracas in Bogota? Are they going to stay on the money trail?"

"About the confrontation, I don't think so. It was just a scuffle. I heard that he may have a case against them for assault, which I doubt he'll pursue. I'm sure they will go after the dough, but where it is and how much effort for how long they will pursue is up to, well, the gods."

"How's the homicide investigation coming along regarding the three individuals on the plane?" Ron asked.

"The FBI is handling it. I heard they don't have any leads or suspects. Almost all the evidence was destroyed in the crash. They're working on it."

"The money." Ron asked again.

"What money? All I was after was Baxter" Sam said.

The money. Three months after the close of the trial. After the Feds went away. After the press and the media went silent, Mark and Alexis boarded a plane for Puerto Vallarta. A month later in Mexico City, Alexis shopped, Mark, watching his back, making sure he was alone in this mega-metropolis, reclaimed his cache from the vault deep underground at the Hotel Revolucion, With the briefcases securely in his grip and under his control, he reunited with Alexis.

Shortly thereafter, somewhere in the Caribbean, on a secluded beach, they sat, side by side, holding onto each other, still deeply in love.

A tropical storm, out in the Western Atlantic began to churn the sea into a tumultuous fit. The oncoming breaking waves pounded hard and noisily onto the firm sandy beach.

Mark looking out across the blue green rolling expanse, offhanded, casually said, "Alexis, how am I ever going to live with myself knowing that the bomb I planted on the plane killed my best friend."

"What was that about your best friend, the surf muffled your words."

"Never mind." He said.

CPSIA information can be obtained at www.ICGtesting.com
Printed in the USA
BVOW02s1850180416

444664BV00002B/56/P